FROM THE DARING IMAGINATION OF RAY BRADBURY

—a deep-sea monster who falls in love with a flirtatious foghorn.

—an atom-blasted land where people are born, live and die, all in the space of eight days.

—a fantastic dinosaur hunt, thousands of years back into time.

—a daring expedition to gather a cupful of the sun.

Ray Bradbury was born in Waukegan, Illinois, and published his first short story in 1941. Bradbury's wonderful writing has taken many forms in television, radio, the novel, and he wrote the script for the great movie, **Moby Dick**. Among other famous books he is the author of **Dandelion Wine, The Illustrated Man,** and **The Martian Chronicles.**

BANTAM PATHFINDER EDITIONS

Bantam Pathfinder Editions provide the best in fiction and nonfiction in a wide variety of subject areas. They include novels by classic and contemporary writers; vivid, accurate histories and biographies; authoritative works in the sciences, collections of short stories, plays and poetry.

Bantam Pathfinder Editions are carefully selected and approved. They are durably bound, printed on specially selected high-quality paper, and presented in a new and handsome format.

R IS FOR ROCKET

BY RAY BRADBURY

BANTAM PATHFINDER EDITIONS
NEW YORK / TORONTO / LONDON

*This low-priced Bantam Book
has been completely reset in a type face
designed for easy reading, and was printed
from new plates. It contains the complete
text of the original hard-cover edition.*
NOT ONE WORD HAS BEEN OMITTED.

📖

RLI: VLM 7.0
IL 7.12

R IS FOR ROCKET

*A Bantam Book / published by arrangement with
Doubleday & Company, Inc.*

PRINTING HISTORY

Doubleday edition published October 1962
2nd printing....November 1962   4th printing........May 1963
3rd printing....December 1962   5th printing....September 1964
Bantam edition published March 1965
2nd printing..........May 1965
Bantam Pathfinder edition published September 1966
4th printing......January 1967   6th printing......October 1968
5th printing....September 1967   7th printing......January 1969
8th printing..........September 1969

9th printing

10th printing

11th printing

12th printing

13th printing

*All rights reserved.
Copyright © 1962 by Ray Bradbury.
This book may not be reproduced in whole or in part, by
mimeograph or any other means, without permission.
For information address: Doubleday & Company, Inc.,
277 Park Avenue, New York, N.Y. 10017.*

Published simultaneously in the United States and Canada

*Bantam Books are published by Bantam Books, Inc., a National
General company. Its trade-mark, consisting of the words "Bantam
Books" and the portrayal of a bantam, is registered in the United
States Patent Office and in other countries. Marca Registrada.
Bantam Books, Inc., 666 Fifth Avenue, New York, N.Y. 10019.*

PRINTED IN THE UNITED STATES OF AMERICA

When I was a boy in the Midwest I used to go out and look at the stars at night and wonder about them.

I guess every boy has done that.

When I wasn't looking at the stars, I was running in my old or my brand-new tennis shoes, on my way to swing in a tree, swim in a lake, or delve in the town library to read about dinosaurs or Time Machines.

I guess every boy has done that, too.

This is a book about those stars and those tennis shoes. Mainly about the stars, because that is the way I grew up, getting more and more involved with rockets and space as I moved toward my twelfth, thirteenth, and fourteenth years.

Not that I have forgotten the tennis shoes and their powerful magic, as you will see in the last story here, which I have included not because it concerns the Future, but because it gives you some sort of idea of the kind of boy I was when I was looking at the stars and thinking of the Years Ahead.

Nor have I forgotten the dinosaurs that all boys love; they are here, too, along with a Machine that travels back in Time to step on a butterfly.

This is a book then by a boy who grew up in a small Illinois town and lived to see the Space Age arrive, as he hoped and dreamt it would.

I dedicate these stories to all boys who wonder about the Past, run swiftly in the Present, and have high hopes for our Future.

The stars are yours, if you have the head, the hands, and the heart for them.

RAY BRADBURY
Los Angeles
March 28, 1962

CONTENTS

R IS FOR ROCKET

There was this fence where we pressed our faces and felt the wind turn warm and held to the fence and forgot who we were or where we came from but dreamed of who we might be and where we might go. . . .

Yet we were boys and liked being boys and lived in a Florida town and liked the town and went to school and fairly liked the school and climbed trees and played football and liked our mothers and fathers. . . .

But some time every hour of every day of every week for a minute or a second when we thought on fire and stars and the fence beyond which they waited . . . we liked the rockets more.

The fence. The rockets.

Every Saturday morning . . .

The guys met at my house . . .

With the sun hardly up, they yelled until the neighbors were moved to brandish paralysis guns out their ventilators commanding the guys to shut up or they'd be frozen statues for the next hour and *then* where would they be?

Aw, climb a rocket, stick your head in the main-jet! the kids always yelled back, but yelled this safe behind our garden fence. Old Man Wickard, next door, is a great shot with the para-gun.

This one dim cool Saturday morning I was lying in bed thinking about how I had flunked my semantics exam the day before at formula-school, when I heard the gang yelling below. It was hardly 7 A.M. and there was still a lot of fog roaming in off the Atlantic, and only now were the weather-control vibrators at each corner starting to hum and shoot out rays to get rid of the stuff; I heard them moaning soft and nice.

Copyright 1943 by Popular Publications, Inc.

I padded to the window and stuck my head out.

"Okay, space-pirates! Motors off!"

"Hey!" shouted Ralph Priory. "We just heard, there's a new schedule today! The Moon Job, the one with the new XL3-motor, is cutting gravity in an *hour!*"

"Buddha, Muhammad, Allah, and other real and semi-mythological figures," I said, and went away from the window so fast the concussion laid all the boys out on my lawn.

I zippered myself into a jumper, yanked on my boots, clipped my food-capsules to my hip-pocket, for I knew there'd be no food or even thought of food today, we'd just stuff with pills when our stomachs barked, and fell down the two-story vacuum elevator.

On the lawn, all five of the guys were chewing their lips, bouncing around, scowling.

"Last one," said I, passing them at 5000 mph, "to the monorail is a bug-eyed Martian!"

On the monorail, with the cylinder hissing us along to Rocket Port, twenty miles from town—a few minutes' ride —I had bugs in my stomach. A guy fifteen doesn't get to see the big stuff often enough, mostly every week it was the small continental cargo rockets coming and going on schedule. But this was big, among the biggest . . . the Moon and be-yond. . . .

"I'm sick," said Priory, and hit me on the arm.

I hit him back. "Me, too. Boy, ain't Saturday the best day in the week!?"

Priory and I traded wide, understanding grins. We got along all Condition Go. The other pirates were okay. Sid Rossen, Mac Leslyn, Earl Marnee, they knew how to jump around like all the kids, and they loved the rockets, too, but I had the feeling they wouldn't be doing what Ralph and I would do some day. Ralph and I wanted the stars for each of us, more than we would want a fistful of clear-cut blue-white diamonds.

We yelled with the yellers, we laughed with the laughers, but at the middle of it all, we were still, Ralph and I, and the cylinder whispered to a stop and we were outside yelling, laughing, running, but quiet and almost in slow motion, Ralph ahead of me, and all of us pointed one way, at the observation fence and grabbing hold, yelling for the slowpokes to catch up, but not looking back for them, and then we were all there together and the big rocket came out of its plastic work canopy like a great interstellar circus tent and moved along its gleaming track out toward the fire point, accompanied by the gigantic gantry like a gathering of prehistoric reptile birds which kept and preened and fed this one big fire monster and led it toward its seizure and birth into a suddenly blast-furnace sky.

I quit breathing. I didn't even suck another breath it seemed until the rocket was way out on the concrete meadow, followed by water-beetle tractors and great cylinders bearing hidden men, and all around, in asbestos suits, praying-mantis mechanics fiddled with machines and buzzed and cawwed and gibbered to each other on invisible, unhearable radiophones, but we could hear it all, in our heads, our minds, our hearts.

"Lord," I said at last.

"The very good Lord," said Ralph Priory at my elbow. The others said this, too, over and over.

It was something to "good Lord" about. It was a hundred years of dreaming all sorted out and chosen and put together to make the hardest, prettiest, swiftest dream of all. Every line was fire solidified and made perfect, it was flame frozen, and ice waiting to thaw there in the middle of a concrete prairie, ready to wake with a roar, jump high and knock its silly fine great head against the Milky Way and knock the stars down in a full return of firefall meteors. You felt it could kick the Coal Sack Nebula square in the midriff and make it stand out of the way.

It got me in the midriff, too—it gripped me in such a way I knew the special sickness of longing and envy and grief for lack of accomplishment. And when the astronauts patrolled the field in the final silent mobile-van, my body went with them in their strange white armor, in their bubble-helmets and insouciant pride, looking as if they were team-parading to a magnetic football game at one of the local mag-fields, for mere practice. But they were going to the Moon, they went every month now, and the crowds that used to come to watch were no longer there, there was just us kids to worry them up and worry them off.

"Gosh," I said. "What wouldn't I give to go with them. What wouldn't I give."

"Me," said Mac, "I'd give my one-year monorail privileges."

"Yeah. Oh, very much yeah."

It was a big feeling for us kids caught half between this morning's toys and this afternoon's very real and powerful fireworks.

And then the preliminaries got over with. The fuel was in the rocket and the men ran away from it on the ground like ants running lickety from a metal god—and the Dream woke up and gave a yell and jumped into the sky. And then it was gone, all the vacuum shouting of it, leaving nothing but a hot trembling in the air, through the ground, and up our legs to our hearts. Where it had been was a blazed, seared pock and a fog of rocket smoke like a cumulus cloud banked low.

"It's gone!" yelled Priory.

And we all began to breathe fast again, frozen there on the ground as if stunned by the passing of a gigantic paralysis gun.

"I want to grow up quick," I said, then. "I want to grow up quick so I can take that rocket."

I bit my lips. I was so darned young, and you cannot apply for space work. You have to be *chosen*. Chosen.

Finally somebody, I guess it was Sidney, said:

"Let's go to the tele-show now."

Everyone said yeah, except Priory and myself. We said no, and the other kids went off laughing breathlessly, talking, and left Priory and me there to look at the spot where the ship had been.

It spoiled everything else for us—that takeoff.

Because of it, I flunked my semantics test on Monday. I didn't care.

At times like that I thanked Providence for concentrates. When your stomach is nothing but a coiled mass of excitement, you hardly feel like drawing a chair to a full hot dinner. A few concen-tabs swallowed, did wonderfully well as substitution, without the urge of appetite.

I got to thinking about it, tough and hard, all day long and late at night. It got so bad I had to use sleep-massage mechs every night, coupled with some of Tschaikovsky's quieter music to get my eyes shut.

"Good Lord, young man," said my teacher, that Monday at class. "If this keeps up I'll have you reclassified at the next psych-board meeting."

"I'm sorry," I replied.

He looked hard at me. "What sort of block have you got? It must be a very simple, and also a conscious, one."

I winced. "It's conscious, sir; but it's not simple. It's multi-tentacular. In brief, though—it's rockets."

He smiled. "R is for Rocket, eh?"

"I guess that's it, sir."

"We can't let it interfere with your scholastic record, though, young man."

"Do you think I need hypnotic suggestion, sir?"

"No, no." He flipped through a small tab of records with my name blocked on it. I had a funny stone in my stomach, just lying there. He looked at me. "You know, Christopher, you're king-of-the-hill here; head of the class." He closed his eyes and mused over it. "We'll have to see about a lot of other things," he concluded. Then he patted me on the shoulder.

"Well—get on with your work. Nothing to worry about."

He walked away.

I tried to get back to work, but I couldn't. During the rest of the day the teacher kept watching me and looking at my tab-record and chewing his lip. About two in the afternoon he dialed a number on his desk-audio and discussed something with somebody for about five minutes.

I couldn't hear what was said.

But when he set the audio into its cradle, he stared straight at me with the funniest light in his eyes.

It was envy and admiration and pity all in one. It was a little sad and it was much of happiness. It had a lot in it, just in his eyes. The rest of his face said nothing.

It made me feel like a saint and a devil sitting there.

Ralph Priory and I slid home from formula-school together early that afternoon. I told Ralph what had happened and he frowned in the dark way he always frowns.

I began to worry. And between the two of us we doubled and tripled the worry.

"You don't think you'll be sent away, do you, Chris?"

Our monorail car hissed. We stopped at our station. We got out. We walked slow. "I don't know," I said.

"That would be plain dirty," said Ralph.

"Maybe I need a good psychiatric laundering, Ralph. I can't go on flubbing my studies this way."

We stopped outside my house and looked at the sky for a long moment. Ralph said something funny.

"The stars aren't out in the daytime, but we can see 'em, can't we, Chris?"

"Yeah," I said. "Darn rights."

"We'll stick it together, huh, Chris? Blast them, they can't take you away now. We're pals. It wouldn't be fair."

I didn't say anything because there was no room in my throat for anything but a hectagonal lump.

"What's the matter with your eyes?" asked Priory.

"Aw, I looked at the sun too long. Come on inside, Ralph."

We yelled under the shower spray in the bath-cubicle, but our yells weren't especially convincing, even when we turned on the ice-water.

While we were standing in the warm-air dryer, I did a lot of thinking. Literature, I figured, was full of people who fought battles against hard, razor-edged opponents. They pitted brain and muscle against obstacles until they won out or were themselves defeated. But here I was with hardly a sign of any outward conflict. It was all running around in spiked boots inside my head, making cuts and bruises where no one could see them except me and a psychologist. But it was just as bad.

"Ralph," I said, as we dressed, "I got a war on."

"All by yourself?" he asked.

"I can't include you," I said. "Because this is personal. How many times has my mother said, 'Don't eat so much, Chris, your eyes are bigger than your stomach?'"

"A million times."

"*Two* million. Well, paraphrase it, Ralph. Change it to 'Don't *see* so much, Chris, your mind is too big for your body.' I got a war on between a mind that wants things my body can't give it."

Priory nodded quietly. "I see what you mean about its being a personal war. In that case, Christopher, I'm at war, too."

"I knew you were," I said. "Somehow I think the other kids'll grow out of it. But I don't think we will, Ralph. I think we'll keep waiting."

We sat down in the middle of the sunlit upper deck of the house, and started checking over some homework on our formula-pads. Priory couldn't get his. Neither could I. Priory put into words the very thing I didn't dare say out loud.

"Chris, the Astronaut Board *selects*. You can't apply for it. You *wait*."

"I know."

"You wait from the time you're old enough to turn cold in the stomach when you see a Moon rocket, until all the years go by, and every month that passes you hope that one morning a blue Astronaut helicopter will come down out of the sky, land on your lawn, and that a neat-looking engineer will ease out, walk up the rampway briskly, and touch the bell.

"You keep waiting for that helicopter until you're twenty-one. And then, on the last day of your twentieth year you drink and laugh a lot and say what the heck, you didn't really care about it, anyway."

We both just sat there, deep in the middle of his words. We both just sat there. Then:

"I don't want that disappointment, Chris. I'm fifteen, just like you. But if I reach my twenty-first year without an Astronaut ringing the bell where I live at the ortho-station, I—"

"I know," I said. "I know. I've talked to men who've waited, all for nothing. And if it happens that way to us, Ralph, well—we'll get good and drunk together and then go out and take jobs loading cargo on a Europe-bound freighter."

Ralph stiffened and his face went pale. "Loading cargo."

There was a soft, quick step on the ramp and my mother was there. I smiled. "Hi, lady!"

"Hello. Hello, Ralph."

"Hello, Jhene."

She didn't look much older than twenty-five, in spite of having birthed and raised me and worked at the Government Statistics House. She was light and graceful and smiled a lot, and I could see how father must have loved her very much when he was alive. One parent is better than none. Poor Priory now, raised in one of those orthopedical stations. . . .

Jhene walked over and put her hand on Ralph's face. "You look ill," she said. "What's wrong?"

Ralph managed a fairly good smile. "Nothing—at all."

Jhene didn't need prompting. She said, "You can stay here tonight, Priory. We want you. Don't we, Chris?"

"Heck, yes."

"I should get back to the station," said Ralph, rather feebly, I observed. "But since you asked and Chris here needs help on his semantics for tomorrow, I'll stick and help him."

"Very generous," I observed.

"First, though, I've a few errands. I'll take the 'rail and be back in an hour, people."

When Ralph was gone my mother looked at me intently, then brushed my hair back with a nice little move of her fingers.

"Something's happening, Chris."

My heart stopped talking because it didn't want to talk any more for a while. It waited.

I opened my mouth, but Jhene went on:

"Something's up somewhere. I had two calls at work today. One from your teacher. One from—I can't say. I don't *want* to say until things happen—"

My heart started talking again, slow and warm.

"Don't tell me, then, Jhene. Those calls—"

She just looked at me. She took my hand between her two soft warm ones. "You're so young, Chris. You're so awfully young."

I didn't speak.

Her eyes brightened. "You never knew your father. I wish you had. You know what he was, Chris?"

I said, "Yeah. He worked in a Chemistry Lab, deep underground most of the time."

And, my mother added, strangely, "He worked deep under the ground, Chris, and never saw the stars."

My heart yelled in my chest. Yelled loud and hard.

"Oh, Mother. Mother—"

It was the first time in years I had called her mother.

When I woke the next morning there was a lot of sunlight in the room, but the cushion where Priory slept when he stayed over, was vacant. I listened. I didn't hear him splashing in the shower-cube, and the dryer wasn't humming. He was gone.

I found his note pinned on the sliding door.

"See you at formula at noon. Your mother wanted me to do some work for her. She got a call this morning, and said she needed me to help. So long. Priory."

Priory out running errands for Jhene. Strange. A call in the early morning to Jhene. I went back and sat down on the cushion.

While I was sitting there a bunch of the kids yelled down on the lawn-court. "Hey, Chris! You're late!"

I stuck my head out the window. "Be right down!"

"No, Chris."

My mother's voice. It was quiet and it had something funny in it. I turned around. She was standing in the doorway behind me, her face pale, drawn, full of some small pain. "No, Chris," she said again, softly. "Tell them to go on to formula without you—today."

The kids were still making noise downstairs, I guess, but I didn't hear them. I just felt myself and my mother, slim and pale and restrained in my room. Far off, the weather-control vibrators started to hum and throb.

I turned slowly and looked down at the kids. The three of them were looking up, lips parted casually, half-smiling, semantic-tabs in their knotty fingers. "Hey—" one of them said. Sidney, it was.

"Sorry, Sid. Sorry, gang. Go on without me. I can't go to formula today. See you later, huh?"

"Aw, Chris!"

"Sick?"

"No. Just— Just go on without me, gang. I'll see you."

I felt numb. I turned away from their upturned, questioning faces and glanced at the door. Mother wasn't there. She had gone downstairs, quietly. I heard the kids moving off, not quite as boisterously, toward the monorail station.

Instead of using the vac-elevator, I walked slowly downstairs. "Jhene," I said, "where's Ralph?"

Jhene pretended to be interested in combing her long light hair with a vibro-toothed comb. "I sent him off. I didn't want him here this morning."

"Why am I staying home from formula, Jhene?"

"Chris, please don't ask."

Before I could say anything else, there was a sound in the air. It cut through the very soundproofed wall of the house, and hummed in my marrow, quick and high as an arrow of glittering music.

I swallowed. All the fear and uncertainty and doubt went away, instantly.

When I heard that note, I thought of Ralph Priory. *Oh, Ralph, if you could be here now.* I couldn't believe the truth of it. Hearing that note and hearing it with my whole body and soul as well as with my ears.

It came closer, that sound. I was afraid it would go away. But it didn't go away. It lowered its pitch and came down outside the house in great whirling petals of light and shadow and I knew it was a helicopter the color of the sky. It stopped humming, and in the silence my mother tensed forward, dropped the vibro-comb and took in her breath.

In that silence, too, I heard booted footsteps walking up the ramp below. Footsteps that I had waited for a long time. Footsteps I was afraid would never come.

Somebody touched the bell.

And I *knew* who it was.

And all I could think was, Ralph, why in heck did you have to go away now, when all this is happening? Blast it, Ralph, why did you?

The man looked as if he had been born in his uniform. It fitted like a second layer of salt-colored skin, touched here and there with a line, a dot of blue. As simple and perfect a uniform as could be made, but with all the muscled power of the universe behind it.

His name was Trent. He spoke firmly, with a natural round perfection, directly to the subject.

I stood there, and my mother was on the far side of the room, looking like a bewildered little girl. I stood listening.

Out of all the talking I remember some of the snatches:

". . . highest grades, high IQ. Perception A-1, curiosity Triple-A. Enthusiasm necessary to the long, eight-year educational grind. . . ."

"Yes, sir."

". . . talks with your semantics and psychology teachers—"

"Yes, sir."

". . . and don't forget, Mr. Christopher . . ."

Mister Christopher!

". . . and don't forget, Mr. Christopher, nobody is to know you have been selected by the Astronaut Board."

"No one?"

"Your mother and teacher know, naturally. But no other person must know. Is that perfectly understood?"

"Yes, sir."

Trent smiled quietly, standing there with his big hands at his sides. "You want to ask why, don't you? Why you can't tell your friends? I'll explain.

"It's a form of psychological protection. We select about ten thousand young men each year from the earth's billions. Out of that number three thousand wind up, eight years later, as spacemen of one sort or another. The others must return to society. They've flunked out, but there's no reason for everyone to know. They usually flunk out, if they're going to flunk, in the first six months. And it's tough to go back and face your friends and say you couldn't make the grade at the biggest job in the world. So we make it easy to go back.

"But there's still another reason. It's psychological, too. Half the fun of being a kid is being able to lord it over the

other guys, by being superior in some way. We take half
the fun out of Astronaut selection by strictly forbidding you
to tell your pals. Then, we'll know if you wanted to go into
space for frivolous reasons, or for space itself. If you're in it
for personal conceit—you're damned. If you're in it
because you can't help being in it and *have* to be in it—
you're blessed."

He nodded to my mother. "Thank you, Mrs. Christopher."

"Sir," I said. "A question. I have a friend. Ralph Priory.
He lives at an ortho-station—"

Trent nodded. "I can't tell you his rating, of course, but
he's on our list. He's your buddy? You want him along, of
course. I'll check his record. Station-bred, you say? That's not
good. But—we'll see."

"If you would, please, thanks."

"Report to me at the Rocket Station Saturday afternoon at
five, Mr. Christopher. Meantime: silence."

He saluted. He walked off. He went away in the helicopter
into the sky, and Mother was beside me quickly, saying, "Oh,
Chris, Chris," over and over, and we held to each other and
whispered and talked and she said many things, how good
this was going to be for us, but especially for me, how fine,
what an honor it was, like the old old days when men fasted
and took vows and joined churches and stopped up their
tongues and were silent and prayed to be worthy and to live
well as monks and priests of many churches in far places,
and came forth and moved in the world and lived as exam-
ples and taught well. It was no different now, this was a
greater priesthood, in a way, she said, she inferred, she knew,
and I was to be some small part of it, I would not be hers
any more, I would belong to all the worlds, I would be all the
things my father wanted to be and never lived or had a
chance to be. . . .

"Darn rights, darn rights," I murmured. "I will, I promise
I will . . ."

I caught my voice. "Jhene—how—how will we tell Ralph?
What about him?"

"You're going away, that's all, Chris. Tell him that. Very
simply. Tell him no more. He'll understand."

"But, Jhene, *you*—"

She smiled softly. "Yes, I'll be lonely, Chris. But I'll have
my work and I'll have Ralph."

"You mean . . ."

"I'm taking him from the ortho-station. He'll live here, when you're gone. That's what you *wanted* me to say, isn't it, Chris?"

I nodded, all paralyzed and strange inside.

"That's exactly what I wanted you to say."

"He'll be a good son, Chris. *Almost* as good as you."

"He'll be *fine!*"

We told Ralph Priory. How I was going away maybe to school in Europe for a year and how Mother wanted him to come live as her son, now, until such time as I came back. We said it quick and fast, as if it burned our tongues. And when we finished, Ralph came and shook my hand and kissed my mother on the cheek and he said:

"I'll be proud. I'll be very proud."

It was funny, but Ralph didn't even ask any more about why I was going, or where, or how long I would be away. All he would say was, "We had a lot of fun, didn't we?" and let it go at that, as if he didn't dare say any more.

It was Friday night, after a concert at the amphitheater in the center of our public circle, and Priory and Jhene and I came home, laughing, ready to go to bed.

I hadn't packed anything. Priory noted this briefly, and let it go. All of my personal supplies for the next eight years would be supplied by someone else. No need for packing.

My semantics teacher called on the audio, smiling and saying a very brief, pleasant good-bye.

Then, we went to bed, and I kept thinking in the hour before I lolled off, about how this was the last night with Jhene and Ralph. The very last night.

Only a kid of fifteen——me.

And then, in the darkness, just before I went to sleep, Priory twisted softly on his cushion, turned his solemn face to me, and whispered, "Chris?" A pause. "Chris. You still awake?" It was like a faint echo.

"Yes," I said.

"Thinking?"

A pause.

"Yes."

He said, "You're—— You're not *waiting* any more, are you, Chris?"

I knew what he meant. I couldn't answer.

I said, "I'm awfully tired, Ralph."

He twisted back and settled down and said, "That's what

I thought. You're not *waiting* any more. Gosh, but that's good, Chris. That's good."

He reached out and punched me in the arm-muscle, lightly. Then we both went to sleep.

It was Saturday morning. The kids were yelling outside. Their voices filled the seven o'clock fog. I heard Old Man Wickard's ventilator flip open and the zip of his para-gun playfully touching around the kids.

"Shut up!" I heard him cry, but he didn't sound grouchy. It was a regular Saturday game with him. And I heard the kids giggle.

Priory woke up and said, "Shall I tell them, Chris, you're not going with them today?"

"Tell them nothing of the sort." Jhene moved from the door. She bent out the window, her hair all light against a ribbon of fog. "Hi, gang! Ralph and Chris will be right down. Hold gravity!"

"Jhene!" I cried.

She came over to both of us. "You're going to spend your Saturday the way you always spend it—with the gang!"

"I planned on sticking with you, Jhene."

"What sort of holiday would *that* be, now?"

She ran us through our breakfast, kissed us on the cheeks, and forced us out the door into the gang's arms.

"Let's not go out to the Rocket Port today, guys."

"Aw, Chris—why not?"

Their faces did a lot of changes. This was the first time in history I hadn't wanted to go. "You're kidding, Chris."

"Sure he is."

"No, he's not. He means it," said Priory. "And I don't want to go either. We go *every* Saturday. It gets tiresome. We can go next week instead."

"Aw . . ."

They didn't like it, but they didn't go off by themselves. It was no fun, they said, without us.

"What the heck—we'll go next week."

"Sure we will. What do you want to do, Chris?"

I told them.

We spent the morning playing Kick the Can and some games we'd given up a long time ago, and we hiked out along some old rusty and abandoned railroad tracks and walked in a small woods outside town and photographed some birds and went swimming raw, and all the time I kept thinking—this is the last day.

We did everything we had ever done before on Saturday. All the silly crazy things, and nobody knew I was going away except Ralph, and five o'clock kept getting nearer and nearer.

At four, I said good-bye to the kids.

"Leaving so soon, Chris? What about tonight?"

"Call for me at eight," I said. "We'll go see the new Sally Gibberts picture!"

"Swell."

"Cut gravity!"

And Ralph and I went home.

Mother wasn't there, but she had left part of herself, her smile and her voice and her words on a spool of audio-film on my bed. I inserted it in the viewer and threw the picture on the wall. Soft yellow hair, her white face and her quiet words:

"I hate good-byes, Chris. I've gone to the laboratory to do some extra work. Good luck. All of my love. When I see you again—you'll be a man."

That was all.

Priory waited outside while I saw it over four times. "I hate good-byes, Chris. I've gone . . . work. . . . luck. All . . . my love. . . ."

I had made a film-spool myself the night before. I spotted it in the viewer and left it there. It only said good-bye.

Priory walked halfway with me. I wouldn't let him get on the Rocket Port monorail with me. I just shook his hand, tight, and said, "It was fun today, Ralph."

"Yeah. Well, see you next Saturday, huh, Chris?"

"I wish I could say yes."

"Say yes anyway. Next Saturday—the woods, the gang, the rockets, and Old Man Wickard and his trusty para-gun."

We laughed. "Sure. Next Saturday, early. Take— Take care of *our* mother, will you, Priory?"

"That's a silly question, you nut," he said.

"It is, isn't it?"

He swallowed. "Chris."

"Yeah?"

"I'll be waiting. Just like you waited and don't have to wait any more. I'll *wait*."

"Maybe it won't be long, Priory. I hope not."

I jabbed him, once, in the arm. He jabbed back.

The monorail door sealed. The car hurled itself away, and Priory was left behind.

I stepped out at the Port. It was a five-hundred-yard walk

down to the Administration building. It took me ten years to walk it.

"Next time I see you you'll be a man—"

"Don't tell anybody—"

"I'll wait, Chris—"

It was all choked in my heart and it wouldn't go away and it swam around in my eyes.

I thought about my dreams. The Moon Rocket. It won't be part of me, part of my *dream* any longer. I'll be part of *it*.

I felt small there, walking, walking, walking.

The afternoon rocket to London was just taking off as I went down the ramp to the office. It shivered the ground and it shivered and thrilled my heart.

I was beginning to grow up awfully fast.

I stood watching the rocket until someone snapped their heels, cracked me a quick salute.

I was numb.

"C. M. Christopher?"

"Yes, sir. Reporting, sir."

"This way, Christopher. Through that gate."

Through that gate and beyond *the* fence . . .

This fence where we had pressed our faces and felt the wind turn warm and held to the fence and forgot who we were or where we came from but dreamed of who we might be and where we might go . . .

This fence where had stood the boys who liked being boys who lived in a town and liked the town and fairly liked school and liked football and liked their fathers and mothers . . .

The boys who some time every hour of every day of every week thought on fire and stars and the fence beyond which they waited. . . . The boys who liked the rockets *more*.

Mother, Ralph, I'll see you. I'll be back.

Mother!

Ralph!

And, walking, I went beyond the fence.

THE END OF THE BEGINNING

He stopped the lawn mower in the middle of the yard, because he felt that the sun at just that moment had gone down and the stars come out. The fresh-cut grass that had showered his face and body died softly away. Yes, the stars were there, faint at first, but brightening in the clear desert sky. He heard the porch screen door tap shut and felt his wife watching him as he watched the night.

"Almost time," she said.

He nodded; he did not have to check his watch. In the passing moments he felt very old, then very young, very cold, then very warm, now this, now that. Suddenly he was miles away. He was his own son talking steadily, moving briskly to cover his pounding heart and the resurgent panics as he felt himself slip into fresh uniform, check food supplies, oxygen flasks, pressure helmet, space-suiting, and turn as every man on earth tonight turned, to gaze at the swiftly filling sky.

Then, quickly, he was back, once more the father of the son, hands gripped to the lawn-mower handle. His wife called, "Come sit on the porch."

"I've got to keep busy!"

She came down the steps and across the lawn. "Don't worry about Robert; he'll be all right."

"But it's all so new," he heard himself say. "It's never been done before. Think of it—a manned rocket going up tonight to build the first space station. Good Lord, it can't be done, it doesn't exist, there's no rocket, no proving ground, no takeoff time, no technicians. For that matter, I don't even have a son named Bob. The whole thing's too much for me!"

Copyright 1956 by Ray Bradbury

16

"Then what are you doing out here, staring?"

He shook his head. "Well, late this morning, walking to the office, I heard someone laugh out loud. It shocked me, so I froze in the middle of the street. It was *me,* laughing! Why? Because finally I really *knew* what Bob was going to do tonight; at last I *believed* it. Holy is a word I never use, but that's how I felt stranded in all that traffic. Then, middle of the afternoon I caught myself humming. You know the song. 'A wheel in a wheel. Way in the middle of the air.' I laughed again. The space station, of course, I thought. The big wheel with hollow spokes where Bob'll live six or eight months, then get on back. Walking home, I remembered more of the song. 'Little wheel run by faith, Big wheel run by the grace of God.' I wanted to jump, yell, and flame-out myself!"

His wife touched his arm. "If we stay out here, let's at least be comfortable."

They placed two wicker rockers in the center of the lawn and sat quietly as the stars dissolved out of darkness in pale crushings of rock salt strewn from horizon to horizon.

"Why," said his wife, at last, "it's like waiting for the fire-works at Sisley Field every year."

"Bigger crowd tonight . . ."

"I keep thinking—a billion people watching the sky right now, their mouths all open at the same time."

They waited, feeling the earth move under their chairs.

"What time is it now?"

"Eleven minutes to eight."

"You're always right; there must be a clock in your head."

"I can't be wrong, tonight. I'll be able to tell you one second before they blast off. Look! The ten-minute warning!"

On the western sky they saw four crimson flares open out, float shimmering down the wind above the desert, then sink silently to the extinguishing earth.

In the new darkness the husband and wife did not rock in their chairs.

After a while he said, "Eight minutes." A pause. "Seven minutes." What seemed a much longer pause. "Six . . ."

His wife, her head back, studied the stars immediately above her and murmured, "Why?" She closed her eyes. "Why the rockets, why tonight? Why all this? I'd like to know."

He examined her face, pale in the vast powdering light of

the Milky Way. He felt the stirring of an answer, but let
his wife continue.

"I mean it's not that old thing again, is it, when people
asked why men climbed Mt. Everest and they said, 'Because
it's there.' I never understood. That was no answer to me."

Five minutes, he thought. Time ticking . . . his wristwatch
. . . a wheel in a wheel . . . little wheel run by . . . big
wheel run by . . . way in the middle of . . . four minutes!
. . . The men snug in the rocket by now, the hive, the control board flickering with light. . . .

His lips moved.

"All I know is it's really the end of the beginning. The
Stone Age, Bronze Age, Iron Age; from now on we'll lump
all those together under one big name for when we walked
on Earth and heard the birds at morning and cried with
envy. Maybe we'll call it the Earth Age, or maybe the Age
of Gravity. Millions of years we fought gravity. When we
were amoebas and fish we struggled to get out of the sea
without gravity crushing us. Once safe on the shore we
fought to stand upright without gravity breaking our new
invention, the spine, tried to walk without stumbling, run
without falling. A billion years Gravity kept us home, mocked
us with wind and clouds, cabbage moths and locusts. That's
what's so really big about tonight . . . it's the end of old man
Gravity and the age we'll remember him by, for once and
all. I don't know where they'll divide the ages, at the Per-
sians, who dreamt of flying carpets, or the Chinese, who
all unknowing celebrated birthdays and New Years with
strung ladyfingers and high skyrockets, or some minute, some
incredible second in the next hour. But we're in at the end
of a billion years trying, the end of something long and to
us humans, anyway, honorable."

Three minutes . . . two minutes fifty-nine seconds . . . two
minutes fifty-eight seconds . . .

"But," said his wife, "I still don't know why."

Two minutes, he thought. *Ready? Ready? Ready?* The far
radio voice calling. *Ready! Ready! Ready!* The quick, faint
replies from the humming rocket. *Check! Check! Check!*

Tonight, he thought, even if we fail with this first, we'll
send a second and a third ship and move on out to all the
planets and later, all the stars. We'll just keep going until
the big words like immortal and forever take on meaning.
Big words, yes, that's what we want. Continuity. Since our
tongues first moved in our mouths we've asked, What does it

all mean? No other question made sense, with death breathing
down our necks. But just let us settle in on ten thousand
worlds spinning around ten thousand alien suns and the
question will fade away. Man will be endless and infinite,
even as space is endless and infinite. Man will go on, as space
goes on, forever. Individuals will die as always, but our
history will reach as far as we'll ever need to see into the
future, and with the knowledge of our survival for all time
to come, we'll know security and thus the answer we've
always searched for. Gifted with life, the least we can do
is preserve and pass on the gift to infinity. That's a goal
worth shooting for.

The wicker chairs whispered ever so softly on the grass.
One minute.

"One minute," he said aloud.

"Oh!" His wife moved suddenly to seize his hands. "I
hope that Bob . . ."

"He'll be all right!"

"Oh, God, take care . . ."

Thirty seconds.

"Watch now."

Fifteen, ten, five . . .

"Watch!"

Four, three, two, one.

"There! There! Oh, there, there!"

They both cried out. They both stood. The chairs toppled
back, fell flat on the lawn. The man and his wife swayed,
their hands struggled to find each other, grip, hold. They
saw the brightening color in the sky and, ten seconds later,
the great uprising comet burn the air, put out the stars, and
rush away in fire flight to become another star in the returning profusion of the Milky Way. The man and wife held
each other as if they had stumbled on the rim of an incredible cliff that faced an abyss so deep and dark there
seemed no end to it. Staring up, they heard themselves
sobbing and crying. Only after a long time were they able
to speak.

"It got away, it did, *didn't* it?"

"Yes . . ."

"It's all right, isn't it?"

"Yes . . . yes . . ."

"It didn't fall back . . . ?"

"No, no, it's all right, Bob's all right, it's all right."

They stood away from each other at last.

He touched his face with his hand and looked at his wet fingers. "I'll be," he said, "I'll be. . . ."

They waited another five and then ten minutes until the darkness in their heads, the retina, ached with a million specks of fiery salt. Then they had to close their eyes.

"Well," she said, "now let's go in."

He could not move. Only his hand reached a long way out by itself to find the lawn-mower handle. He saw what his hand had done and said, "There's just a little more to do. . . ."

"But you can't see."

"Well enough," he said. "I must finish this. Then we'll sit on the porch awhile before we turn in."

He helped her put the chairs on the porch and sat her down and then walked back out to put his hands on the guide bar of the lawn mower. The lawn mower. A wheel in a wheel. A simple machine which you held in your hands, which you sent on ahead with a rush and a clatter while you walked behind with your quiet philosophy. Racket, followed by warm silence. Whirling wheel, then soft footfall of thought.

I'm a billion years old, he told himself; I'm one minute old. I'm one inch, no, ten thousand *miles,* tall. I look down and can't see my feet they're so far off and gone away below.

He moved the lawn mower. The grass showering up fell softly around him; he relished and savored it and felt that he was all mankind bathing at last in the fresh waters of the fountain of youth.

Thus bathed, he remembered the song again about the wheels and the faith and the grace of God being way up there in the middle of the sky where that single star, among a million motionless stars, dared to move and keep on moving.

Then he finished cutting the grass.

THE FOG HORN

Out there in the cold water, far from land, we waited every night for the coming of the fog, and it came, and we oiled the brass machinery and lit the fog light up in the stone tower. Feeling like two birds in the gray sky, McDunn and I sent the light touching out, red, then white, then red again, to eye the lonely ships. And if they did not see our light, then there was always our Voice, the great deep cry of our Fog Horn shuddering through the rags of mist to startle the gulls away like decks of scattered cards and make the waves turn high and foam.

"It's a lonely life, but you're used to it now, aren't you?" asked McDunn.

"Yes," I said. "You're a good talker, thank the Lord."

"Well, it's your turn on land tomorrow," he said, smiling, "to dance the ladies and drink gin."

"What do you think, McDunn, when I leave you out here alone?"

"On the mysteries of the sea." McDunn lit his pipe. It was a quarter past seven of a cold November evening, the heat on, the light switching its tail in two hundred directions, the Fog Horn bumbling in the high throat of the tower. There wasn't a town for a hundred miles down the coast, just a road which came lonely through dead country to the sea, with few cars on it, a stretch of two miles of cold water out to our rock, and rare few ships.

"The mysteries of the sea," said McDunn thoughtfully. "You know, the ocean's the most confounded big snowflake ever? It rolls and swells a thousand shapes and colors, no two alike. Strange. One night, years ago, I was here alone, when all of the fish of the sea surfaced out there. Something

Copyright 1951 by The Curtis Publishing Company.

made them swim in and lie in the bay, sort of trembling and staring up at the tower light going red, white, red, white across them so I could see their funny eyes. I turned cold. They were like a big peacock's tail, moving out there until midnight. Then, without so much as a sound, they slipped away, the million of them was gone. I kind of think maybe, in some sort of way, they came all those miles to worship. Strange. But think how the tower must look to them, standing seventy feet above the water, the God-light flashing out from it, and the tower declaring itself with a monster voice. They never came back, those fish, but don't you think for a while they thought they were in the Presence?"

I shivered. I looked out at the long gray lawn of the sea stretching away into nothing and nowhere.

"Oh, the sea's full." McDunn puffed his pipe nervously, blinking. He had been nervous all day and hadn't said why. "For all our engines and so-called submarines, it'll be ten thousand centuries before we set foot on the real bottom of the sunken lands, in the fairy kingdoms there, and know *real* terror. Think of it, it's still the year 300,000 Before Christ down under there. While we've paraded around with trumpets, lopping off each other's countries and heads, they have been living beneath the sea twelve miles deep and cold in a time as old as the beard of a comet."

"Yes, it's an old world."

"Come on. I got something special I been saving up to tell you."

We ascended the eighty steps, talking and taking our time. At the top, McDunn switched off the room lights so there'd be no reflection in the plate glass. The great eye of the light was humming, turning easily in its oiled socket. The Fog Horn was blowing steadily, once every fifteen seconds.

"Sounds like an animal, don't it?" McDunn nodded to himself. "A big lonely animal crying in the night. Sitting here on the edge of ten billion years called out to the Deeps, I'm here, I'm here, I'm here. And the Deeps do answer, yes, they do. You been here now for three months, Johnny, so I better prepare you. About this time of year," he said, studying the murk and fog, "something comes to visit the lighthouse."

"The swarms of fish like you said?"

"No, this is something else. I've put off telling you because you might think I'm daft. But tonight's the latest I can put it off for if my calendar's marked right from last year, to-night's the night it comes. I won't go into detail, you'll have to see it yourself. Just sit down there. If you want, tomorrow you can pack your duffel and take the motorboat in to land and get your car parked there at the dinghy pier on the cape and drive on back to some little inland town and keep your lights burning nights. I won't question or blame you. It's happened three years now, and this is the only time anyone's been here with me to verify it. You wait and watch."

Half an hour passed with only a few whispers between us. When we grew tired waiting, McDunn began describing some of his ideas to me. He had some theories about the Fog Horn itself.

"One day many years ago a man walked along and stood in the sound of the ocean on a cold sunless shore and said, 'We need a voice to call across the water, to warn ships; I'll make one. I'll make a voice like all of time and all of that fog that ever was; I'll make a voice that is like an empty bed beside you all night long, and like an empty house when you open the door, and like trees in autumn with no leaves. A sound like the birds flying south, crying, and a sound like November wind and the sea on the hard, cold shore. I'll make a sound that's so alone that no one can miss it, that whoever hears it will weep in their souls, and hearths will seem warmer, and being inside will seem better to all who hear it in the distant towns. I'll make me a sound and an apparatus and they'll call it a Fog Horn and whoever hears it will know the sadness of eternity and the briefness of life."

The Fog Horn blew.

"I made up that story," said McDunn quietly, "to try to explain why this thing keeps coming back to the lighthouse every year. The Fog Horn calls it, I think, and it comes. . . ."

"But—" I said.

"Sssst!" said McDunn. "There!" He nodded out to the Deeps.

Something was swimming toward the lighthouse tower.

It was a cold night, as I have said; the high tower was cold, the light coming and going, and the Fog Horn calling and calling through the raveling mist. You couldn't see far and you couldn't see plain, but there was the deep sea moving on its way about the night earth, flat and quiet, the color of gray mud, and here were the two of us alone in the high tower, and there, far out at first, was a ripple, followed by a wave, a rising, a bubble, a bit of froth. And then, from the surface of the cold sea came a head, a large head, dark-colored, with immense eyes, and then a neck. And then—not a body—but more neck and more! The head rose a full forty feet above the water on a slender and beautiful dark neck. Only then did the body, like a little island of black coral and shells and crayfish, drip up from the subterranean. There was a flicker of tail. In all, from head to tip of tail, I estimated the monster at ninety or a hundred feet.

I don't know what I said. I said something.

"Steady, boy, steady," whispered McDunn.

"It's impossible!" I said.

"No, Johnny, *we're* impossible. *It's* like it always was ten million years ago. *It* hasn't changed. It's *us* and the land that've changed, become impossible. *Us!*"

It swam slowly and with a great dark majesty out in the icy waters, far away. The fog came and went about it, momentarily erasing its shape. One of the monster eyes caught and held and flashed back our immense light, red, white, red, white, like a disk held high and sending a message in primeval code. It was as silent as the fog through which it swam.

"It's a dinosaur of some sort!" I crouched down, holding to the stair rail.

"Yes, one of the tribe."

"But they died out!"

"No, only hid away in the Deeps. Deep, deep down in the deepest Deeps. Isn't *that* a word now, Johnny, a real word, it says so much: the Deeps. There's all the coldness and darkness and deepness in the world in a word like that."

"What'll we do?"

"Do? We got our job, we can't leave. Besides, we're safer here than in any boat trying to get to land. That thing's as big as a destroyer and almost as swift."

"But here, why does it come *here?*"

The next moment I had my answer.

The Fog Horn blew.

And the monster answered.

A cry came across a million years of water and mist. A cry so anguished and alone that it shuddered in my head and my body. The monster cried out at the tower. The Fog Horn blew. The monster roared again. The Fog Horn blew. The monster opened its great toothed mouth and the sound that came from it was the sound of the Fog Horn itself. Lonely and vast and far away. The sound of isolation, a viewless sea, a cold night, apartness. That was the sound.

"Now," whispered McDunn, "do you know why it comes here?"

I nodded.

"All year long, Johnny, that poor monster there lying far out, a thousand miles at sea, and twenty miles deep maybe, biding its time, perhaps it's a million years old, this one creature. Think of it, waiting a million years; could *you* wait that long? Maybe it's the last of its kind. I sort of think that's true. Anyway, here come men on land and build this lighthouse, five years ago. And set up their Fog Horn and sound it and sound it out toward the place where you bury yourself in sleep and sea memories of a world where there were thousands like yourself, but now you're alone, all alone in a world not made for you, a world where you have to hide.

"But the sound of the Fog Horn comes and goes, comes and goes, and you stir from the muddy bottom of the Deeps, and your eyes open like the lenses of two-foot cameras and you move, slow, slow, for you have the ocean sea on your shoulders, heavy. But that Fog Horn comes through a thousand miles of water, faint and familiar, and the furnace in your belly stokes up, and you begin to rise, slow, slow. You feed yourself on great slakes of cod and minnow, on rivers of jellyfish, and you rise slow through the autumn months, through September when the fogs started, through October with more fog and the horn still calling you on, and then, late in November, after pressurizing yourself day by day, a few feet higher every hour, you are near the surface and still alive. You've got to go slow; if you surfaced all at once you'd explode. So it takes you all of three months to surface, and then a number of days to swim through the cold waters to the lighthouse. And there you are, out there, in the night, Johnny, the biggest damn monster in creation. And here's the lighthouse calling to you, with a long neck like your neck sticking way up out of the water, and a body like your body, and, most important of all, a voice like your voice. Do you understand now, Johnny, do you understand?"

The Fog Horn blew.

The monster answered.

I saw it all, I knew it all—the million years of waiting alone, for someone to come back who never came back. The million years of isolation at the bottom of the sea, the insanity of time there, while the skies cleared of reptile-birds, the

swamps dried on the continental lands, the sloths and saber-
tooths had their day and sank in tar pits, and men ran like
white ants upon the hills.

The Fog Horn blew.

"Last year," said McDunn, "that creature swam round and
round, round and round, all night. Not coming too near,
puzzled, I'd say. Afraid, maybe. And a bit angry after coming
all this way. But the next day, unexpectedly, the fog lifted,
the sun came out fresh, the sky was as blue as a painting.
And the monster swam off away from the heat and the silence and didn't come back. I suppose it's been brooding on it
for a year now, thinking it over from every which way."

The monster was only a hundred yards off now, it and the
Fog Horn crying at each other. As the lights hit them, the
monster's eyes were fire and ice, fire and ice.

"That's life for you," said McDunn. "Someone always waiting for someone who never comes home. Always someone
loving some thing more than that thing loves them. And after
a while you want to destroy whatever that thing is, so it can't
hurt you no more."

The monster was rushing at the lighthouse.

The Fog Horn blew.

"Let's see what happens," said McDunn.

He switched the Fog Horn off.

The ensuing minute of silence was so intense that we
could hear our hearts pounding in the glassed area of the
tower, could hear the slow greased turn of the light.

The monster stopped and froze. Its great lantern eyes
blinked. Its mouth gaped. It gave a sort of rumble, like a
volcano. It twitched its head this way and that, as if to seek
the sounds now dwindled off into the fog. It peered at the
lighthouse. It rumbled again. Then its eyes caught fire. It
reared up, threshed the water, and rushed at the tower, its
eyes filled with angry torment.

"McDunn!" I cried. "Switch on the horn!"

McDunn fumbled with the switch. But even as he flicked
it on, the monster was rearing up. I had a glimpse of its
gigantic paws, fishskin glittering in webs between the finger-
like projections, clawing at the tower. The huge eyes on the
right side of its anguished head glittered before me like a
caldron into which I might drop, screaming. The tower shook.
The Fog Horn cried; the monster cried. It seized the tower
and gnashed at the glass, which shattered in upon us.

McDunn seized my arm. "Downstairs!"

The tower rocked, trembled, and started to give. The Fog Horn and the monster roared. We stumbled and half fell down the stairs. "Quick!"

We reached the bottom as the tower buckled down toward us. We ducked under the stairs into the small stone cellar. There were a thousand concussions as the rocks rained down; the Fog Horn stopped abruptly. The monster crashed upon the tower. The tower fell. We knelt together, McDunn and I, holding tight, while our world exploded.

Then it was over, and there was nothing but darkness and the wash of the sea on the raw stones.

That and the other sound.

"Listen," said McDunn quietly. "Listen."

We waited a moment. And then I began to hear it. First a great vacuumed sucking of air, and then the lament, the bewilderment, the loneliness of the great monster, folded over and upon us, above us, so that the sickening reek of its body filled the air, a stone's thickness away from our cellar. The monster gasped and cried. The tower was gone. The light was gone. The thing that had called to it across a million years was gone. And the monster was opening its mouth and sending out great sounds. The sounds of a Fog Horn, again and again. And ships far at sea, not finding the light, not seeing anything, but passing and hearing late that night, must've thought: There it is, the lonely sound, the Lonesome Bay horn. All's well. We've rounded the cape.

And so it went for the rest of that night.

The sun was hot and yellow the next afternoon when the rescuers came out to dig us from our stoned-under cellar.

"It fell apart, is all," said Mr. McDunn gravely. "We had a few bad knocks from the waves and it just crumbled." He pinched my arm.

There was nothing to see. The ocean was calm, the sky blue. The only thing was a great algaic stink from the green matter that covered the fallen tower stones and the shore rocks. Flies buzzed about. The ocean washed empty on the shore.

The next year they built a new lighthouse, but by that time I had a job in the little town and a wife and a good small warm house that glowed yellow on autumn nights, the doors locked, the chimney puffing smoke. As for McDunn, he was master of the night lighthouse, built to his own specifications, out of still-reinforced concrete. "Just in case," he said.

The new lighthouse was ready in November. I drove down alone one evening late and parked my car and looked across the gray waters and listened to the new horn sounding, once, twice, three, four times a minute far out there, by itself.

The monster?

It never came back.

"It's gone away," said McDunn. "It's gone back to the Deeps. It's learned you can't love anything too much in this world. It's gone into the deepest Deeps to wait another million years. Ah, the poor thing! Waiting out there, and waiting out there, while man comes and goes on this pitiful little planet. Waiting and waiting."

I sat in my car, listening. I couldn't see the lighthouse or the light standing out in Lonesome Bay. I could only hear the Horn, the Horn, the Horn. It sounded like the monster calling.

I sat there wishing there was something I could say.

THE ROCKET

Many nights Fiorello Bodoni would awaken to hear the rockets sighing in the dark sky. He would tiptoe from bed, certain that his kind wife was dreaming, to let himself out into the night air. For a few moments he would be free of the smells of old food in the small house by the river. For a silent moment he would let his heart soar alone into space, following the rockets.

Now, this very night, he stood half naked in the darkness, watching the fire fountains murmuring in the air. The rockets on their long wild way to Mars and Saturn and Venus!

"Well, well, Bodoni."

Bodoni started.

On a milk crate, by the silent river, sat an old man who also watched the rockets through the midnight hush.

"Oh, it's you, Bramante!"

"Do you come out every night, Bodoni?"

"Only for the air."

"So? I prefer the rockets myself," said old Bramante. "I was a boy when they started. Eighty years ago, and I've never been on one yet."

"I will ride up in one someday," said Bodoni.

"Fool!" cried Bramante. "You'll never go. This is a rich man's world." He shook his gray head, remembering. "When I was young they wrote it in fiery letters: THE WORLD OF THE FUTURE! Science, Comfort, and New Things for All! Ha! Eighty years. The Future becomes Now! Do *we* fly rockets? No! We live in shacks like our ancestors before us."

"Perhaps my *sons*—" said Bodoni.

Copyright 1950 by Fictioneers, Inc.

"No, nor *their* sons!" the old man shouted. "It's the rich who have dreams and rockets!"

Bodoni hesitated. "Old man, I've saved three thousand dollars. It took me six years to save it. For my business, to invest in machinery. But every night for a month now I've been awake. I hear the rockets. I think. And tonight I've made up my mind. One of us will fly to Mars!" His eyes were shining and dark.

"Idiot," snapped Bramante. "How will you choose? Who will go? If you go, your wife will hate you, for you will be just a bit nearer God, in space. When you tell your amazing trip to her, over the years, won't bitterness gnaw at her?"

"No, no!"

"Yes! And your children? Will their lives be filled with the memory of Papa, who flew to Mars while they stayed here? What a senseless task you will set your boys. They will think of the rocket all their lives. They will lie awake. They will be sick with wanting it. Just as you are sick now. They will want to die if they cannot go. Don't set that goal, I warn you. Let them be content with being poor. Turn their eyes down to their hands and to your junkyard, not up to the stars."

"But—"

"Suppose your wife went? How would you feel, knowing she had *seen* and you had not? She would become holy. You would think of throwing her in the river. No, Bodoni, buy a new wrecking machine, which you need, and pull your dreams apart with it, and smash them to pieces."

The old man subsided, gazing at the river in which, drowned, images of rockets burned down the sky.

"Good night," said Bodoni.

"Sleep well," said the other.

When the toast jumped from its silver box, Bodoni almost screamed. The night had been sleepless. Among his nervous children, beside his mountainous wife, Bodoni had twisted and stared at nothing. Bramante was right. Better to invest the money. Why save it when only one of the family could ride the rocket, while the others remained to melt in frustration?

"Fiorello, eat your toast," said his wife, Maria.

"My throat is shriveled," said Bodoni.

The children rushed in, the three boys fighting over a toy rocket, the two girls carrying dolls which duplicated the inhabitants of Mars, Venus, and Neptune, green mannequins with three yellow eyes and twelve fingers.

"I saw the Venus rocket!" cried Paolo.

"It took off, *whoosh!*" hissed Antonello.

"Children!" shouted Bodoni, hands to his ears.

They stared at him. He seldom shouted.

Bodoni arose. "Listen, all of you," he said. "I have enough money to take one of us on the Mars rocket."

Everyone yelled.

"You understand?" he asked. "Only *one* of us. Who?"

"Me, me, me!" cried the children.

"You," said Maria.

"You," said Bodoni to her.

They all fell silent.

The children reconsidered. "Let Lorenzo go—he's oldest."

"Let Miriamne go—she's a girl!"

"Think what you would see," said Bodoni's wife to him. But her eyes were strange. Her voice shook. "The meteors, like fish. The universe. The Moon. Someone should go who could tell it well on returning. You have a way with words."

"Nonsense. So have you," he objected.

Everyone trembled.

"Here," said Bodoni unhappily. From a broom he broke straws of various lengths. "The short straw wins." He held out his tight fist. "Choose."

Solemnly each took his turn.

"Long straw."

"Long straw."

Another.

"Long straw."

The children finished. The room was quiet.

Two straws remained. Bodoni felt his heart ache in him. "Now," he whispered. "Maria."

She drew.

"The short straw," she said.

"Ah," sighed Lorenzo, half happy, half sad. "Mama goes to Mars."

Bodoni tried to smile. "Congratulations. I will buy your ticket today."

"Wait, Fiorello—"

"You can leave next week," he murmured.

She saw the sad eyes of her children upon her, with the smiles beneath their straight, large noses. She returned the straw slowly to her husband. "I cannot go to Mars.

"But why not?"

"I will be busy with another child."

"What!"

She would not look at him. "It wouldn't do for me to travel in my condition."

He took her elbow. "Is this the truth?"

"Draw again. Start over."

"Why didn't you tell me before?" he said incredulously.

"I didn't remember."

"Maria, Maria," he whispered, patting her face. He turned to the children. "Draw again."

Paolo immediately drew the short straw.

"I go to Mars!" He danced wildly. "Thank you, Father!" The other children edged away. "That's swell, Paolo."

Paolo stopped smiling to examine his parents and his brothers and sisters. "I *can* go, can't I?" he asked uncertainly.

"Yes."

"And you'll *like* me when I come back?"

"Of course."

Paolo studied the precious broomstraw on his trembling hand and shook his head. He threw it away. "I forgot. School starts. I can't go. Draw again."

But no one would draw. A full sadness lay on them.

"None of us will go," said Lorenzo.

"That's best," said Maria.

"Bramante was right," said Bodoni.

With his breakfast curdled within him, Fiorello Bodoni worked in his junkyard, ripping metal, melting it, pouring out usable ingots. His equipment flaked apart; competition had kept him on the insane edge of poverty for twenty years.

It was a very bad morning.

In the afternoon a man entered the junkyard and called up to Bodoni on his wrecking machine. "Hey, Bodoni, I got some metal for you!"

"What is it, Mr. Mathews?" asked Bodoni, listlessly.

"A rocket ship. What's wrong? Don't you want it?"

"Yes, yes!" He seized the man's arm, and stopped, bewildered.

"Of course," said Mathews, "it's only a mockup. *You* know. When they plan a rocket they build a full-scale model first, of aluminum. You might make a small profit boiling her down. Let you have her for two thousand—"

Bodoni dropped his hand. "I haven't the money."

"Sorry. Thought I'd help you. Last time we talked you said how everyone outbid you on junk. Thought I'd slip this to you on the q.t. Well—"

"I need new equipment. I saved money for that."

"I understand."

"If I bought your rocket, I wouldn't even be able to melt it down. My aluminum furnace broke down last week—"

"Sure."

"I couldn't possibly use the rocket if I bought it from you."

"I know."

Bodoni blinked and shut his eyes. He opened them and looked at Mr. Mathews. "But I am a great fool. I will take my money from the bank and give it to you."

"But if you can't melt the rocket down—"

"Deliver it," said Bodoni.

"All right, if you say so. Tonight?"

"Tonight," said Bodoni, "would be fine. Yes, I would like to have a rocket ship tonight."

There was a moon. The rocket was white and big in the junkyard. It held the whiteness of the moon and the blueness of the stars. Bodoni looked at it and loved all of it. He wanted to pet it and lie against it, pressing it with his cheek, telling it all the secret wants of his heart.

He stared up at it. "You are all mine," he said. "Even if you never move or spit fire, and just sit there and rust for fifty years, you are mine."

The rocket smelled of time and distance. It was like walking into a clock. It was finished with Swiss delicacy. One might wear it on one's watch fob. "I might even sleep here tonight," Bodoni whispered excitedly.

He sat in the pilot's seat.

He touched a lever.

He hummed in his shut mouth, his eyes closed.

The humming grew louder, louder, higher, higher, wilder, stranger, more exhilarating, trembling in him and leaning him forward and pulling him and the ship in a roaring silence and in a kind of metal screaming, while his fists flew over the controls, and his shut eyes quivered, and the sound grew and grew until it was a fire, a strength, a lifting and a pushing of power that threatened to tear him in half. He gasped. He hummed again and again, and did not stop, for it could not be stopped, it could only go on, his eyes tighter, his heart furious. "Taking off!" he screamed. *The jolting concussion! The thunder!* "The Moon!" he cried, eyes blind, tight. "The meteors!" *The silent rush in volcanic light.* "Mars. Oh, Yes! Mars! Mars!"

He fell back, exhausted and panting. His shaking hands came loose of the controls and his head tilted wildly. He sat for a long time, breathing out and in, his heart slowing.

Slowly, slowly, he opened his eyes.

The junkyard was still there.

He sat motionless. He looked at the heaped piles of metal for a minute, his eyes never leaving them. Then, leaping up, he kicked the levers. "Take off, blast you!"

The ship was silent.

"I'll show you!" he cried.

Out in the night air, stumbling, he started the fierce motor of his terrible wrecking machine and advanced upon the rocket. He maneuvered the massive weights into the moon-lit sky. He readied his trembling hands to plunge the weights, to smash, to rip apart this insolently false dream, this silly thing for which he had paid his money, which would not move, which would not do his bidding. "I'll teach you!" he shouted.

But his hand stayed.

The silver rocket lay in the light of the moon. And beyond the rocket stood the yellow lights of his home, a block away, burning warmly. He heard the family radio playing some distant music. He sat for half an hour considering the rocket and the house lights, and his eyes narrowed and grew wide. He stepped down from the wrecking machine and began to walk, and as he walked he began to laugh, and when he reached the back door of his house he took a deep breath and called, "Maria, Maria, start packing. We're going to Mars!"

"Oh!"

"Ah!"

"I can't *believe* it!"

"You will, you will."

The children balanced in the windy yard, under the glowing rocket, not touching it yet. They started to cry.

Maria looked at her husband. "What have you done?" she said. "Taken our money for this? It will never fly."

"It will fly," he said, looking at it.

"Rocket ships cost millions. Have you millions?"

"It will fly," he repeated steadily. "Now, go to the house, all of you. I have phone calls to make, work to do. Tomorrow we leave! Tell no one, understand? It is a secret."

The children edged off from the rocket, stumbling. He saw their small, feverish faces in the house windows, far away.

Maria had not moved. "You have ruined us," she said. "Our money used for this—this thing. When it should have been spent on equipment."

"You will see," he said.

Without a word she turned away.

"God help me," he whispered, and started to work.

Through the midnight hours trucks arrived, packages were delivered, and Bodoni, smiling, exhausted his bank account. With blowtorch and metal stripping he assaulted the rocket, added, took away, worked fiery magics and secret insults upon it. He bolted nine ancient automobile motors into the rocket's empty engine room. Then he welded the engine room shut, so none could see his hidden labor.

At dawn he entered the kitchen. "Maria," he said, "I'm ready for breakfast."

She would not speak to him.

At sunset he called to the children. "We're ready! Come on!" The house was silent.

"I've locked them in the closet," said Maria.

"What do you mean?" he demanded.

"You'll be killed in that rocket," she said. "What kind of rocket can you buy for two thousand dollars? A bad one!"

"Listen to me, Maria."

"It will blow up. Anyway, you are no pilot."

"Nevertheless, I can fly *this* ship. I have fixed it."

"You have gone mad," she said.

"Where is the key to the closet?"

"I have it here."

He put out his hand. "Give it to me."

She handed it to him. "You will kill them."

"No, no."

"Yes, you will. I *feel* it."

He stood before her. "You won't come along?"

"I'll stay here," she said.

"You will understand; you will see then," he said, and smiled. He unlocked the closet. "Come, children. Follow your father."

"Good-bye, good-bye, Mama!"

She stayed in the kitchen window, looking out at them, very straight and silent.

At the door of the rocket the father said, "Children, this is a swift rocket. We will be gone only a short while. You must come back to school, and I to my business." He took each of their hands in turn. "Listen. This rocket is very old and will fly only *one* more journey. It will not fly again. This will be the one trip of your life. Keep your eyes wide."

"Yes, Papa."

"Listen, keep your ears clean. Smell the smells of a rocket. *Feel. Remember.* So when you return you will talk of it all the rest of your lives."

"Yes, Papa."

The ship was quiet as a stopped clock. The airlock hissed shut behind them. He strapped them all, like tiny mummies, into rubber hammocks. "Ready?" he called.

"Ready!" all replied.

"Blast-off!" He jerked ten switches. The rocket thundered and leaped. The children danced in their hammocks, screaming. "We're moving! We're off! Look!"

"Here comes the Moon!"

The moon dreamed by. Meteors broke into fireworks. Time flowed away in a serpentine of gas. The children shouted. Released from their hammocks, hours later, they peered from the ports. "There's Earth!" "There's Mars!"

The rocket dropped pink petals of fire while the hour dials spun; the child eyes dropped shut. At last they hung like drunken moths in their cocoon hammocks.

"Good," whispered Bodoni, alone.

He tiptoed from the control room to stand for a long moment, fearful, at the airlock door.

He pressed a button. The airlock door swung wide. He stepped out. Into space? Into inky tides of meteor and gaseous torch? Into swift mileages and infinite dimensions?

No. Bodoni smiled.

All about the quivering rocket lay the junkyard.

Rusting, unchanged, there stood the padlocked junkyard gate, the little silent house by the river, the kitchen window lighted, and the river going down to the same sea. And in the center of the junkyard, manufacturing a magic dream, lay the quivering, purring rocket. Shaking and roaring, bouncing the netted children like flies in a web.

Maria stood in the kitchen window.

He waved to her and smiled.

He could not see if she waved or not. A small wave, perhaps. A small smile.

The sun was rising.

Bodoni withdrew hastily into the rocket. Silence. All still slept. He breathed easily. Tying himself into a hammock, he closed his eyes. To himself he prayed, Oh, let nothing happen to the illusion in the next six days. Let all of space come and go, and red Mars come up under our ship, and the moons of Mars, and let there be no flaws in the color film. Let there be three dimensions; let nothing go wrong with the hidden mirrors and screens that mold the fine illusion. Let time pass without crisis.

He awoke.

Red Mars floated near the rocket.

"Papa!" The children thrashed to be free.

Bodoni looked and saw red Mars and it was good and there was no flaw in it and he was very happy.

At sunset on the seventh day the rocket stopped shuddering.

"We are home," said Bodoni.

They walked across the junkyard from the open door of the rocket, their blood singing, their faces glowing. Perhaps they knew what he had done. Perhaps they guessed his wonderful magic trick. But if they knew, if they guessed, they never said. Now they only laughed and ran.

"I have ham and eggs for all of you," said Maria, at the kitchen door.

"Mama, Mama, you should have come, to see it, to see Mars, Mama, and meteors, and everything!"

"Yes," she said.

At bedtime the children gathered before Bodoni. "We want to thank you, Papa."

"It was nothing."

"We will remember it for always, Papa. We will never forget."

Very late in the night Bodoni opened his eyes. He sensed that his wife was lying beside him, watching him. She did not move for a very long time, and then suddenly she kissed his cheeks and his forehead. "What's this?" he cried.

"You're the best father in the world," she whispered.

"Why?"

"Now I see," she said. "I understand."

She lay back and closed her eyes, holding his hand. "Is it a very lovely journey?" she asked.

"Yes," he said.

"Perhaps," she said, "perhaps, some night, you might take me on just a little trip, do you think?"

"Just a little one, perhaps," he said.

"Thank you," she said. "Good night."

"Good night," said Fiorello Bodoni.

THE ROCKET MAN

The electrical fireflies were hovering above Mother's dark hair to light her path. She stood in her bedroom door looking out at me as I passed in the silent hall. "You *will* help me keep him here this time, won't you?" she asked.

"I guess so," I said.

"Please." The fireflies cast moving bits of light on her white face. "This time he mustn't go away again."

"All right," I said, after standing there a moment. "But it won't do any good; it's no use."

She went away, and the fireflies, on their electric circuits, fluttered after her like an errant constellation, showing her how to walk in darkness. I heard her say, faintly, "We've got to try, anyway."

Other fireflies followed me to my room. When the weight of my body cut a circuit in the bed, the fireflies winked out. It was midnight, and my mother and I waited, our rooms separated by darkness, in bed. The bed began to rock me and sing to me. I touched a switch; the singing and rocking stopped. I didn't want to sleep. I didn't want to sleep at all.

This night was no different from a thousand others in our time. We would wake nights and feel the cool air turn hot, feel the fire in the wind, or see the walls burned a bright color for an instant, and then we knew *his* rocket was over our house—his rocket, and the oak trees swaying from the concussion. And I would lie there, eyes wide, panting, and Mother in her room. Her voice would come to me over the interroom radio:

"Did you feel it?"

And I would answer, "That was him, all right."

That was my father's ship passing over our town, a small town where space rockets never came, and we would lie awake for the next two hours, thinking. "Now Dad's landed

39

in Springfield, now he's on the tarmac, now he is signing the papers, now he's in the helicopter, now he's over the river, now the hills, now he's settling the helicopter in at the little airport at Green Village here. . . ." And the night would be half over when, in our separate cool beds, Mother and I would be listening, listening. "Now he's walking down Bell Street. He always walks . . . never takes a cab . . . now across the park, now turning the corner of Oakhurst and now . . ."

I lifted my head from my pillow. Far down the street, coming closer and closer, smartly, quickly, briskly—footsteps. Now turning in at our house, up the porch steps. And we were both smiling in the cool darkness, Mom and I, when we heard the front door open in recognition, speak a quiet word of welcome, and shut, downstairs. . . .

Three hours later I turned the brass knob to their room quietly, holding my breath, balancing in a darkness as big as the space between the planets, my hand out to reach the small black case at the foot of my parents' sleeping bed. Taking it, I ran silently to my room, thinking. He won't tell me, he doesn't want me to *know*.

And from the opened case spilled his black uniform, like a black nebula, stars glittering here or there, distantly, in the material. I kneaded the dark stuff in my warm hands; I smelled the planet Mars, an iron smell, and the planet Venus, a green ivy smell, and the planet Mercury, a scent of sulfur and fire; and I could smell the milky moon and the hardness of stars. I pushed the uniform into a centrifuge machine I'd built in my ninth-grade shop that year, set it whirling. Soon a fine powder precipitated into a retort. This I slid under a microscope. And while my parents slept unaware, and while our house was asleep, all the automatic bakers and servers and robot cleaners in an electric slumber, I stared down upon brilliant motes of meteor dust, comet tail, and loam from far Jupiter glistening like worlds themselves which drew me down the tube a billion miles into space, at terrific accelerations.

At dawn, exhausted with my journey and fearful of discovery, I returned the boxed uniform to their sleeping room.

Then I slept, only to waken at the sound of the horn of the dry-cleaning car which stopped in the yard below. They took the black uniform box with them. It's good I didn't wait, I thought. For the uniform would be back in an hour, clean of all its destiny and travel.

I slept again, with the little vial of magical dust pajama pocket, over my beating heart.

When I came downstairs, there was Dad at the breakfast table, biting into his toast. "Sleep good, Doug?" he said, as if he had been here all the time, and hadn't been gone for three months.

"All right," I said.

"Toast?"

He pressed a button and the breakfast table made me four pieces, golden brown.

I remember my father that afternoon, digging and digging in the garden, like an animal after something, it seemed. There he was with his long dark arms moving swiftly, planting, tamping, fixing, cutting, pruning, his dark face always down to the soil, his eyes always down to what he was doing, never up to the sky, never looking at me, or Mother, even, unless we knelt with him to feel the earth soak up through the overalls at our knees, to put our hands into the black dirt and not look at the bright, crazy sky. Then he would glance to either side, to Mother or me, and give us a gentle wink, and go on, bent down, face down, the sky staring at his back.

That night we sat on the mechanical porch swing which swung us and blew a wind upon us and sang to us. It was summer and moonlight and we had lemonade to drink, and we held the cold glasses in our hands, and Dad read the stereo-newspapers inserted into the special hat you put on your head and which turned the microscopic page in front of the magnifying lens if you blinked three times in succession. Dad smoked cigarettes and told me about how it was when he was a boy in the year 1997. After a while he said, "Why aren't you out playing kick-the-can, Doug?"

I didn't say anything, but Mom said, "He does, on nights when you're not here."

Dad looked at me and then, for the first time that day, at the sky. Mother always watched him when he glanced at the stars. The first day and night when he got home he wouldn't look at the sky much. I thought about him gardening and gardening so furiously, his face almost driven into the earth. But the second night he looked at the stars a little more. Mother wasn't afraid of the sky in the day so much, but it was the night stars that she wanted to turn off, and sometimes I could almost see her reaching for a switch in her mind, but never finding it. And by the third night maybe Dad'd be out here on the porch until way after we were all ready for bed, and then I'd hear Mom call him in, almost like she called me from the street at times. And then I would hear Dad fitting the electric-eye door lock in place, with a sigh. And the next morning at breakfast I'd glance down and see his little black case near his feet as he buttered his toast and Mother slept late.

"Well, be seeing you, Doug," he'd say, and we'd shake hands.

"In about three months?"

"Right."

And he'd walk away down the street, not taking a helicopter or beetle or bus, just walking with his uniform hidden in his small underarm case; he didn't want anyone to think he was vain about being a Rocket Man.

Mother would come out to eat breakfast, one piece of dry toast, about an hour later.

But now it was tonight, the first night, the good night, and he wasn't looking at the stars much at all.

"Let's go to the television carnival," I said.

"Fine," said Dad.

Mother smiled at me.

And we rushed off to town in a helicopter and took Dad through a thousand exhibits, to keep his face and head down with us and not looking anywhere else. And as we laughed at the funny things and looked serious at the serious ones, I thought, My father goes to Saturn and Neptune and Pluto, but he never brings me presents. Other boys whose fathers go into space bring back bits of ore from Callisto and hunks of black meteor or blue sand. But I have to get my own collection, trading from other boys, the Martian rocks and Mercurian sands which filled my room, but about which Dad would never comment.

On occasion, I remembered, he brought something for Mother. He planted some Martian sunflowers once in our yard, but after he was gone a month and the sunflowers grew large, Mom ran out one day and cut them all down.

Without thinking, as we paused at one of the three-dimensional exhibits, I asked Dad the question I always asked:

"What's it like, out in space?"

Mother shot me a frightened glance. It was too late.

Dad stood there for a full half minute trying to find an answer, then he shrugged.

"It's the best thing in a lifetime of best things." Then he caught himself. "Oh, it's really nothing at all. Routine. You wouldn't like it." He looked at me, apprehensively.

"But *you* always go back."

"Habit."

"Where're you going next?"

"I haven't decided yet. I'll think it over."

He always thought it over. In those days rocket pilots were rare and he could pick and choose, work when he liked. On the third night of his homecoming you could see him picking and choosing among the stars.

"Come on," said Mother, "let's go home."

It was still early when we got home. I wanted Dad to put on his uniform. I shouldn't have asked—it always made Mother unhappy—but I could not help myself. I kept at him, though he had always refused. I had never seen him in it, and at last he said, "Oh, all right."

We waited in the parlor while he went upstairs in the air flue. Mother looked at me dully, as if she couldn't believe that her own son could do this to her. I glanced away. "I'm sorry," I said.

"You're not helping at all," she said. "At all."

There was a whisper in the air flue a moment later.

"Here I am," said Dad quietly.

We looked at him in his uniform.

It was glossy black with silver buttons and silver rims to the heels of the black boots, and it looked as if someone had cut the arms and legs and body from a dark nebula, with little faint stars glowing through it. It fit as close as a glove fits to a slender long hand, and it smelled like cool air and metal and space. It smelled of fire and time.

Father stood, smiling awkwardly, in the center of the room.

"Turn around," said Mother.

Her eyes were remote, looking at him.

When he was gone, she never talked of him. She never said anything about anything but the weather or the condition of my neck and the need of a washcloth for it, or the fact that she didn't sleep nights. Once she said the light was too strong at night.

"But there's no moon this week," I said.

"There's starlight," she said.

I went to the store and bought her some darker, greener shades. As I lay in bed at night, I could hear her pull them down tight to the bottom of the windows. It made a long rustling noise.

Once I tried to mow the lawn.

"No." Mom stood in the door. "Put the mower away."

So the grass went three months at a time without cutting. Dad cut it when he came home.

She wouldn't let me do anything else either, like repairing the electrical breakfast maker or the mechanical book reader. She saved everything up, as if for Christmas. And then I would see Dad hammering or tinkering, and always smiling at his work, and Mother smiling over him, happy.

No, she never talked of him when he was gone. And as for Dad, he never did anything to make a contact across the millions of miles. He said once, "If I called you, I'd want to be with you. I wouldn't be happy."

Once Dad said to me, "Your mother treats me, sometimes, as if I weren't here—as if I were invisible."

I had seen her do it. She would look just beyond him, over his shoulder, at his chin or hands, but never into his eyes. If she did look at his eyes, her eyes were covered with a film, like an animal going to sleep. She said yes at the right times, and smiled, but always a half second later than expected.

"I'm not there for her," said Dad.

But other days she would be there and he would be there for her, and they would hold hands and walk around the block, or take rides, with Mom's hair flying like a girl's behind her, and she would cut off all the mechanical devices in the kitchen and bake him incredible cakes and pies and cookies, looking deep into his face, her smile a real smile. But at the end of such days when he was there to her, she would always cry. And Dad would stand helpless, gazing about the room as if to find the answer but never finding it.

Dad turned slowly, in his uniform, for us to see.

"Turn around again," said Mom.

The next morning Dad came rushing into the house with handfuls of tickets. Pink rocket tickets for California, blue tickets for Mexico.

"Come on!" he said. "We'll buy disposable clothes and burn them when they're soiled. Look, we take the noon rocket to L.A., the two-o'clock helicopter to Santa Barbara, the nine-o'clock plane to Ensenada, sleep overnight!"

And we went to California and up and down the Pacific

Coast for a day and a half, settling at last on the sands of Malibu to cook wieners at night. Dad was always listening or singing or watching things on all sides of him, holding onto things as if the world were a centrifuge going so swiftly that he might be flung off away from us at any instant.

The last afternoon at Malibu Mom was up in the hotel room. Dad lay on the sand beside me for a long time in the hot sun. "Ah," he sighed, "this is it." His eyes were gently closed; he lay on his back, drinking the sun. "You *miss* this," he said.

He meant "on the rocket," of course. But he never said "the rocket" or mentioned the rocket and all the things you couldn't have on the rocket. You couldn't have a salt wind on the rocket or a blue sky or a yellow sun or Mom's cooking. You couldn't talk to your fourteen-year-old boy on a rocket.

"Let's hear it," he said at last.

And I knew that now we would talk, as we had always talked, for three hours straight. All afternoon we would murmur back and forth in the lazy sun about my school grades, how high I could jump, how fast I could swim.

Dad nodded each time I spoke and smiled and slapped my chest lightly in approval. We talked. We did not talk of rockets or space, but we talked of Mexico, where we had driven once in an ancient car, and of the butterflies we had caught in the rain forests of green warm Mexico at noon, seeing the hundred butterflies sucked to our radiator, dying there, beating their blue and crimson wings, twitching, beautiful, and sad. We talked of such things instead of the things I wanted to talk about. And he listened to me. That was the thing he did, as if he was trying to fill himself up with all the sound he could hear. He listened to the wind and the falling ocean and my voice, always with a rapt attention, a concentration that almost excluded physical bodies themselves and kept only the sounds. He shut his eyes to listen. I would see him listening to the lawn mower as he cut the grass by hand instead of using the remote-control device, and I would see him smelling the cut grass as it sprayed up at him behind the mower in a green fount.

"Doug," he said, about five in the afternoon, as we were picking up our towels and heading back along the beach near the surf, "I want you to promise me something."

"What?"

"Don't ever be a Rocket Man."

I stopped.

"I mean it," he said. "Because when you're out there you want to be here, and when you're here you want to be out there. Don't start that. Don't let it get hold of you."

"But—"

"You don't know what it is. Every time I'm out there I think, 'If I ever get back to Earth I'll stay there; I'll never go out again.' But I go out, and I guess I'll always go out."

"I've thought about being a Rocket Man for a long time," I said.

He didn't hear me. "I *try* to stay here. Last Saturday when I got home I started trying so darned hard to *stay* here."

I remembered him in the garden, sweating, and all the traveling and doing and listening, and I knew that he did this to convince himself that the sea and the towns and the land and his family were the only real things and the good things. But I knew where he would be tonight: looking at the jewelry in Orion from our front porch.

"Promise you won't be like me," he said.

I hesitated awhile. "Okay," I said.

He shook my hand. "Good boy," he said.

The dinner was fine that night. Mom had run about the kitchen with handfuls of cinnamon and dough and pots and pans tinkling, and now a great turkey fumed on the table, with dressing, cranberry sauce, peas, and pumpkin pie.

"In the middle of August?" said Dad, amazed.

"You won't be here for Thanksgiving."

"So I won't."

He sniffed it. He lifted each lid from each tureen and let the flavor steam over his sunburned face. He said "Ah" to each. He looked at the room and his hands. He gazed at the pictures on the wall, the chairs, the table, me, and Mom. He cleared his throat. I saw him make up his mind. "Lilly?"

"Yes?" Mom looked across her table which she had set like a wonderful silver trap, a miraculous gravy pit into which, like a struggling beast of the past caught in a tar pool, her husband might at last be caught and held, gazing out through a jail of wishbones, safe forever. Her eyes sparkled.

"Lilly," said Dad.

Go on, I thought crazily. Say it quick: say you'll stay home this time, for good, and never go away; say it!

Just then a passing helicopter jarred the room and the windowpane shook with a crystal sound. Dad glanced at the window.

The blue stars of evening were there, and the red planet Mars was rising in the East.

Dad looked at Mars a full minute. Then he put his hand out blindly toward me. "May I have some peas," he said.

"Excuse me," said Mother. "I'm going to get some bread." She rushed out into the kitchen.

"But there's bread on the table," I said.

Dad didn't look at me as he began his meal.

I couldn't sleep that night. I came downstairs at one in the morning and the moonlight was like ice on all the house-tops, and dew glittered in a snow field on our grass. I stood in the doorway in my pajamas, feeling the warm night wind, and then I knew that Dad was sitting in the mechanical porch swing, gliding gently. I could see his profile tilted back, and he was watching the stars wheel over the sky. His eyes were like gray crystal there, the moon in each one.

I went out and sat beside him.

We glided awhile in the swing.

At last I said, "How many ways are there to die in space?"

"A million."

"Name some."

"The meteors hit you. The air goes out of your rocket. Or comets take you along with them. Concussion. Strangula-tion. Explosion. Centrifugal force. Too much acceleration. Too little. The heat, the cold, the sun, the moon, the stars, the planets, the asteroids, the planetoids, radiation . . ."

"And do they bury you?"

"They never find you."

"Where do you go?"

"A billion miles away. Traveling graves, they call them. You become a meteor or a planetoid traveling forever through space."

I said nothing.

"One thing," he said later, "it's quick in space. Death. It's over like that. You don't linger. Most of the time you don't even know it. You're dead and that's it."

We went up to bed.

It was morning.

Standing in the doorway, Dad listened to the yellow canary singing in its golden cage.

"Well, I've decided," he said. "Next time I come home, I'm home to stay."

"Dad!" I said.

"Tell your mother that when she gets up," he said.

"You *mean* it!"

He nodded gravely. "See you in about three months."

And there he went off down the street, carrying his uniform in its secret box, whistling and looking at the tall green trees and picking chinaberries off the chinaberry bush as he brushed by, tossing them ahead of him as he walked away into the bright shade of early morning. . . .

I asked Mother about a few things that morning after Father had been gone a number of hours. "Dad said that sometimes you don't act as if you hear or see him," I said.

And then she explained everything to me quietly.

"When he went off into space ten years ago, I said to myself, 'He's dead.' Or as good as dead. So think of him dead. And when he comes back, three or four times a year, it's not him at all, it's only a pleasant little memory or a dream. And if a memory stops or a dream stops, it can't hurt half as much. So most of the time I think of him dead—"

"But other times—"

"Other times I can't help myself. I bake pies and treat him as if he were alive, and then it hurts. No, it's better to think he hasn't been here for ten years and I'll never see him again. It doesn't hurt as much."

"Didn't he say next time he'd settle down?"

She shook her head slowly. "No, he's dead. I'm very sure of that."

"He'll come alive again, then," I said.

"Ten years ago," said Mother, "I thought, What if he dies on Venus? Then we'll never be able to see Venus again. What if he dies on Mars? We'll never be able to look at Mars again, all red in the sky, without wanting to go in and lock the door. Or what if he dies on Jupiter or Saturn or Neptune? On those nights when those planets were high in the sky, we wouldn't want to have anything to do with the stars."

"I guess not," I said.

The message came the next day.

The messenger gave it to me and I read it standing on the porch. The sun was setting. Mom stood in the screen door behind me, watching me fold the message and put it in my pocket.

"Mom," I said.

"Don't tell me anything I don't already know," she said. She didn't cry.

Well, it wasn't Mars, and it wasn't Venus, and it wasn't Jupiter or Saturn that killed him. We wouldn't have to think of him every time Jupiter or Saturn or Mars lit up the evening sky.

This was different.

His ship had fallen into the sun.

And the sun was big and fiery and merciless, and it was always in the sky and you couldn't get away from it.

So for a long time after my father died my mother slept through the days and wouldn't go out. We had breakfast at midnight and lunch at three in the morning, and dinner at the cold dim hour of 6 A.M. We went to all-night shows and went to bed at sunrise, with all the green dark shades pulled tight down on all the windows.

And, for a long while, the only days we ever went out to walk were the days when it was raining and there was no sun.

THE GOLDEN APPLES OF
THE SUN

"South," said the captain.

"But," said his crew, "there are no directions out here in space."

"When you travel on down toward the sun," replied the captain, "and everything gets yellow and warm and lazy, then you're going in one direction only." He shut his eyes and thought about the smouldering, warm, faraway land, his breath moving gently in his mouth. "South." He nodded slowly to himself. "South."

Their rocket was the *Copa de Oro*, also named the *Prometheus* and the *Icarus*, and their destination in all reality was the blazing noonday sun. In high good spirits they might almost have packed along two thousand sour lemonades and a thousand white-capped beers for this journey to the wide Sahara. But now as the sun boiled up at them they remembered a score of verses and quotations:

" 'The golden apples of the sun?' "

"Yeats."

" 'Fear no more the heat of the sun?' "

"Shakespeare, of course!"

" 'Cup of Gold?' Steinbeck. 'The Crock of Gold?' Stephens. And what about the pot of gold at the rainbow's end? *There's* a name for our trajectory! Rainbow!"

"Temperature?"

"One thousand degrees Fahrenheit!"

The captain stared from the huge dark-lensed port, and there indeed was the sun, and to go to that sun and touch it and steal part of it forever away was his quiet and single idea. In this ship were combined the coolly delicate and the coldly practical. Through corridors of ice and milk-frost, am-

Copyright 1953 by Ray Bradbury

moniated winter and storming snowflakes blew. Any spark from that vast hearth burning out there beyond the callous hull of this ship, any small fire-breath that might seep through would find winter, slumbering here like all the coldest hours of February.

The audio-thermometer murmured in the arctic silence: "Temperature: two thousand degrees!"

Falling, thought the captain, like a snowflake into the lap of June, warm July, and the sweltering dog-mad days of August.

"Three thousand degrees Fahrenheit!"

Under the snow fields engines raced, refrigerants pumped ten thousand miles per hour in rimed boa-constrictor coils.

"Four thousand degrees Fahrenheit."

Noon. Summer. July.

"Five thousand Fahrenheit!"

And at last the captain spoke with all the quietness of the journey in his voice:

"Now, we are touching the sun."

Their eyes, thinking it, were melted gold.

"Seven thousand degrees!"

Strange how a mechanical thermometer could sound excited, though it possessed only an emotionless steel voice.

"What *time* is it?" asked someone.

Everyone had to smile.

For now there was only the sun and the sun and the sun. It was every horizon, it was every direction. It burned the minutes, the seconds, the hourglasses, the clocks; it burned all time and eternity away. It burned the eyelids and the serum of the dark world behind the lids, the retina, the hidden brain; and it burned sleep and the sweet memories of sleep and cool nightfall.

"Watch it!"

"Captain!"

Bretton, the first mate, fell flat to the winter deck. His protective suit whistled where, burst open, his warmness, his oxygen, and his life bloomed out in a frosted steam.

"Quick!"

Inside Bretton's plastic face-mask, milk crystals had already gathered in blind patterns. They bent to see.

"A structural defect in his suit, Captain. Dead."

"Frozen."

They stared at that other thermometer which showed how winter lived in this snowing ship. One thousand degrees below zero. The captain gazed down upon the frosted statue and the twinkling crystals that iced over it as he watched. Irony of the coolest sort, he thought; a man afraid of fire and killed by frost.

The captain turned away. "No time. No time. Let him lie." He felt his tongue move. "Temperature?"

The dials jumped four thousand degrees.

"Look. Will you look? Look."

Their icicle was melting.

The captain jerked his head to look at the ceiling.

As if a motion-picture projector had jammed a single clear memory frame in his head, he found his mind focused ridiculously on a scene whipped out of childhood.

Spring mornings as a boy he had leaned from his bedroom window into the snow-smelling air to see the sun sparkle the last icicle of winter. A dripping of white wine, the blood of cool but warming April fell from that clear crystal blade. Minute by minute, December's weapon grew less dangerous. And then at last the icicle fell with the sound of a single chime to the graveled walk below.

"Auxiliary pump's broken, sir. Refrigeration. We're losing our ice!"

A shower of warm rain shivered down upon them. The captain jerked his head right and left. "Can you see the trouble? Quick!"

The men rushed; the captain bent in the warm air, cursing, felt his hands run over the cold machine, felt them burrow and search, and while he worked he saw a future which was removed from them by the merest breath. He saw the skin peel from the rocket beehive, men thus revealed running, running, mouths shrieking, soundless. Space was a black mossed well where life drowned its roars and terrors. Scream a big scream, but space snuffed it out before it was half up your throat. Men scurried, ants in a flaming matchbox; the ship was dripping lava, gushing steam, nothing!

"Captain?"

The nightmare flicked away.

"Here." He worked in the soft warm rain that fell from the upper decks. He fumbled at the auxiliary pump. "Damn it!" He jerked the feed line. When it came, it'd be the quickest death in the history of dying. One moment, yelling; a warm flash later only a billion billion tons of space-fire would whisper, unheard, in space. Popped like strawberries in a furnace, their thoughts would linger on the scorched air a long breath after their bodies were charred roast and fluorescent gas.

"There!" He stabbed the auxiliary pump with a screw driver. "So!" He shuddered. The complete annihilation of it. He clamped his eyes tight, teeth tight. Lord, he thought, we're used to more leisurely dyings, measured in minutes and hours. Even twenty seconds now would be a slow death compared to this hungry idiot thing waiting to eat us!

"Captain, do we pull out or stay?"

"Get the Cup ready. Take over, finish this. Now!"

He turned and put his hand to the working mechanism of the huge Cup; shoved his fingers into the robot Glove. A twitch of his hand here moved a gigantic hand, with gigantic metal fingers, from the bowels of the ship. Now, now, the great metal hand slid out holding the huge *Copa de Oro,* breathless, into the chemical furnace, the bodiless body and the fleshless flesh of the sun.

A million years ago, thought the captain, quickly, quickly, as he moved the hand and the Cup, a million years ago a naked man on a lonely northern trail saw lightning strike a tree. And while his clan fled, with bare hands he plucked a limb of fire, broiling the flesh of his fingers, to carry it, running in triumph, shielding it from the rain with his body, to his cave, where he shrieked out a laugh and tossed it full on a mound of leaves and gave his people summer. And the tribe crept at last, trembling, near the fire, and they put out their flinching hands and felt the new season in their cave, this small yellow spot of changing weather, and they, too, at last, nervously, smiled. And the gift of fire was theirs.

"Captain!"

It took all of four seconds for the huge hand to push the empty Cup to the fire. So here we are again, to-day, on another trail, he thought, reaching for a cup of precious gas and vacuum, a handful of different fire with which to run back up cold space, lighting our way, and take to Earth a gift of fire that might burn forever. Why?

He knew the answer before the question.

Because the atoms we work with our hands, on Earth, are pitiful; the atomic bomb is pitiful and small and our knowledge is pitiful and small, and only the sun really knows what we want to know, and only the sun has the secret. And besides, it's grand, it's a chance, it's a great thing coming here, playing tag, hitting and running. There is no reason, really, except the pride and vanity of little insect men hoping to sting the lion and escape the maw. Look! See! We'll cry we *did* it! And here is our cup of energy, fire, vibration, call it what you will, that may well power our cities and sail our ships and light our libraries and tan our children and bake our daily breads and simmer the knowledge of our universe for us for a thousand years until it is well done. Here, from this cup, all good men of science and religion: drink! Warm yourselves against the night of ignorance, the long snows of superstition, the cold winds of disbelief, and from the great fear of darkness in each man. So: we stretch out our hand with the beggar's cup . . .

"Ah."

The Cup dipped into the sun. It scooped up a bit of the flesh of God, the blood of the universe, the blazing thought, the blinding philosophy that set out and mothered a galaxy, that idled and swept planets in their fields and summoned or laid to rest lives and livelihoods.

"What'll happen when we pull it inside? That extra heat now, at this time, Captain?"

"Only the good Lord knows. . . ."

"Now, *slow*," whispered the captain.

"Auxiliary pump all repaired, sir."

"Start it!"

The pump leaped on.

"Close the lid of the Cup and inside now, slow, slow." The beautiful hand outside the ship trembled, a tremendous image of his own gesture, sank with oiled silence into the ship body. The Cup, lid shut, dripped yellow flowers and white stars, slid deep. The audio-thermometer screamed. The refrigerator system kicked; ammoniated fluids banged the walls like blood in the head of a shrieking idiot.

He shut the outer air-lock door.

"Now."

They waited. The ship's pulse ran. The heart of the ship rushed, beat, rushed, the Cup of gold in it. The cold blood raced around about down through, around about down through.

The captain exhaled slowly.

The ice stopped dripping from the ceiling. It froze again.

"Let's get out of here."

The ship turned and ran.

"Listen!"

The heart of the ship was slowing, slowing. The dials spun on down through the thousands; the needles whirred, invisible. The thermometer voice chanted the change of seasons. They were all thinking now, together: Pull away and away from the fire and the flame, the heat and the melting, the yellow and the white. Go on out now to cool and dark. In twenty hours perhaps they might even dismantle some refrigerators, let winter die. Soon they would move in night so cold it might be necessary to use the ship's new furnace, draw heat from the shielded fire they carried now like an unborn child.

They were going home.

They were going home and there was some little time, even as he tended to the body of Bretton lying in a bank of white winter snow, for the captain to remember a poem he had written many years before:

> Sometimes I see the sun a burning Tree,
> Its golden fruit swung bright in airless air,
> Its apples wormed with man and gravity,
> Their worship breathing from them everywhere,
> As man sees Sun as burning Tree . . .

The captain sat for a long while by the body, feeling many separate things. I feel sad, he thought, and I feel good, and I feel like a boy coming home from school with a handful of wild flowers.

"Well," said the captain, sitting, eyes shut, sighing. "Well, where do we go now, eh, where are we going?" He felt his men sitting or standing all about him, the terror dead in them, their breathing quiet. "When you've gone a long, long way down to the sun and touched it and lingered and jumped around and streaked away from it, where are you going then? When you go away from the heat and the noonday light and the laziness, where do you go?"

His men waited for him to say it out. They waited for him to gather all of the coolness and the whiteness and the welcome and refreshing climate of the word in his mind, and they saw him settle the word, like a bit of ice cream, in his mouth, rolling it gently.

"There's only one direction in space from here on out," he said at last.

They waited. They waited as the ship moved swiftly into cold darkness away from the light.

"North," murmured the captain. "North."

And they all smiled, as if a wind had come up suddenly in the middle of a hot afternoon.

A SOUND OF THUNDER

The sign on the wall seemed to quaver under a film of sliding warm water. Eckels felt his eyelids blink over his stare, and the sign burned in this momentary darkness:

> TIME SAFARI, INC.
> SAFARIS TO ANY YEAR IN THE PAST.
> YOU NAME THE ANIMAL.
> WE TAKE YOU THERE.
> YOU SHOOT IT.

A warm phlegm gathered in Eckels' throat; he swallowed and pushed it down. The muscles around his mouth formed a smile as he put his hand slowly out upon the air, and in that hand waved a check for ten thousand dollars to the man behind the desk.

"Does this safari guarantee I come back alive?"

"We guarantee nothing," said the official, "except the dinosaurs." He turned. "This is Mr. Travis, your Safari Guide in the Past. He'll tell you what and where to shoot. If he says no shooting, no shooting. If you disobey instructions, there's a stiff penalty of another ten thousand dollars, plus possible government action, on your return."

Eckels glanced across the vast office at a mass and tangle, a snaking and humming of wires and steel boxes, at an aurora that flickered now orange, now silver, now blue. There was a sound like a gigantic bonfire burning all of Time, all the years and all the parchment calendars, all the hours piled high and set aflame.

A touch of the hand and this burning would, on the instant, beautifully reverse itself. Eckels remembered the wording in the advertisements to the letter. Out of chars and ashes, out of dust and coals, like golden salamanders, the

Copyright 1952 by The Crowell-Collier Publishing Company

old years, the green years, might leap; roses sweeten the air, white hair turn Irish-black, wrinkles vanish; all, everything fly back to seed, flee death, rush down to their beginnings, suns rise in western skies and set in glorious easts, moons eat themselves opposite to the custom, all and everything cupping one in another like Chinese boxes, rabbits into hats, all and everything returning to the fresh death, the seed death, the green death, to the time before the beginning. A touch of a hand might do it, the merest touch of a hand.

"Unbelievable." Eckels breathed, the light of the Machine on his thin face. "A real Time Machine." He shook his head. "Makes you think. If the election had gone badly yesterday, I might be here now running away from the results. Thank God Keith won. He'll make a fine President of the United States."

"Yes," said the man behind the desk. "We're lucky. If Deutscher had gotten in, we'd have the worst kind of dictatorship. There's an anti-everything man for you, a militarist, anti-Christ, anti-human, anti-intellectual. People called us up, you know, joking but not joking. Said if Deutscher became President they wanted to go live in 1492. Of course it's not our business to conduct Escapes, but to form Safaris. Anyway, Keith's President now. All you got to worry about is—"

"Shooting my dinosaur," Eckels finished it for him.

"A *Tyrannosaurus rex*. The Tyrant Lizard, the most incredible monster in history. Sign this release. Anything happens to you, we're not responsible. Those dinosaurs are hungry."

Eckels flushed angrily. "Trying to scare me!"

"Frankly, yes. We don't want anyone going who'll panic at the first shot. Six Safari leaders were killed last year, and a dozen hunters. We're here to give you the severest thrill a *real* hunter ever asked for. Traveling you back sixty million years to bag the biggest game in all of Time. Your personal check's still there. Tear it up."

Mr. Eckels looked at the check. His fingers twitched.

"Good luck," said the man behind the desk. "Mr. Travis, he's all yours."

They moved silently across the room, taking their guns with them, toward the Machine, toward the silver metal and the roaring light.

First a day and then a night and then a day and then a

night, then it was day-night-day-night-day. A week, a month, a year, a decade! A.D. 2055. A.D. 2019. 1999! 1957! Gone! The Machine roared.

They put on their oxygen helmets and tested the intercoms.

Eckels swayed on the padded seat, his face pale, his jaw stiff. He felt the trembling in his arms and he looked down and found his hands tight on the new rifle. There were four other men in the Machine. Travis, the Safari Leader, his assistant, Lesperance, and two other hunters, Billings and Kramer. They sat looking at each other, and the years blazed around them.

"Can these guns get a dinosaur cold?" Eckels felt his mouth saying.

"If you hit them right," said Travis on the helmet radio. "Some dinosaurs have two brains, one in the head, another far down the spinal column. We stay away from those. That's stretching luck. Put your first two shots into the eyes, if you can, blind them, and go back into the brain."

The Machine howled. Time was a film run backward. Suns fled and ten million moons fled after them. "Think," said Eckels. "Every hunter that ever lived would envy us today. This makes Africa seem like Illinois."

The Machine slowed; its scream fell to a murmur. The Machine stopped.

The sun stopped in the sky.

The fog that had enveloped the Machine blew away and they were in an old time, a very old time indeed, three hunters and two Safari Heads with their blue metal guns across their knees.

"Christ isn't born yet," said Travis. "Moses has not gone to the mountain to talk with God. The Pyramids are still in the earth, waiting to be cut out and put up. *Remember* that. Alexander, Caesar, Napoleon, Hitler—none of them exists."

The man nodded.

"That"—Mr. Travis pointed—"is the jungle of sixty million two thousand and fifty-five years before President Keith."

He indicated a metal path that struck off into green wilderness, over streaming swamp, among giant ferns and palms.

"And that," he said, "is the Path, laid by Time Safari for your use. It floats six inches above the earth. Doesn't touch so much as one grass blade, flower, or tree. It's an antigravity metal. Its purpose is to keep you from touching this world of the past in any way. Stay on the Path. Don't go off it. I repeat. *Don't go off.* For *any* reason! If you fall off, there's a penalty. And don't shoot any animal we don't okay."

"Why?" asked Eckels.

They sat in the ancient wilderness. Far birds' cries blew on a wind, and the smell of tar and an old salt sea, moist grasses, and flowers the color of blood.

"We don't want to change the Future. We don't belong here in the Past. The government doesn't *like* us here. We have to pay big graft to keep our franchise. A Time Machine is finicky business. Not knowing it, we might kill an important animal, a small bird, a roach, a flower even, thus destroying an important link in a growing species."

"That's not clear," said Eckels.

"All right," Travis continued, "say we accidentally kill one mouse here. That means all the future families of this one particular mouse are destroyed, right?"

"Right."

"And all the families of the families of the families of that one mouse! With a stamp of your foot, you annihilate first one, then a dozen, then a thousand, a million, a *billion* possible mice!"

"So they're dead," said Eckels. "So what?"

"So what?" Travis snorted quietly. "Well, what about the foxes that'll need those mice to survive? For want of ten mice, a fox dies. For want of ten foxes, a lion starves. For want of a lion, all manner of insects, vultures, infinite billions of life forms are thrown into chaos and destruction. Eventually it all boils down to this: fifty-nine million years later, a caveman, one of a dozen on the *entire world*, goes hunting wild boar or saber-toothed tiger for food. But you, friend, have *stepped* on all the tigers in that region. By stepping on *one* single mouse. So the caveman starves. And the caveman, please note, is not just *any* expendable man, no! He is an *entire future nation*. From his loins would have sprung ten sons. From *their* loins one hundred sons, and thus onward to a civilization. Destroy this one man, and you destroy a race, a people, an entire history of life. It is comparable to slaying some of Adam's grandchildren. The stomp of your foot, on one mouse, could start an earthquake, the effects of which could shake our earth and destinies down through Time, to their very foundations. With the death of that one caveman, a billion others yet unborn are throttled in the womb. Perhaps Rome never rises on its seven hills. Perhaps Eruope is forever a dark forest, and only Asia waxes healthy and teeming. Step on a mouse and you crush the Pyramids. Step on a mouse and you leave your print, like a Grand Canyon, across Eternity. Queen Elizabeth might never be born, Washington might not cross the Delaware, there might never be a United States at all. So be careful. Stay on the Path. *Never* step off!"

"I see," said Eckels. "Then it wouldn't pay for us even to touch the *grass?*"

"Correct. Crushing certain plants could add up infinitesimally. A little error here would multiply in sixty million years, all out of proportion. Of course maybe our theory is wrong. Maybe Time *can't* be changed by us. Or maybe it can be changed only in little subtle ways. A dead mouse here makes an insect imbalance there, a population disproportion later, a bad harvest further on, a depression, mass starvation, and, finally, a change in *social* temperament in far-flung countries. Something much more subtle, like that. Perhaps only a soft breath, a whisper, a hair, pollen on the air, such a slight, slight change that unless you looked close you wouldn't see it. Who knows? Who really can say he knows? We don't know. We're guessing. But until we do know for certain whether our messing around in Time *can* make a big roar or a little rustle in history, we're being careful. This Machine, this Path, your clothing and bodies, were sterilized, as you know, before the journey. We wear these oxygen helmets so we can't introduce our bacteria into an ancient atmosphere."

"How do we know which animals to shoot?"

"They're marked with red paint," said Travis. "Today, before our journey, we sent Lesperance here back with the Machine. He came to this particular era and followed certain animals."

"Studying them?"

"Right," said Lesperance. "I track them through their entire existence, noting which of them lives longest. Very few. How many times they mate. Not often. Life's short. When I find one that's going to die when a tree falls on him, or one that drowns in a tar pit, I note the exact hour, minute, and second. I shoot a paint bomb. It leaves a red patch on his side. We can't miss it. Then I correlate our arrival in the Past so that we meet the Monster not more than two minutes before he would have died anyway. This way, we kill only animals with no future, that are never going to mate again. You see how *careful* we are?"

"But if you came back this morning in Time," said Eckels eagerly, "you must've bumped into *us,* our Safari! How did it turn out? Was it successful? Did all of us get through—alive?"

Travis and Lesperance gave each other a look.

"That'd be a paradox," said the latter. "Time doesn't permit that sort of mess—a man meeting himself. When such occasions threaten, Time steps aside. Like an airplane hitting an air pocket. You felt the Machine jump just before we stopped? That was us passing ourselves on the way back to the Future. We saw nothing. There's no way of telling *if* this expedition was a success, *if we* got our monster, or whether all of us—meaning *you,* Mr. Eckels—got out alive."

Eckels smiled palely.

"Cut that," said Travis sharply. "Everyone on his feet!"

They were ready to leave the Machine.

The jungle was high and the jungle was broad and the jungle was the entire world forever and forever. Sounds like music and sounds like flying tents filled the sky, and those were pterodactyls soaring with cavernous gray wings, gigantic bats of delirium and night fever. Eckels, balanced on the narrow Path, aimed his rifle playfully.

"Stop that!" said Travis. "Don't even aim for fun, blast you! If your guns should go off—"

Eckels flushed. "Where's our *Tyrannosaurus?*"

Lesperance checked his wristwatch. "Up ahead. We'll bisect his trail in sixty seconds. Look for the red paint! Don't shoot till we give the word. Stay on the path. *Stay on the Path!*"

They moved forward in the wind of morning.

"Strange," murmured Eckels. "Up ahead, sixty million years, Election Day over. Keith made President. Everyone celebrating. And here we are, a million years lost, and they don't exist. The things we worried about for months, a lifetime, not even born or thought of yet."

"Safety catches off, everyone!" ordered Travis. "You, first shot, Eckels. Second, Billings. Third, Kramer."

"I've hunted tiger, wild boar, buffalo, elephant, but now, this is *it,*" said Eckels. "I'm shaking like a kid."

"Ah," said Travis.

Everyone stopped.

Travis raised his hand. "Ahead," he whispered. "In the mist. There he is. There's His Royal Majesty now."

The jungle was wide and full of twitterings, rustlings, murmurs, and sighs.

Suddenly it all ceased, as if someone had shut a door. Silence.

A sound of thunder.

Out of the mist, one hundred yards away, came *Tyrannosaurus rex.*

"It," whispered Eckels. "It . . ."

"Sh!"

It came on great oiled, resilient, striding legs. It towered thirty feet above half of the trees, a great evil god, folding its delicate watchmaker's claws close to its oily reptilian chest. Each lower leg was a piston, a thousand pounds of white bone, sunk in thick ropes of muscle, sheathed over in a gleam of pebbled skin like the mail of a terrible warrior. Each thigh was a ton of meat, ivory, and steel mesh. And from the great breathing cage of the upper body those two delicate arms dangled out front, arms with hands which might pick up and examine men like toys, while the snake neck coiled. And the head itself, a ton of sculptured stone, lifted easily upon the sky. Its mouth gaped, exposing a fence of teeth like daggers. Its eyes rolled, ostrich eggs, empty of all expression save hunger. It closed its mouth in a death grin. It ran, its pelvic bones crushing aside trees and bushes, its taloned feet clawing damp earth, leaving prints six inches deep wherever it settled its weight. It ran with a gliding ballet step, far too poised and balanced for its ten tons. It moved into a sunlit arena warily, its beautifully reptilian hands feeling the air.

"Why, why," Eckels twitched his mouth. "It could reach up and grab the moon."

"Sh!" Travis jerked angrily. "He hasn't seen us yet."

"It can't be killed." Eckels pronounced this verdict quietly, as if there could be no argument. He had weighed the evidence and this was his considered opinion. The rifle in his hands seemed a cap gun. "We were fools to come. This is impossible."

"Shut up!" hissed Travis.

"Nightmare."

"Turn around," commanded Travis. "Walk quietly to the Machine. We'll remit one half your fee."

"I didn't realize it would be this *big*," said Eckels. "I miscalculated, that's all. And now I want out."

"It *sees* us!"

"There's the red paint on its chest!"

The Tyrant Lizard raised itself. Its armored flesh glittered like a thousand green coins. The coins, crusted with slime, steamed. In the slime, tiny insects wriggled, so that the entire body seemed to twitch and undulate, even while the monster itself did not move. It exhaled. The stink of raw flesh blew down the wilderness.

"Get me out of here," said Eckels. "It was never like this before. I was always sure I'd come through alive. I had good guides, good safaris, and safety. This time, I figured wrong. I've met my match and admit it. This is too much for me to get hold of."

"Don't run," said Lesperance. "Turn around. Hide in the Machine."

"Yes." Eckels seemed to be numb. He looked at his feet as if trying to make them move. He gave a grunt of helplessness.

"Eckels!"

He took a few steps, blinking, shuffling.

"Not *that* way!"

The Monster, at the first motion, lunged forward with a terrible scream. It covered one hundred yards in six seconds. The rifles jerked up and blazed fire. A windstorm from the beast's mouth engulfed them in the stench of slime and old blood. The Monster roared, teeth glittering with sun.

Eckels, not looking back, walked blindly to the edge of the Path, his gun limp in his arms, stepped off the Path, and walked, not knowing it, in the jungle. His feet sank into green moss. His legs moved him, and he felt alone and remote from the events behind.

The rifles cracked again. Their sound was lost in shriek and lizard thunder. The great level of the reptile's tail swung up, lashed sideways. Trees exploded in clouds of leaf and branch. The Monster twitched its jeweler's hands down to fondle at the men, to twist them in half, to crush them like berries, to cram them into its teeth and its screaming throat. Its boulder-stone eyes leveled with the men. They saw themselves mirrored. They fired at the metallic eyelids and the blazing black iris.

Like a stone idol, like a mountain avalanche, *Tyrannosaurus* fell. Thundering, it clutched trees, pulled them with it. It wrenched and tore the metal Path. The men flung themselves back and away. The body hit, ten tons of cold flesh and stone. The guns fired. The Monster lashed its armored tail, twitched its snake jaws, and lay still. A fount of blood spurted from its throat. Somewhere inside, a sac of fluids burst. Sickening gushes drenched the hunters. They stood, red and glistening.

The thunder faded.

The jungle was silent. After the avalanche, a green peace. After the nightmare, morning.

Billings and Kramer sat on the pathway and threw up. Travis and Lesperance stood with smoking rifles, cursing steadily.

In the Time Machine, on his face, Eckels lay shivering. He had found his way back to the Path, climbed into the Machine.

Travis came walking, glanced at Eckels, took cotton gauze from a metal box, and returned to the others, who were sitting on the Path.

"Clean up."

They wiped the blood from their helmets. They began to curse too. The Monster lay, a hill of solid flesh. Within, you could hear the sighs and murmurs as the furthest chambers of it died, the organs malfunctioning, liquids running a final instant from pocket to sac to spleen, everything shutting off, closing up forever. It was like standing by a wrecked locomotive or a steam shovel at quitting time, all valves being released or levered tight. Bones cracked; the tonnage of its own flesh, off balance, dead weight, snapped the delicate forearms, caught underneath. The meat settled, quivering.

Another cracking sound. Overhead, a gigantic tree branch broke from its heavy mooring, fell. It crashed upon the dead beast with finality.

"There." Lesperance checked his watch. "Right on time. That's the giant tree that was scheduled to fall and kill this animal originally." He glanced at the two hunters. "You want the trophy picture?"

"What?"

"We can't take a trophy back to the Future. The body has to stay right here where it would have died originally, so the insects, birds, and bacteria can get at it, as they were intended to. Everything in balance. The body stays. But we *can* take a picture of you standing near it."

The two men tried to think, but gave up, shaking their heads.

They let themselves be led along the metal Path. They sank wearily into the Machine cushions. They gazed back at the ruined Monster, the stagnating mound, where already strange reptilian birds and golden insects were busy at the steaming armor.

A sound on the floor of the Time Machine stiffened them. Eckels sat there, shivering.

"I'm sorry," he said at last.

"Get up!" cried Travis.

Eckels got up.

"Go out on that Path alone," said Travis. He had his rifle pointed. "You're not coming back in the Machine. We're leaving you here!"

Lesperance seized Travis's arm. "Wait——"

"Stay out of this!" Travis shook his hand away. "This fool nearly killed us. But it isn't *that* so much, no. It's his *shoes!* Look at them! He ran off the Path. That *ruins* us! We'll forfeit! Thousands of dollars of insurance! We guarantee no one leaves the Path. He left it. Oh, the fool! I'll have to report to the government. They might revoke our licence to travel. Who knows *what* he's done to Time, to History!"

"Take it easy, all he did was kick up some dirt."

"How do we *know?*" cried Travis. "We don't know anything! It's all a mystery! Get out here, Eckels!"

Eckels fumbled his shirt. "I'll pay anything. A hundred thousand dollars!"

Travis glared at Eckels' checkbook and spat. "Go out there. The Monster's next to the Path. Stick your arms up to your elbows in his mouth. Then you can come back with us."

"That's unreasonable!"

"The Monster's dead, you idiot. The bullets! The bullets can't be left behind. They don't belong in the Past; they might change anything. Here's my knife. Dig them out!"

The jungle was alive again, full of the old tremorings and bird cries. Eckels turned slowly to regard the primeval garbage dump, that hill of nightmares and terror. After a long time, like a sleepwalker he shuffled out along the Path.

He returned, shuddering, five minutes later, his arms soaked and red to the elbows. He held out his hands. Each held a number of steel bullets. Then he fell. He lay where he fell, not moving.

"You didn't have to make him do that," said Lesperance.

"Didn't I? It's too early to tell." Travis nudged the still body. "He'll live. Next time he won't go hunting game like this. Okay." He jerked his thumb wearily at Lesperance. "Switch on. Let's go home."

1492. 1776. 1812.

They cleaned their hands and faces. They changed their caking shirts and pants. Eckels was up and around again, not speaking. Travis glared at him for a full ten minutes.

"Don't look at me," cried Eckels. "I haven't done anything."

"Who can tell?"

"Just ran off the Path, that's all, a little mud on my shoes —what do you want me to do—get down and pray?"

"We might need it. I'm warning you, Eckels, I might kill you yet. I've got my gun ready."

"I'm innocent. I've done nothing!"

1999. 2000. 2055.

The Machine stopped.

"Get out," said Travis.

The room was there as they had left it. But not the same as they had left it. The same man sat behind the same desk. But the same man did not quite sit behind the same desk.

Travis looked around swiftly. "Everything okay here?" he snapped.

"Fine. Welcome home!"

Travis did not relax. He seemed to be looking at the very atoms of the air itself, at the way the sun poured through the one high window.

"Okay, Eckels, get out. Don't ever come back."

Eckels could not move.

"You heard me," said Travis. "What're you *staring* at?"

Eckels stood smelling of the air, and there was a thing to the air, a chemical taint so subtle, so slight, that only a faint cry of his sublimal senses warned him it was there. The colors, white, gray, blue, orange, in the wall, in the furniture, in the sky beyond the window, were . . . were . . . And there was a *feel*. His flesh twitched. His hands twitched. He stood drinking the oddness with the pores of his body. Somewhere, someone must have been screaming one of those whistles that only a dog can hear. His body screamed silence in return. Beyond this room, beyond this wall, beyond this man who was not quite the same man seated at this desk that was not quite the same desk . . . lay an entire world of streets and people. What sort of world it was now, there was no telling. He could feel them moving there, beyond the walls, almost, like so many chess pieces blown in a dry wind. . . .

But the immediate thing was the sign painted on the office wall, the same sign he had read earlier today on first entering.

Somehow, the sign had changed:

TYME SEFARI INC.

SEFARIS TU ANY YEER EN THE PAST.

YU NAIM THE ANIMALL.

WEE TAEKYUTHAIR.

YU SHOOT ITT.

Eckels felt himself fall into a chair. He fumbled crazily at the thick slime on his boots. He held up a clod of dirt, trembling, "No, it *can't* be. Not a *little* thing like that. No!"

Embedded in the mud, glistening green and gold and black, was a butterfly, very beautiful and very dead.

"Not a little thing like *that!* Not a butterfly!" cried Eckels.

It fell to the floor, an exquisite thing, a small thing that could upset balances and knock down a line of small dominoes and then big dominoes and then gigantic dominoes, all down the years across Time. Eckels' mind whirled. It *couldn't* change things. Killing one butterfly couldn't be *that* important! Could it?

His face was cold. His mouth trembled, asking: "Who— Who won the presidential election yesterday?"

The man behind the desk laughed. "You joking? You know very well. Deutscher, of course! Who else? Not that fool weakling Keith. We got an iron man now, a man with guts!" The official stopped. "What's wrong?"

Eckels moaned. He dropped to his knees. He scrabbled at the golden butterfly with shaking fingers. "Can't we," he pleaded to the world, to himself, to the officials, to the Machine, "can't we take it *back,* can't we *make* it alive again? Can't we start over? Can't we—"

He did not move. Eyes shut, he waited, shivering. He heard Travis breathe loud in the room; he heard Travis shift his rifle, click the safety catch, and raise the weapon.

There was a sound of thunder.

THE LONG RAIN

The rain continued. It was a hard rain, a perpetual rain, a sweating and steaming rain; it was a mizzle, a downpour, a fountain, a whipping at the eyes, an undertow at the ankles; it was a rain to drown all rains and the memory of rains. It came by the pound and the ton, it hacked at the jungle and cut the trees like scissors and shaved the grass and tunneled the soil and molted the bushes. It shrank men's hands into the hands of wrinkled apes; it rained a solid glassy rain, and it never stopped.

"How much farther, Lieutenant?"

"I don't know. A mile, ten miles, a thousand."

"Aren't you sure?"

"How can I be sure?"

"I don't like this rain. If we only knew how far it is to the Sun Dome, I'd feel better."

"Another hour or two from here."

"You really think so, Lieutenant?"

"Of course."

"Or are you lying to keep us happy?"

"I'm lying to keep you happy. Shut up!"

The two men sat together in the rain. Behind them sat two other men who were wet and tired and slumped like clay that was melting.

The lieutenant looked up. He had a face that once had been brown and now the rain had washed it pale, and the rain had washed the color from his eyes and they were white, as were his teeth, and as was his hair. He was all white. Even his uniform was beginning to turn white, and perhaps a little green with fungus.

The lieutenant felt the rain on his cheeks. "How many

Copyright 1950 by Love Romances Publishing Co., Inc.

million years since the rain stopped raining here on Venus?"

"Don't be crazy," said one of the two other men. "It never stops raining on Venus. It just goes on and on. I've lived here for ten years and I never saw a minute, or even a second, when it wasn't pouring."

"It's like living under water," said the lieutenant, and rose up, shrugging his guns into place. "Well, we'd better get going. We'll find that Sun Dome yet."

"Or we won't find it," said the cynic.

"It's an hour or so."

"Now you're lying to me, Lieutenant."

"No, now I'm lying to myself. This is one of those times when you've got to lie. I can't take much more of this."

They walked down the jungle trail, now and then looking at their compasses. There was no direction anywhere, only what the compass said. There was a gray sky and rain falling and jungle and a path, and, far back behind them somewhere, a rocket in which they had ridden and fallen. A rocket in which lay two of their friends, dead and dripping rain.

They walked in single file, not speaking. They came to a river which lay wide and flat and brown, flowing down to the great Single Sea. The surface of it was stippled in a billion places by the rain.

"All right, Simmons."

The lieutenant nodded and Simmons took a small packet from his back which, with a pressure of hidden chemical, inflated into a large boat. The lieutenant directed the cutting of wood and the quick making of paddles and they set out into the river, paddling swiftly across the smooth surface in the rain.

The lieutenant felt the cold rain on his cheeks and on his neck and on his moving arms. The cold was beginning to seep into his lungs. He felt the rain on his ears, on his eyes, on his legs

"I didn't sleep last night," he said.

"Who could? Who has? When? How many nights have we slept? Thirty nights, thirty days! Who can sleep with rain slamming their head, banging away. . . . I'd give anything for a hat. Anything at all, just so it wouldn't hit my head any more. I get headaches. My head is sore; it hurts all the time."

"I'm sorry I came to China," said one of the others.

"First time I ever head Venus called China."

"Sure, China. Chinese water cure. Remember the old torture? Rope you against a wall. Drop one drop of water on your head every half-hour. You go crazy waiting for the next one. Well, that's Venus, but on a big scale. We're not made for water. You can't sleep, you can't breathe right, and you're crazy from just being soggy. If we'd been ready for a crash, we'd have brought waterproofed uniforms and hats. It's this beating rain on your head gets you, most of all. It's so heavy. It's like BB shot. I don't know how long I can take it."

"Boy, me for the Sun Dome! The man who thought *them* up, thought of something."

They crossed the river, and in crossing they thought of the Sun Dome, somewhere ahead of them, shining in the jungle rain. A yellow house, round and bright as the sun. A house forty feet high by one hundred feet in diameter, in which was warmth and quiet and hot food and freedom from rain. And in the center of the Sun Dome, of course, was a sun. A small floating free globe of yellow fire, drifting in a space at the top of the building where you could look at it from where you sat, smoking or reading a book or drinking your hot chocolate crowned with marshmallow dollops or drinking something else. There it would be, the yellow sun, just the size of the Earth sun, and it was warm and continuous, and the rain world of Venus would be forgotten as long as you stayed in that house and idled your time.

The lieutenant turned and looked back at the three men using their oars and gritting their teeth. They were as white as mushrooms, as white as he was. Venus bleached everything away in a few months. Even the jungle was an immense cartoon nightmare, for how could the jungle be green with no sun, with always rain falling and always dusk? The white, white jungle with the pale cheese-colored leaves, and the earth carved of wet Camembert, and the tree boles like immense toadstools—everything black and white. And how often could you see the soil itself? Wasn't it mostly a creek, a stream, a puddle, a pool, a lake, a river, and then, at last, the sea?

"Here we are!"

They leaped out on the farthest shore, splashing and sending up showers. The boat was deflated and stored in a cigar-box packet. Then, standing on the rainy shore, they tried to light up a few smokes for themselves, and it was five minutes or so before, shuddering, they worked the inverted lighter and, cupping their hands, managed a few drags upon cigarettes that all too quickly were limp and beaten away from their lips by a sudden slap of rain.

They walked on.

"Wait just a moment," said the lieutenant. "I thought I saw something ahead."

"The Sun Dome?"

"I'm not sure. The rain closed in again."

Simmons began to run. "The Sun Dome!"

"Come back, Simmons!"

"The Sun Dome!"

Simmons vanished in the rain. The others ran after him.

They found him in a little clearing, and they stopped and looked at him and what he had discovered.

The rocket ship.

It was lying where they had left it. Somehow they had circled back and were where they had started. In the ruin of the ship green fungus was growing out of the mouths of the two dead men. As they watched, the fungus took flower, the petals broke away in the rain, and the fungus died.

"How did we do it?"

"An electrical storm must be nearby. Threw our compasses off. That explains it."

"You're right."

"What'll we do now?"

"Start out again."

"Good Lord, we're not any closer to anywhere!"

"Let's try to keep calm about it, Simmons."

"Calm, calm! This rain's driving me wild!"

"We've enough food for another two days if we're careful."

The rain danced on their skin, on their wet uniforms; the rain streamed from their noses and ears, from their fingers and knees. They looked like stone fountains frozen in the jungle, issuing forth water from every pore.

And, as they stood, from a distance they heard a roar.

And the monster came out of the rain.

The monster was supported upon a thousand electric blue legs. It walked swiftly and terribly. It struck down a leg with a driving blow. Everywhere a leg struck a tree fell and burned. Great whiffs of ozone filled the rainy air, and smoke blew away and was broken up by the rain. The monster was a half mile wide and a mile high and it felt of the ground like a great blind thing. Sometimes, for a moment, it had no legs at all. And then, in an instant, a thousand whips would fall out of its belly, white-blue whips, to sting the jungle.

"There's the electrical storm," said one of the men. "There's the thing ruined our compasses. And it's coming this way."

"Lie down, everyone," said the lieutenant.

"Run!" cried Simmons.

"Don't be a fool. Lie down. It hits the highest points. We may get through unhurt. Lie down about fifty feet from the rocket. It may very well spend its force there and leave us be. Get down!"

The men flopped.

"Is it coming?" they asked each other, after a moment.

"Coming."

"Is it nearer?"

"Two hundred yards off."

"Nearer?"

"Here she is!"

The monster came and stood over them. It dropped down ten blue bolts of lightning which struck the rocket. The rocket flashed like a beaten gong and gave off a metal ringing. The monster let down fifteen more bolts which danced about in a ridiculous pantomime, feeling of the jungle and the watery soil.

"No, no!" One of the men jumped up.

"Get down, you fool!" said the lieutenant.

"No!"

The lightning struck the rocket another dozen times. The lieutenant turned his head on his arm and saw the blue blazing flashes. He saw trees split and crumple into ruin. He saw the monstrous dark cloud turn like a black disk overhead and hurl down a hundred other poles of electricity.

The man who had leaped up was now running, like someone in a great hall of pillars. He ran and dodged between the pillars and then at last a dozen of the pillars slammed down and there was the sound a fly makes when landing upon the grill wires of an exterminator. The lieutenant remembered this from his childhood on a farm. And there was a smell of a man burned to a cinder.

The lieutenant lowered his head. "Don't look up," he told the others. He was afraid that he too might run at any moment.

The storm above them flashed down another series of bolts and then moved on away. Once again there was only the rain, which rapidly cleared the air of the charred smell, and in a moment the three remaining men were sitting and waiting for the beat of their hearts to subside into quiet once more.

They walked over to the body, thinking that perhaps they could still save the man's life. They couldn't believe that there wasn't some way to help the man. It was the natural act of men who have not accepted death until they have touched it and turned it over and made plans to bury it or leave it there for the jungle to bury in an hour of quick growth.

The body was twisted steel, wrapped in burned leather. It looked like a wax dummy that had been thrown into an incinerator and pulled out after the wax had sunk to the charcoal skeleton. Only the teeth were white, and they shone like a strange white bracelet dropped half through a clenched black fist.

"He shouldn't have jumped up." They said it almost at the same time.

Even as they stood over the body it began to vanish, for the vegetation was edging in upon it, little vines and ivy and creepers, and even flowers for the dead.

At a distance the storm walked off on blue bolts of lightning and was gone.

They crossed a river and a creek and a stream and a dozen others rivers and creeks and streams. Before their eyes rivers appeared, rushing, new rivers, while old rivers changed their courses—rivers the color of mercury, rivers the color of silver and milk.

They came to the sea.

The Single Sea. There was only one continent on Venus. This land was three thousand miles long by a thousand miles wide, and about this island was the Single Sea, which covered the entire raining planet. The Single Sea, which lay upon the pallid shore with little motion . . .

"This way." The lieutenant nodded south. "I'm sure there are two Sun Domes down that way."

"While they were at it, why didn't they build a hundred more?"

"There're a hundred and twenty of them now, aren't there?"

"One hundred and twenty-six, as of last month. They tried to push a bill through Congress back on Earth a year ago to provide for a couple dozen more, but oh no, you know how *that* is. They'd rather a few men went crazy with the rain."

They started south.

The lieutenant and Simmons and the third man, Pickard, walked in the rain, in the rain that fell heavily and lightly, heavily and lightly; in the rain that poured and hammered and did not stop falling upon the land and the sea and the walking people.

Simmons saw it first. "There it is!"

"There's what?"

"The Sun Dome!"

The lieutenant blinked the water from his eyes and raised his hands to ward off the stinging blows of the rain.

At a distance there was a yellow glow on the edge of the jungle by the sea. It was, indeed, the Sun Dome.

The men smiled at each other.

"Looks like you were right, Lieutenant."

"Luck."

"Brother, that puts muscle in me, just seeing it. Come on!" Simmons began to trot. The others automatically fell in with this, gasping, tired, but keeping pace.

"A big pot of coffee for me," panted Simmons, smiling. "And a pan of cinnamon buns. Boy! And just lie there and let the old sun hit you. The guy that invented the Sun Domes, he should have got a medal!"

They ran faster. The yellow glow grew brighter.

"Guess a lot of men went crazy before they figured out the cure. Think it'd be obvious! Right off." Simmons panted the words in cadence to his running "Rain, rain! Years ago. Found a friend. Of mine. Out in the jungle. Wandering around. In the rain. Saying over and over, 'Don't know enough, to come in, outta the rain. Don't know enough, to come in, outta the rain. Don't know enough—' On and on. Like that. Poor crazy fool."

"Save your breath!"

They ran.

They all laughed. They reached the door of the Sun Dome, laughing.

Simmons yanked the door wide. "Hey!" he yelled. "Bring on the coffee!"

There was no reply.

They stepped through the door.

The Sun Dome was empty and dark. There was no synthetic yellow sun floating in a high gaseous whisper at the center of the blue ceiling. There was no food waiting. It was cold as a vault. And through a thousand holes which had been newly punctured in the ceiling water streamed, the rain fell down, soaking into the thick rugs and the heavy modern furniture and splashing on the glass tables. The jungle was growing up like a moss in the room, on top of the bookcases and the divans. The rain slashed through the holes and fell upon the three men's faces.

Pickard began to laugh quietly.

"Shut up, Pickard!"

"Ye gods, look what's here for us—no food, no sun, nothing. The Venusians—they did it! Of course!"

Simmons nodded, with the rain funneling down on his face. The water ran in his silvered hair and on his white eyebrows. "Every once in a while the Venusians come up out of the sea and attack a Sun Dome. They know if they ruin the Sun Dòmes they can ruin us."

"But aren't the Sun Domes protected with guns?"

"Sure." Simmons stepped aside to a place that was relatively dry. "But it's been five years since the Venusians tried anything. Defense relaxes. They caught this Dome unaware."

"Where are the bodies?"

"The Venusians took them all down into the sea. I hear they have a delightful way of drowning you. It takes about eight hours to drown the way they work it. Really delightful."

"I bet there isn't any food here at all." Pickard laughed.

The lieutenant frowned at him, nodded at him so Simmons could see. Simmons shook his head and went back to a room at one side of the oval chamber. The kitchen was strewn with soggy loaves of bread, and meat that had grown a faint green fur. Rain came through a hundred holes in the kitchen roof.

"Brilliant." The lieutenant glanced up at the holes. "I don't suppose we can plug up all those holes and get snug here."

"Without food, sir?" Simmons snorted. "I notice the sun machine's dismantled. Our best bet is to make our way to the next Sun Dome. How far is that from here?"

"Not far. As I recall, they built two rather close together here. Perhaps if we waited, a rescue mission from the other might—"

"It's probably been here and gone already, some days ago. They'll send a crew to repair this place in about six months, when they get the money from Congress. I don't think we'd better wait."

"All right then, we'll eat what's left of our rations and get on to the next Dome."

Pickard said, "If only the rain wouldn't hit my head, just for a few minutes. If I could only remember what it's like not to be bothered." He put his hands on his skull and held it tight. "I remember when I was in school a bully used to sit in back of me and pinch me and pinch me and pinch me every five minutes, all day long. He did that for weeks and months. My arms were sore and black and blue all the time. And I thought I'd go crazy from being pinched. One day I must have gone a little mad from being hurt and hurt, and I turned around and took a metal trisquare I used in mechanical drawing and I almost cut his lousy head off. I almost scalped him before they dragged me out of the room, and I kept yelling, 'Why don't he leave me alone? Why don't he leave me alone?' Brother!" His hands clenched the bone of his head, shaking, tightening, his eyes shut. "But what do I do *now*? Who do I hit, who do I tell to lay off, stop bothering me, this damn rain, like the pinching, always *on* you, that's all you hear, that's all you feel!"

"We'll be at the other Sun Dome by four this afternoon."

"Sun Dome? Look at this one! What if all the Sun Domes on Venus are gone? What then? What if there are holes in all the ceilings, and the rain coming in!"

"We'll have to chance it."

"I'm tired of chancing it. All I want is a roof and some quiet. I want to be alone."

"That's only eight hours off, if you hold on."

"Don't worry, I'll hold on all right." And Pickard laughed, not looking at them.

"Let's eat," said Simmons, watching him.

They set off down the coast, southward again. After four hours they had to cut inland to go around a river that was a mile wide and so swift it was not navigable by boat. They had to walk inland six miles to a place where the river boiled out of the earth, suddenly, like a mortal wound. In the rain, they walked on solid ground and returned to the sea.

"I've got to sleep," said Pickard at last. He slumped. "Haven't slept in four weeks. Tried, but couldn't. Sleep here."

The sky was getting darker. The night of Venus was

setting in and it was so completely black that it was dangerous to move. Simmons and the lieutenant fell to their knees
also, and the lieutenant said, "All right, we'll see what we
can do. We've tried it before, but I don't know. Sleep doesn't
seem one of the things you can get in this weather."

They lay out full, propping their heads so the water
wouldn't come to their mouths, and they closed their eyes.

The lieutenant twitched.

He did not sleep.

There were things that crawled on his skin. Things grew
upon him in layers. Drops fell and touched other drops and
they became streams that trickled over his body, and
while these moved down his flesh, the small growths of the
forest took root in his clothing. He felt the ivy cling and
make a second garment over him; he felt the small flowers
bud and open and petal away, and still the rain pattered on
his body and on his head. In the luminous night—for the
vegetation glowed in the darkness—he could see the other
two men outlined, like logs that had fallen and taken upon
themselves velvet coverings of grass and flowers. The rain
hit his face. He covered his face with his hands. The rain
hit his neck. He turned over on his stomach in the mud,
on the rubbery plants, and the rain hit his back and hit his
legs.

Suddenly he leaped up and begun to brush the water from
himself. A thousand hands were touching him and he no
longer wanted to be touched. He no longer could stand
being touched. He floundered and struck something else
and knew that it was Simmons, standing up in the rain,
sneezing moisture, coughing and choking. And then Pickard
was up, shouting, running about.

"Wait a minute, Pickard!"

"Stop it, stop it!" Pickard screamed. He fired his gun six
times at the night sky. In the flashes of powdery illumi-
nation they could see armies of raindrops, suspended as in
a vast motionless amber, for an instant, hesitating as if shocked
by the explosion, fifteen billion droplets, fifteen billion tears,
fifteen billion ornaments, jewels standing out against a white
velvet viewing board. And then, with the light gone, the
drops which had waited to have their pictures taken, which
had suspended their downward rush, fell upon them, stinging, in an insect cloud of coldness and pain.

"Stop it! Stop it!"

"Pickard!"

But Pickard was only standing now, alone. When the lieutenant switched on a small hand lamp and played it over Pickard's wet face, the eyes of the man were dilated, and his mouth was open, his face turned up, so the water hit and splashed on his tongue, and hit and drowned the wide eyes, and bubbled in a whispering froth on the nostrils.

"Pickard!"

The man would not reply. He simply stood there for a long while with the bubbles of rain breaking out in his whitened hair and manacles of rain jewels dripping from his wrists and his neck.

"Pickard! We're leaving. We're going on. Follow us."

The rain dripped from Pickard's ears.

"Do you hear me, Pickard!"

It was like shouting down a well.

"Pickard!"

"Leave him alone," said Simmons.

"We can't go on without him."

"What'll we do, carry him?" Simmons spat. "He's no good to us or himself. You know what he'll do? He'll just stand here and drown."

"What?"

"You ought to know that by now. Don't you know the story? He'll just stand here with his head up and let the rain come in his nostrils and his mouth. He'll breathe the water."

"No."

"That's how they found General Mendt that time. Sitting on a rock with his head back, breathing the rain. His lungs were full of water."

The lieutenant turned the light back to the unblinking face. Pickard's nostrils gave off a tiny whispering wet sound.

"Pickard!" The lieutenant slapped the face.

"He can't even feel you," said Simmons. "A few days in this rain and you don't have any face or any legs or hands."

The lieutenant looked at his own hand in horror. He could no longer feel it.

"But we can't leave Pickard here."

"I'll show you what we can do." Simmons fired his gun.

Pickard fell into the raining earth.

Simmons said, "Don't move, Lieutenant. I've got my gun ready for you too. Think it over; he would only have stood or sat there and drowned. It's quicker this way."

The lieutenant blinked at the body. "But you killed him."

"Yes, because he'd have killed us by being a burden. You saw his face. Insane."

After a moment the lieutenant nodded.

They walked off into the rain.

It was dark and their hand lamps threw a beam that pierced the rain for only a few feet. After a half hour they had to stop and sit through the rest of the night, aching with hunger, waiting for the dawn to come; when it did come it was gray and continually raining as before, and they began to walk again.

"We've miscalculated," said Simmons.

"No. Another hour."

"Speak louder. I can't hear you." Simmons stopped and smiled. He touched his ears. "My ears. They've gone out on me. All the rain pouring finally numbed me right down to the bone."

"Can't you hear anything?" said the lieutenant.

"What?" Simmons' eyes were puzzled.

"Nothing. Come on."

"I think I'll wait here. You go on ahead."

"You can't do that."

"I can't hear you. You go on. I'm tired. I don't think the Sun Dome is down this way. And, if it is, it's probably got holes in the roof, like the last one. I think I'll just sit here."

"Get up from there!"

"So long, Lieutenant."

"You can't give up now."

"I've got a gun here that says I'm staying. I just don't care any more. I'm not crazy yet, but I'm the next thing to it. I don't want to go out that way. As soon as you get out of sight I'm going to use this gun on myself."

"Simmons!"

"You said my name. I can read that much off your lips."

"Simmons."

"Look, it's a matter of time. Either I die now or in a few hours. Wait'll you get to that next Dome, if you ever get there, and find rain coming in through the roof. Won't that be nice?"

The lieutenant waited and then splashed off in the rain. He turned and called back once, but Simmons was only sitting there with the gun in his hands, waiting for him to get out of sight. He shook his head and waved the lieutenant on.

The lieutenant didn't even hear the sound of the gun.

He began to eat the flowers as he walked. They stayed down for a time, and weren't poisonous; neither were they particularly sustaining, and he vomited them up, sickly, a minute or so later.

Once he took some leaves and tried to make himself a hat, but he had tried that before; the rain melted the leaves from his head. Once picked, the vegetation rotted quickly and fell away into gray masses in his fingers.

"Another five minutes," he told himself. "Another five minutes and then I'll walk into the sea and keep walking. We weren't made for this; no Earthman was or ever will be able to take it. Your nerves, your nerves."

He floundered his way through a sea of slush and foliage and came to a small hill.

At a distance there was a faint yellow smudge in the cold veils of water.

The next Sun Dome.

Through the trees, a long round yellow building, far away. For a moment he only stood, swaying, looking at it.

He began to run and then he slowed down, for he was afraid. He didn't call out. What if it's the same one? What if it's the dead Sun Dome, with no sun in it? he thought.

He slipped and fell. Lie here, he thought; it's the wrong one. Lie here. It's no use. Drink all you want.

But he managed to climb to his feet again and crossed several creeks, and the yellow light grew very bright, and he began to run again, his feet crashing into mirrors and glass, his arms flailing at diamonds and precious stones.

He stood before the yellow door. The printed letters over it said THE SUN DOME. He put his numb hand up to feel it. Then he twisted the doorknob and stumbled in.

He stood for a moment looking about. Behind him the rain whirled at the door. Ahead of him, upon a low table, stood a silver pot of hot chocolate, steaming, and a cup, full, with a marshmallow in it. And beside that, on another tray, stood thick sandwiches of rich chicken meat and fresh-cut tomatoes and green onions. And on a rod just before his eyes was a great thick green Turkish towel, and a bin in which to throw wet clothes, and, to his right, a small cubicle in which heat rays might dry you instantly. And upon a chair, a fresh change of uniform, waiting for anyone—himself, or any lost one—to make use of it. And farther over, coffee in steaming copper urns, and a phonograph from which music would soon play quietly, and books bound in red

and brown leather. And near the books a cot, a soft deep
cot upon which one might lie, exposed and bare, to drink
in the rays of the one great bright thing which dominated
the long room.

He put his hands to his eyes. He saw other men moving
toward him, but said nothing to them. He waited, and opened
his eyes, and looked. The water from his uniform pooled at
his feet, and he felt it drying from his hair and his face and
his chest and his arms and his legs.

He was looking at the sun.

It hung in the center of the room, large and yellow and
warm. It made not a sound, and there was no sound in the
room. The door was shut and the rain only a memory to his
tingling body. The sun hung high in the blue sky of the
room, warm, hot, yellow, and very fine.

He walked forward, tearing off his clothes as he went.

THE EXILES

Their eyes were fire and the breath flamed out the witches'
mouths as they bent to probe the caldron with greasy stick
and bony finger.

> *"When shall we three meet again*
> *In thunder, lightning, or in rain?"*

They danced drunkenly on the shore of an empty sea,
fouling the air with their three tongues, and burning it with
their cats' eyes malevolently aglitter:

> *"Round about the cauldron go:*
> *In the poison'd entrails throw. . . .*
> *Double, double toil and trouble;*
> *Fire burn and cauldron bubble."*

They paused and cast a glance about. "Where's the
crystal? Where the needles?"

"Here!"

"Good!"

"Is the yellow wax thickened?"

"Yes!"

"Pour it in the iron mold!"

"Is the wax figure done?" They shaped it like molasses
adrip on their green hands.

"Shove the needle through the heart!"

"The crystal, the crystal; fetch it from the tarot bag. Dust
it off; have a look!"

They bent to the crystal, their faces white.

> *"See, see, see . . ."*

Copyright 1950 by Fantasy Fiction, Inc.

A rocket ship moved through space from the planet Earth to the planet Mars. On the rocket ship men were dying.

The captain raised his head, tiredly. "We'll have to use the morphine."

"But, Captain—"

"You see yourself this man's condition." The captain lifted the wool blanket and the man restrained beneath the wet sheet moved and groaned. The air was full of sulfurous thunder.

"I saw it—I saw it." The man opened his eyes and stared at the port where there were only black spaces, reeling stars, Earth far removed, and the planet Mars rising large and red. "I saw it—a bat, a huge thing, a bat with a man's face, spread over the front port. Fluttering and fluttering, fluttering and fluttering."

"Pulse?" asked the captain.

The orderly measured it. "One hundred and thirty."

"He can't go on with that. Use the morphine. Come along, Smith."

They moved away. Suddenly the floor plates were laced with bone and white skulls that screamed. The captain did not dare look down, and over the screaming he said, "Is this where Perse is?" turning in at a hatch.

A white-smocked surgeon stepped away from a body. "I just don't understand it."

"How did Perse die?"

"We don't know, Captain. It wasn't his heart, his brain, or shock. He just—died."

The captain felt the doctor's wrist, which changed to a hissing snake and bit him. The captain did not flinch. "Take care of yourself. You've a pulse too."

The doctor nodded. "Perse complained of pains—needles, he said—in his wrists and legs. Said he felt like wax, melting. He fell. I helped him up. He cried like a child. Said he had a silver needle in his heart. He died. Here he is. We can repeat the autopsy for you. Everything's physically normal."

"That's impossible! He died of *something!*"

The captain walked to a port. He smelled of menthol and iodine and green soap on his polished and manicured hands. His white teeth were dentifriced, and his ears scoured to a pinkness, as were his cheeks. His uniform was the color of new salt, and his boots were black mirrors shining below him. His crisp crew-cut hair smelled of sharp alcohol. Even his breath was sharp and new and clean. There was no spot to him. He was a fresh instrument, honed and ready, still hot from the surgeon's oven.

The men with him were from the same mold. One expected huge brass keys spiraling slowly from their backs. They were expensive, talented, well-oiled toys, obedient and quick.

The captain watched the planet Mars grow very large in space.

"We'll be landing in an hour on that blasted place. Smith, did you see any bats, or have other nightmares?"

"Yes, sir. The month before our rocket took off from New York, sir. White rats biting my neck, drinking my blood. I didn't tell. I was afraid you wouldn't let me come on this trip."

"Never mind," sighed the captain. "I had dreams too. In all of my fifty years I never had a dream until that week before we took off from Earth. And then every night I dreamed I was a white wolf. Caught on a snowy hill. Shot with a silver bullet. Buried with a stake in my heart." He moved his head toward Mars. "Do you think, Smith, *they* know we're coming?"

"We don't know if there *are* Martian people, sir."

"Don't we? They began frightening us off eight weeks ago, before we started. They've killed Perse and Reynolds now. Yesterday they made Grenville go blind. How? I don't know. Bats, needles, dreams, men dying for no reason. I'd call it witchcraft in another day. But this is the year 2120, Smith. We're rational men. This all can't be happening. But it is! Whoever they are, with their needles and their bats, they'll try to finish us all." He swung about. "Smith, fetch those books from my file. I want them when we land."

Two hundred books were piled on the rocket deck.

"Thank you, Smith. Have you glanced at them? Think I'm insane? Perhaps. It's a crazy hunch. At that last moment I ordered these books from the Historical Museum. Because of my dreams. Twenty nights I was stabbed, butchered, a screaming bat pinned to a surgical mat, a thing rotting underground in a black box; bad, wicked dreams. Our whole crew dreamed of witch-things and were-things, vampires and phantoms, things they *couldn't* know anything about. Why? Because books on such ghastly subjects were destroyed a century ago. By law. Forbidden for anyone to own the grisly volumes. These books you see here are the *last* copies, kept for historical purposes in the locked museum vaults."

Smith bent to read the dusty titles:

"*Tales of Mystery and Imagination*, by Edgar Allan Poe. *Dracula*, by Bram Stoker. *Frankenstein*, by Mary Shelley. *The Turn of the Screw*, by Henry James. *The Legend of Sleepy Hollow*, by Washington Irving. *Rappaccini's Daughter*, by Nathaniel Hawthorne. *An Occurrence at Owl Creek Bridge*, by Ambrose Bierce. *Alice's Adventures in Wonderland*, by Lewis Carroll. *The Willows*, by Algernon Blackwood. *The Wizard of Oz*, by L. Frank Baum. *The Weird Shadow over Innsmouth*, by H. P. Lovecraft. And more! Books by Walter de la Mare, Wakefield, Harvey, Wells, Asquith, Huxley—all forbidden authors. All burned in the same year that Halloween was outlawed and Christmas was banned! But, sir, what good are these to us on the rocket?"

"I don't know," sighed the captain, "yet."

The three hags lifted the crystal where the captain's image flickered, his tiny voice tinkling out of the glass:

"I don't know," sighed the captain, "yet."

The three witches glared redly into one another's faces.

"We haven't much time," said one.

"Better warn *Them* in the City."

"They'll want to know about the books. It doesn't look good. That fool of a captain!"

"In an hour they'll land their rocket."

The three hags shuddered and blinked up at the Emerald City by the edge of the dry Martian sea. In its highest window a small man held a blood-red drape aside. He watched the wastelands where the three witches fed their caldron and shaped the waxes. Farther along, ten thousand other blue fires and laurel incenses, black tobacco smokes and fir weeds, cinnamons and bone dusts rose soft as moths through the Martian night. The man counted the angry, magical fires. Then, as the three witches stared, he turned. The crimson drape, released, fell, causing the distant portal to wink, like a yellow eye.

Mr. Edgar Allan Poe stood in the tower window, a faint vapor of spirits upon his breath. "Hecate's friends are busy tonight," he said, seeing the witches, far below.

A voice behind him said, "I saw Will Shakespeare at the

shore, earlier, whipping them on. All along the sea Shakespeare's army alone, tonight, numbers thousands: the three witches, Oberon, Hamlet's father, Puck—all, all of them— thousands! Good Lord, a regular sea of people."

"Good William." Poe turned. He let the crimson drape fall shut. He stood for a moment to observe the raw stone room, the black-timbered table, the candle flame, the other man, Mr. Ambrose Bierce, sitting very idly there, lighting matches and watching them burn down, whistling under his breath, now and then laughing to himself.

"We'll have to tell Mr. Dickens now," said Mr. Poe. "We've put it off too long. It's a matter of hours. Will you go down to his home with me, Bierce?"

Bierce glanced up merrily. "I've just been thinking—what'll happen to us?"

"If we can't kill the rocket men off, frighten them away, then we'll have to leave, of course. We'll go on to Jupiter, and when they come to Jupiter, we'll go on to Saturn, and when they come to Saturn, we'll go to Uranus, or Neptune, and then on out to Pluto—"

"Where then?"

Mr. Poe's face was weary; there were fire coals remaining, fading, in his eyes, and a sad wildness in the way he talked, and a uselessness of his hands and the way his hair fell lankly over his amazing white brow. He was like a satan of some lost dark cause, a general arrived from a derelict invasion. His silky, soft, black mustache was worn away by his musing lips. He was so small his brow seemed to float, vast and phosphorescent, by itself, in the dark room.

"We have the advantages of superior forms of travel," he said. "We can always hope for one of their atomic wars, dissolution, the dark ages come again. The return of superstition. We could go back then to Earth, all of us, in one night." Mr. Poe's black eyes brooded under his round and luminant brow. He gazed at the ceiling. "So they're coming to ruin *this* world too? They won't leave *anything* undefiled, will they?"

"Does a wolf pack stop until it's killed its prey and eaten the guts?" said Bierce. "It should be quite a war. I shall sit on the side lines and be the scorekeeper. So many Earthmen boiled in oil, so many Mss. Found in Bottles burnt, so many Earthmen stabbed with needles, so many Red Deaths put to flight by a battery of hypodermic syringes—ha!"

Poe swayed angrily, faintly drunk with wine. "What did

we do? Be *with* us, Bierce, in the name of God! Did we have a fair trial before a company of literary critics? No! Our books were plucked up by neat, sterile, surgeon's pliers, and flung into vats, to boil, to be killed of all their mortuary germs. Damn them all!"

"I find our situation amusing," said Bierce.

They were interrupted by a hysterical shout from the tower stair.

"Mr. Poe! Mr. Bierce!"

"Yes, yes, we're coming!" Poe and Bierce descended to find a man gasping against the stone passage wall.

"Have you heard the news?" he cried immediately, clawing at them like a man about to fall over a cliff. "In an hour they'll land! They're bringing books with them—*old* books, the witches said! What're you doing in the tower at a time like this? Why aren't you acting?"

Poe said: "We're doing everything we can, Blackwood. You're new to all this. Come along, we're going to Mr. Charles Dickens' place—"

"—to contemplate our doom, our black doom," said Mr. Bierce, with a wink.

They moved down the echoing throats of the castle, level after dim green level, down into mustiness and decay and spiders and dreamlike webbing. "Don't worry," said Poe, his brow like a huge white lamp before them, descending, sinking. "All along the dead sea tonight I've called the others. Your friends and mine, Blackwood—Bierce. They're all there. The animals and the old women and the tall men with the sharp white teeth. The traps are waiting; the pits, yes, and the pendulums. The Red Death." Here he laughed quietly. "Yes, even the Red Death. I never thought—no, I never thought the time would come when a thing like the Red Death would actually *be*. But *they* asked for it, and they shall have it!"

"But are we strong enough?" wondered Blackwood.

"How strong is strong? They won't be prepared for us, at least. They haven't the imagination. Those clean young rocket men with their antiseptic bloomers and fish-bowl helmets, with their new religion. About their necks, on gold chains, scalpels. Upon their heads, a diadem of microscopes. In their holy fingers, steaming incense urns which in reality are only germicidal ovens for steaming out superstition. The names of Poe, Bierce, Hawthorne, Blackwood—blasphemy to their clean lips."

Outside the castle they advanced through a watery space, a tarn that was not a tarn, which misted before them like the stuff of nightmares. The air filled with wing sounds and whirring, a motion of winds and blacknesses. Voices changed, figures swayed at campfires. Mr. Poe watched the needles knitting, knitting, knitting, in the firelight; knitting pain and misery, knitting wickedness into wax marionettes, clay puppets. The caldron smells of wild garlic and cayenne and saffron hissed up to fill the night with evil pungency.

"Get on with it!" said Poe. "I'll be back!"

All down the empty seashore black figures spindled and waned, grew up and blew into black smoke on the sky. Bells rang in mountain towers and licorice ravens spilled out with the bronze sounds and spun away to ashes.

Over a lonely moor and into a small valley Poe and Bierce hurried, and found themselves quite suddenly on a cobbled street, in cold, bleak, biting weather, with people stomping up and down stony courtyards to warm their feet; foggy withal, and candles flaring in the windows of offices and shops where hung the Yuletide turkeys. At a distance some boys, all bundled up, snorting their pale breaths on the wintry air, were trilling, "God Rest Ye Merry, Gentlemen," while the immense tones of a great clock continuously sounded midnight. Children dashed by from the baker's with dinners all asteam in their grubby fists, on trays and under silver bowls.

At a sign which read SCROOGE, MARLEY AND DICKENS, Poe gave the Marley-faced knocker a rap, and from within, as the door popped open a few inches, a sudden gust of music almost swept them into a dance. And there, beyond the shoulder of the man who was sticking a trim goatee and mustaches at them, was Mr. Fezziwig clapping his hands, and Mrs. Fezziwig, one vast substantial smile, dancing and colliding with other merrymakers, while the fiddle chirped and laughter ran about a table like chandelier crystals given a sudden push of wind. The large table was heaped with brawn and turkey and holly and geese; with mince pies, suckling pigs, wreaths of sausages, oranges and apples; and there was Bob Cratchit and Little Dorrit and Tiny Tim and Mr. Fagin himself, and a man who looked as if he might be an undigested bit of beef, a blot of mustard, a crumb of cheese, a fragment of underdone potato—who else but Mr. Marley, chains and all, while the wine poured and the brown turkeys did their excellent best to steam!

"What do you want?" demanded Mr. Charles Dickens.

"We've come to plead with you again, Charles; we need your help," said Poe.

"Help? Do you think I would help you fight against those good men coming in the rocket? I don't belong here, anyway. My books were burned by mistake. I'm no supernaturalist, no writer of horrors and terrors like you, Poe; you, Bierce, or the others. I'll have nothing to do with you terrible people!"

"You are a persuasive talker," reasoned Poe. "You could go to meet the rocket men, lull them, lull their suspicions and then—then we would take care of them."

Mr. Dickens eyed the folds of the black cape which hid Poe's hands. From it, smiling, Poe drew forth a black cat. "For *one* of our visitors."

"And for the others?"

Poe smiled again, well pleased. "The Premature Burial?"

"You are a grim man, Mr. Poe."

"I am a frightened and an angry man. I am a god, Mr. Dickens, even as you are a god, even as we all are gods, and our inventions—our people, if you wish—have not only been threatened, but banished and burned, torn up and censored, ruined and done away with. The worlds we created are falling into ruin. Even gods must fight!"

"So?" Mr. Dickens tilted his head, impatient to return to the party, the music, the food. "Perhaps you can explain why we are here? How did we come here?"

"War begets war. Destruction begets destruction. On Earth, in the last half of the twentieth century they began to outlaw our books. Oh, what a horrible thing—to destroy our literary creations that way! It summoned us out of—what? Death? The Beyond? I don't like abstract things. I don't know. I only know that our worlds and our creations called us and we tried to save them, and the only saving thing we could do was wait out the century here on Mars, hoping Earth might overweight itself with these scientists and their doubtings; but now they're coming to clean us out of here, us and our dark things, and all the alchemists, witches, vampires, and were-things that, one by one, retreated across space as science made inroads through every country on Earth and finally left no alternative at all but exodus. You must help us. You have a good speaking manner. We need you."

"I repeat, I am not of you, I don't approve of you and the others," cried Dickens angrily. "I was no player with witches and vampires and midnight things."

"What of *A Christmas Carol?*"

"Ridiculous! *One* story. Oh, I wrote a few others about ghosts, perhaps, but what of that? My basic works had none of that nonsense!"

"Mistaken or not, they grouped you with us. They destroyed your books—your worlds too. You must hate them, Mr. Dickens!"

"I admit they are stupid and rude, but that is all. Good day!"

"Let Mr. Marley come, at least!"

"No!"

The door slammed. As Poe turned away, down the street, skimming over the frosty ground, the coachman playing a lively air on a bugle, came a great coach, out of which, cherry-red, laughing and singing, piled the Pickwickians, banging on the door, shouting Merry Christmas good and loud, when the door was opened by the fat boy.

Mr. Poe hurried along the midnight shore of the dry sea. By fires and smoke he hesitated, to shout orders, to check the bubbling caldrons, the poisons and the chalked pentagrams. "Good!" he said, and ran on. "Fine!" he shouted, and ran again. People joined him and ran with him. Here were Mr. Coppard and Mr. Machen running with him now. And there were hating serpents and angry demons and fiery bronze dragons and spitting vipers and trembling witches like the barbs and nettles and thorns and all the vile flotsam and jetsam of the retreating sea of imagination, left on the melancholy shore, whining and frothing and spitting.

Mr. Machen stopped. He sat like a child on the cold sand. He began to sob. They tried to soothe him, but he would not listen. "I just thought," he said. "What happens to us on the day when the *last* copies of our books are destroyed?"

The air whirled.

"Don't speak of it!"

"We must," wailed Mr. Machen. "Now, now, as the rocket comes down, you, Mr. Poe; you, Coppard; you, Bierce—all of you grow faint. Like wood smoke. Blowing away. Your faces melt—"

"Death! *Real* death for all of us."

"We exist only through Earth's sufferance. If a final edict tonight destroyed our last few works we'd be like lights put out."

Coppard brooded gently. "I wonder who I am. In what Earth mind tonight do I exist? In some African hut? Some hermit reading my tales? Is he the lonely candle in the wind of time and science? The flickering orb sustaining me here in rebellious exile? Is it him? Or some boy in a discarded attic finding me, only just in time! Oh, last night I felt ill, ill, ill to the marrows of me, for there is a body of the soul as well as a body of the body, and this soul body ached in all of its glowing parts, and last night I felt myself a candle, guttering. When suddenly I sprang up, given new light, as some child, sneezing with dust, in some yellow garret on Earth once more found a worn, time-specked copy of me! And so I'm given a short respite!"

A door banged wide in a little hut by the shore. A thin short man, with flesh hanging from him in folds, stepped out and, paying no attention to the others, sat down and stared into his clenched fists.

"There's the one I'm sorry for," whispered Blackwood. "Look at him, dying away. He was once more real than we, who were men. They took him, a skeleton thought, and clothed him in centuries of pink flesh and snow beard and red velvet suit and black boot; made him reindeers, tinsel, holly. And after centuries of manufacturing him they drowned him in a vat of Lysol, you might say."

The men were silent.

"What must it be on Earth?" wondered Poe. "Without Christmas? No hot chestnuts, no tree, no ornaments or drums or candles—nothing; nothing but the snow and wind and the lonely, factual people. . . ."

They all looked at the thin little old man with the scraggly beard and faded red velvet suit.

"Have you heard his story?"

"I can imagine it. The glitter-eyed psychiatrist, the clever sociologist, the resentful, froth-mouthed educationalist, the antiseptic parents—"

"A regrettable situation," said Bierce, smiling, "for the Yuletide merchants who, toward the last there, as I recall, were beginning to put up holly and sing Noel the day before

Halloween. With any luck at all this year they might have started on Labor Day!"

Bierce did not continue. He fell forward with a sigh. As he lay upon the ground he had time to say only, "How interesting." And then, as they all watched, horrified, his body burned into blue dust and charred bone, the ashes of which fled through the air in black tatters.

"Bierce, Bierce!"

"Gone!"

"His last book gone. Someone on Earth just now burned it."

"God rest him. Nothing of him left now. For what are we but books, and when those are gone, nothing's to be seen."

A rushing sound filled the sky.

They cried out, terrified, and looked up. In the sky, dazzling it with sizzling fire clouds, was the rocket! Around the men on the seashore lanterns bobbed; there was a squealing and a bubbling and an odor of cooked spells. Candle-eyed pumpkins lifted into the cold clear air. Thin fingers clenched into fists and a witch screamed from her withered mouth:

> *"Ship, ship, break, fall!*
> *Ship, ship, burn all!*
> *Crack, flake, shake, melt!*
> *Mummy dust, cat pelt!"*

"Time to go," murmured Blackwood. "On to Jupiter, on to Saturn or Pluto."

"Run away?" shouted Poe in the wind. "Never!"

"I'm a tired old man!"

Poe gazed into the old man's face and believed him. He climbed atop a huge boulder and faced the ten thousand gray shadows and green lights and yellow eyes on the hissing wind.

"The powders!" he shouted.

A thick hot smell of bitter almond, civet, cumin, wormseed and orris!

The rocket came down—steadily down, with the shriek of a damned spirit! Poe raged at it! He flung his fists up and the orchestra of heat and smell and hatred answered in symphony! Like stripped tree fragments, bats flew upward! Burning hearts, flung like missiles, burst in bloody fireworks

on the singed air. Down, down, relentlessly down, like a
pendulum the rocket came. And Poe howled, furiously, and
shrank back with every sweep and sweep of the rocket
cutting and ravening the air! All the dead sea seemed a pit in
which, trapped, they waited the sinking of the dread machinery, the glistening ax; they were people under the avalanche!

"The snakes!" screamed Poe.

And luminous serpentines of undulant green hurtled toward the rocket. But it came down, a sweep, a fire, a motion,
and it lay panting out exhaustions of red plumage on the
sand, a mile away.

"At it!" shrieked Poe. "The plan's changed! Only one
chance! Run! At it! At it! Drown them with our bodies!
Kill them!"

And as if he had commanded a violent sea to change its
course, to suck itself free from primeval beds, the whirls and
savage gouts of fire spread and ran like wind and rain and
stark lightning over the sea sands, down empty river deltas,
shadowing and screaming, whistling and whining, sputtering
and coalescing toward the rocket which, extinguished, lay
like a clean metal torch in the farthest hollow. As if a great
charred caldron of sparkling lava had been overturned, the
boiling people and snapping animals churned down the dry
fathoms.

"Kill them!" screamed Poe, running.

The rocket men leaped out of their ship, guns ready. They
stalked about, sniffing the air like hounds. They saw nothing.
They relaxed.

The captain stepped forth last. He gave sharp commands.
Wood was gathered, kindled, and a fire leapt up in an instant. The captain beckoned his men into a half circle about
him.

"A new world," he said, forcing himself to speak deliber-
ately, though he glanced nervously, now and again, over his
shoulder at the empty sea. "The old world left behind. A new
start. What more symbolic than that we here dedicate ourselves all the more firmly to science and progress." He nodded
crisply to his lieutenant. "The books."

Firelight limned the faded gilt titles: *The Willows, The
Outsider, Behold This Dreamer, Dr. Jekyll and Mr. Hyde, The
Land of Oz, Pellucidar, The Land That Time Forgot, A Mid-
summer Night's Dream,* and the monstrous names of Machen

and Edgar Allan Poe and Cabell and Dunsany and Black-wood and Lewis Carroll; the names, the old names, the evil names.

"A new world. With a gesture, we burn the last of the old."

The captain ripped pages from the books. Leaf by seared leaf, he fed them into the fire.

A scream!

Leaping back, the men stared beyond the firelight at the edges of the encroaching and uninhabited sea.

Another scream! A high and wailing thing, like the death of a dragon and the thrashing of a bronzed whale left gasping when the waters of a leviathan's sea drain down the shingles and evaporate.

It was the sound of air rushing in to fill a vacuum, where, a moment before, there had been *something!*"

The captain neatly disposed of the last book by putting it into the fire.

The air stopped quivering.

Silence!

The rocket men leaned and listened.

"Captain, did you hear it?"

"No."

"Like a wave, sir. On the sea bottom! I thought I saw something. Over there. A black wave. Big. Running at us."

"You were mistaken."

"There, sir!"

"What?"

"See it? There! The city! Way over! That green city near the lake! It's splitting in half. It's falling!"

The men squinted and shuffled forward.

Smith stood trembling among them. He put his hand to his head as if to find a thought there. "I remember. Yes, now I do. A long time back. When I was a child. A book I read. A story. Oz, I think it was. Yes. Oz. *The Emerald City of Oz . . .*"

"Oz?"

"Yes, Oz, that's what it was. I saw it just now, like in the story. I saw it fall."

"Smith!"

"Yes, sir?"

"Report to the ship's doctor."

"Yes, sir!" A brisk salute.

"Be careful."

The men tiptoed, guns alert, beyond the ship's aseptic light to gaze at the long sea and the low hills.

"Why," whispered Smith, disappointed, "there's no one here at all, is there? No one here at all."

The wind blew sand over his shoes, whining.

HERE THERE BE TYGERS

"You have to beat a planet at its own game," said Chatterton. "Get in and rip it up, kill its snakes, poison its animals, dam its rivers, sow its fields, depollinate its air, mine it, nail it down, hack away at it, and get the blazes out from under when you have what you want. Otherwise, a planet will fix you good. You can't trust planets. They're bound to be different, bound to be bad, bound to be out to get you, especially this far out, a billion miles from nowhere, so you get them first. Tear their skin off, I say. Drag out the minerals and run away before the nightmare world explodes in your face. That's the way to treat them."

The rocket ship sank down toward planet 7 of star system 84. They had traveled millions upon millions of miles; Earth was far away, her system and her sun forgotten, her system settled and investigated and profited on, and other systems rummaged through and milked and tidied up, and now the rockets of these tiny men from an impossibly remote planet were probing out to far universes. In a few months, a few years, they could travel anywhere, for the speed of their rocket was the speed of a god, and now for the ten-thousandth time one of the rockets of the far-circling hunt was feathering down toward an alien world.

"No," said Captain Forester. "I have too much respect for other worlds to treat them the way you want to, Chatterton. It's not my business to rape or ruin, anyway, thank God. I'm glad I'm just a rocket man. You're the anthropologist-mineralogist. Go ahead, do your mining and ripping and scraping. I'll just watch. I'll just go around looking at this new world, whatever it is, however it seems. I like to look. All rocket men are lookers or they wouldn't be rocket men. You

Copyright 1951 by Ray Bradbury

like to smell new airs, if you're a rocket man, and see new oceans and islands."

"Take your gun along," said Chatterton.

"In my holster," said Forester.

They turned to the port together and saw the green world rising to meet their ship. "I wonder what *it* thinks of us?" said Forester.

"It won't like me," said Chatterton. "I'll see to it it won't like me. And I don't care, you know, I'm out for the money. Land us over there, will you, Captain; that looks like rich country if I ever saw it."

It was the freshest green color they had seen since childhood.

Lakes lay like clear blue water droplets through the soft hills; there were no loud highways, signboards or cities. It's a sea of green golf links, thought Forester, which goes on forever. Putting greens, driving greens, you could walk ten thousand miles in any direction and never finish your game. A Sunday planet, a croquet-lawn world, where you could lie on your back, clover in your lips, eyes half shut, smiling at the sky, smelling the grass, drowse through an eternal Sabbath, rousing only on occasion to turn the Sunday paper or crack the red-striped wooden ball through the wicket.

"If ever a planet was a woman, this one is."

"Woman on the outside, man on the inside," said Chatterton. "All hard underneath, all male iron, copper, uranium, black sod. Don't let the cosmetics fool you."

He walked to the bin where the Earth Drill waited. Its great screw-snout glittered bluely, ready to stab seventy feet deep and suck out corks of earth, deeper still with extensions into the heart of the planet. Chatterton winked at it. "We'll fix your planet, Forester, but good."

"Yes, I know you will," said Forester, quietly.

The rocket landed.

"It's too green, too peaceful," said Chatterton. "I don't like it." He turned to the captain. "We'll go out with our rifles."

"I give orders, if you don't mind."

"Yes, and my company pays our way with millions of dollars of machinery we must protect; quite an investment."

The air on the new planet 7 in star system 84 was good. The port swung wide. The men filed out into the greenhouse world.

The last man to emerge was Chatterton, gun in hand.

As Chatterton set foot to the green lawn, the earth trembled. The grass shook. The distant forest rumbled. The sky seemed to blink and darken imperceptibly. The men were watching Chatterton when it happened.

"An earthquake!"

Chatterton's face paled. Everyone laughed.

"It doesn't like you, Chatterton!"

"Nonsense!"

The trembling died away at last.

"Well," said Captain Forester, "It didn't quake for us, so it must be that it doesn't approve of your philosophy."

"Coincidence," Chatterton smiled weakly. "Come on now, on the double, I want the Drill out here in a half hour for a few samplings."

"Just a moment." Forester stopped laughing. "We've got to clear the area first, be certain there're no hostile people or animals. Besides, it isn't every year you hit a planet like this, very nice; can you blame us if we want to have a look at it?"

"All right." Chatterton joined them. "Let's get it over with."

They left a guard at the ship and they walked away over fields and meadows, over small hills and into little valleys. Like a bunch of boys out hiking on the finest day of the best summer in the most beautiful year in history, walking in the croquet weather where if you listened you could hear the whisper of the wooden ball across grass, the click through the wicket, the gentle undulations of voices, a sudden high drift of women's laughter from some ivy-shaded porch, the tinkle of ice in the summer tea pitcher.

"Hey," said Driscoll, one of the younger crewmen, sniffing the air. "I brought a baseball and bat; we'll have a game later. What a diamond!"

The men laughed quietly in the baseball season, in the good quiet wind for tennis, in the weather for bicycling and picking wild grapes.

"How'd you like the job of mowing all this?" asked Driscoll.

The men stopped.

"I *knew* there was something wrong!" cried Chatterton. "This grass; it's freshly cut!"

"Probably a species of dichondra; always short."

Chatterton spat on the green grass and rubbed it in with his boot. "I don't like it. I don't like it. If anything happened to us, no one on Earth would ever know. Silly policy: if a rocket fails to return, we never send a second rocket to check the reason why."

"Natural enough," explained Forester. "We can't waste time on a thousand hostile worlds, fighting futile wars. Each rocket represents years, money, lives. We can't afford to waste *two* rockets if one rocket proves a planet hostile. We go on to peaceful planets. Like this one."

"I often wonder," said Driscoll, "what happened to all those lost expeditions on worlds we'll never try again."

Chatterton eyed the distant forest. "They were shot, stabbed, broiled for dinner. Even as we may be, any minute. It's time we got back to work, Captain!"

They stood at the top of a little rise.

"Feel," said Driscoll, his hands and arms out loosely. "Remember how you used to run when you were a kid, and how the wind felt. Like feathers on your arms. You ran and thought any minute you'd fly, but you never quite did."

The men stood remembering. There was a smell of pollen and new rain drying upon a million grass blades.

Driscoll gave a little run. "Feel it, by God, the wind. You know, we never have *really* flown by ourselves. We have to sit inside tons of metal, away from flying, really. We've never flown like birds fly, to themselves. Wouldn't it be nice to put your arms out like this——" He extended his arms. "And run." He ran ahead of them, laughing at his idiocy. "And fly!" he cried.

He flew.

Time passed on the silent gold wristwatches of the men standing below. They stared up. And from the sky came a high sound of almost unbelievable laughter.

"Tell him to come down now," whispered Chatterton. "He'll be killed."

Nobody heard. Their faces were raised away from Chatterton; they were stunned and smiling.

At last Driscoll landed at their feet. "Did you *see* me? I flew!"

They had seen.

"Let me sit down, oh, Lord, Lord." Driscoll slapped his knees, chuckling. "I'm a sparrow, I'm a hawk, God bless me. Go on, all of you, try it!"

"It's the wind, it picked me up and flew me!" he said, a moment later, gasping, shivering with delight.

"Let's get out of here." Chatterton started turning, slowly in circles, watching the blue sky. "It's a trap, it wants us all to fly in the air. Then it'll drop us all at once and kill us. I'm going back to the ship."

"You'll wait for my order on that," said Forester.

The men were frowning, standing in the warm-cool air, while the wind sighed about them. There was a kite sound in the air, a sound of eternal March.

"I *asked* the wind to fly me," said Driscoll. "And it *did!*"

Forester waved the others aside. "I'll chance it next. If I'm killed, back to the ship, all of you."

"I'm sorry, I can't allow this, you're the captain," said Chatterton. "We can't risk you." He took out his gun. "I should have some sort of authority or force here. This game's gone on too long; I'm ordering us back to the ship."

"Holster your gun," said Forester, quietly.

"Stand still, you idiot!" Chatterton blinked now at this man, now at that. "Haven't you *felt* it? This world's alive, it has a look to us, it's playing with us, biding its time."

"I'll be the judge of that," said Forester. "You're going back to the ship, in a moment, under arrest, if you don't put up that gun."

"If you fools won't come with me, you can die out here. I'm going back, get my samples, and get out."

"Chatterton!"

"Don't try to stop me!"

Chatterton started to run. Then, suddenly, he gave a cry. Everyone shouted and looked up.

"There he goes," said Driscoll.

Chatterton was up in the sky.

Night had come on like the closing of a great but gentle eye. Chatterton sat stunned on the side of the hill. The other men sat around him, exhausted and laughing. He would not look at them, he would not look at the sky, he would only feel of the earth, and his arms and his legs and his body, tightening in on himself.

"Oh, wasn't it perfect!" said a man named Koestler.

They had all flown, like orioles and eagles and sparrows, and they were all happy.

"Come out of it, Chatterton, it was fun, wasn't it?" said Koestler.

"It's impossible." Chatterton shut his eyes, tight, tight.

"There's only one way for it to do it; it's alive. The air's alive. Like a fist it picked me up. Any minute now, it can kill us all. It's alive."

"All right," said Koestler, "say it's alive. And a living thing must have purpose. Suppose the purpose of this world is to make us happy."

As if to add to this, Driscoll came flying up, canteens in each hand. "I found a creek, tested and found pure water, wait'll you try it!"

Forester took a canteen, nudged Chatterton with it, offering a drink. Chatterton shook his head and drew hastily away. He put his hands over his face. "It's the blood of this planet. Living blood. Drink that, put that inside and you put this world inside you to peer out your eyes and listen through your ears. No thanks!"

Forester shrugged and drank.

"Wine!" he said.

"It can't be!"

"It *is*! Smell it, taste it! A rare white wine!"

"French domestic." Driscoll sipped his.

"Poison," said Chatterton.

They passed the canteens around.

They had idled on through the gentle afternoon, not wanting to do anything to disturb the peace that lay all about them. They were like very young men in the presence of great beauty, of a fine and famous woman, afraid that by some word, some gesture, they might turn her face away, avert her loveliness and her kindly attentions. They had felt the earthquake that had greeted Chatterton, and they did not want earthquake. Let them enjoy this Day After School Lets Out, this fishing weather. Let them sit under the shade trees or walk on the tender hills, but let them drill no drillings, test no testings, contaminate no contaminations.

They found a small stream which poured into a boiling water pool. Fish, swimming in the cold creek above, fell glittering into the hot spring and floated, minutes later, cooked, to the surface.

Chatterton reluctantly joined the others, eating.

"It'll poison us all. There's always a trick to things like this. I'm sleeping in the rocket tonight. You can sleep out if you want. To quote a map I saw in medieval history: 'Here there be tygers.' Some time tonight when you're sleeping, the tigers and cannibals will show up."

Forester shook his head. "I'll go along with you, this planet is alive. It's a race itself. But it needs us to show off to, to appreciate its beauty. What's the use of a stage full of miracles if there's no audience?"

But Chatterton was busy. He was bent over, being sick. "I'm poisoned! Poisoned!"

They held his shoulders until the sickness passed. They gave him water. The others were feeling fine.

"Better eat nothing but ship's food from now on," advised Forester. "It'd be safer."

"We're starting work right now." Chatterton swayed, wiping his mouth. "We've wasted a whole day. I'll work alone if I have to. I'll show this infernal place!"

He staggered away toward the rocket.

"He doesn't know when he's well off," murmured Driscoll. "Can't we stop him, Captain?"

"He practically owns the expedition. We don't have to help him, there's a clause in our contract that guarantees refusal to work under dangerous conditions. So . . . do unto this Picnic Ground as you would have it do unto you. No initial-cutting on the trees. Replace the turf on the greens. Clean up your banana peels after you."

Now, below, in the ship there was an immense humming. From the storage port rolled the great shining Drill. Chatterton followed it, calling directions to its robot radio. "This way, here!"

"The fool."

"Now!" cried Chatterton.

The Drill plunged its long screw-bore into the green grass. Chatterton waved up at the other men. "Watch this!"

The sky trembled.

The Drill stood in the center of a little sea of grass. For a moment it plunged away, bringing up moist corks of sod which it spat unceremoniously into a shaking analysis bin.

Now the Drill gave a wrenched, metallic squeal like a monster interrupted at its feed. From the soil beneath it slow bluish liquids bubbled up.

Chatterton shouted, "Get back, you fool!"

The Drill lumbered in a prehistoric dance. It shrieked like a mighty train turning on a sharp curve, throwing out red sparks. It was sinking. The black slime gave under it in a dark convulsion.

With a coughing sigh, a series of pants and churnings, the

Drill sank into a black scum like an elephant shot and dying, trumpeting, like a mammoth at the end of an Age, vanishing limb by ponderous limb into the pit.

"Fool, Fool," said Forester under his breath, fascinated with the scene. "You know what that is, Driscoll? It's tar. The fool machine hit a tar pit!"

"Listen, listen!" cried Chatterton at the Drill, running about on the edge of the oily lake. "*This* way, over here!"

But like the old tyrants of the earth, the dinosaurs with their tubed and screaming necks, the Drill was plunging and thrashing in the one lake from where there was no returning to bask on the firm and understandable shore.

Chatterton turned to the other men far away. "Do something, someone!"

The Drill was gone.

The tar pit bubbled and gloated, sucking the hidden monster bones. The surface of the pool was silent. A huge bubble, the last, rose, expelled a scent of ancient petroleum, and fell apart.

The men came down and stood on the edge of the little black sea.

Chatterton stopped yelling.

After a long minute of staring into the silent tar pool, Chatterton turned and looked at the hills, blindly, at the green rolling lawns. The distant trees were growing fruit now and dropping it, softly, to the ground.

"I'll show it," he said quietly.

"Take it easy, Chatterton."

"I'll fix it," he said.

"Sit down, have a drink."

"I'll fix it good, I'll show it it can't do this to me."

Chatterton started off back to the ship.

"Wait a minute now," said Forester.

Chatterton ran. "I know what to do, I know how to fix it!"

"Stop him!" said Forester. He ran, then remembered he could fly. "The A-Bomb's on the ship, if he should get to that . . ."

The other men had thought of that and were in the air. A small grove of trees stood between the rocket and Chatterton as he ran on the ground, forgetting that he could fly, or afraid to fly, or not allowed to fly, yelling. The crew headed for the rocket to wait for him, the captain with them. They arrived, formed a line, and shut the rocket port. The last they saw of Chatterton he was plunging through the edge of the tiny forest.

The crew stood waiting.

"That fool, that crazy guy."

Chatterton didn't come out on the other side of the small woodland.

"He's turned back, waiting for us to relax our guard."

"Go bring him in," said Forester.

Two men flew off.

Now, softly, a great and gentle rain fell upon the green world.

"The final touch," said Driscoll. "We'd never have to build houses here. Notice it's not raining *on* us. It's raining all around, ahead, behind us. What a world!"

They stood dry in the middle of the blue, cool rain. The sun was setting. The moon, a large one the color of ice, rose over the freshened hills.

"There's only one more thing this world needs."

"Yes," said everyone, thoughtfully, slowly.

"We'll have to go looking," said Driscoll. "It's logical. The wind flies us, the trees and streams feed us, everything is alive. Perhaps if we asked for companionship . . ."

"I've thought a long time, today and other days," said Koestler. "We're all bachelors, been traveling for years, and tired of it. Wouldn't it be nice to settle down somewhere? Here, maybe. On Earth you sweat just to save enough to buy a house, pay taxes; the cities stink. Here, you won't even need a house, with this weather. If it gets monotonous you can ask for rain, clouds, snow, changes. You don't have to work here for anything."

"It'd be boring. We'd go crazy."

"No," Koestler said, smiling. "If life got too soft, all we'd have to do is repeat a few times what Chatterton said: *'Here there be tygers.'* Listen!"

Far away, wasn't there the faintest roar of a giant cat, hidden in the twilight forests?

The men shivered.

"A versatile world," said Koestler dryly. "A woman who'll do anything to please her guests, as long as we're kind to her. Chatterton wasn't kind."

"Chatterton. What about him?"

As if to answer this, someone cried from a distance. The

two men who had flown off to find Chatterton were waving at the edge of the woods.

Forester, Driscoll, and Koestler flew down alone.

"What's up?"

The men pointed into the forest. "Thought you'd want to see this, Captain. It's eerie." One of the men indicated a pathway. "Look here, sir."

The marks of great claws stood on the path, fresh and clear.

"And over here."

A few drops of blood.

A heavy smell of some feline animal hung in the air. "Chatterton?"

"I don't think we'll ever find him, Captain."

Faintly, faintly, moving away, now gone in the breathing silence of twilight, came the roar of a tiger.

The men lay on the resilient grass by the rocket and the night was warm. "Reminds me of nights when I was a kid," said Driscoll. "My brother and I waited for the hottest night in July and then we slept on the Court House lawn, counting the stars, talking; it was a great night, the best night of my life." Then he added, "Not counting tonight, of course."

"I keep thinking about Chatterton," said Koestler.

"Don't," said Forester. "We'll sleep a few hours and take off. We can't chance staying here another day. I don't mean the danger that got Chatterton. No. I mean, if we stayed on we'd get to liking this world too much. We'd never want to leave."

A soft wind blew over them.

"I don't want to leave now." Driscoll put his hands behind his head, lying quietly. "And it doesn't want us to leave."

"If we go back to Earth and tell everyone what a lovely planet it is, what then, Captain? They'll come smashing in here and ruin it."

"No," said Forester idly. "First, this planet wouldn't put up with a full-scale invasion. I don't know what it'd do, but it could probably think of some interesting things. Secondly, I like this planet too much; I respect it. We'll go back to Earth and lie about it. Say it's hostile. Which it would be to the average man, like Chatterton, jumping in here to hurt it. I guess we won't be lying after all."

"Funny thing," said Koestler. "I'm not afraid. Chatterton vanishes, is killed most horribly, perhaps, yet we lie here, no one runs, no one trembles. It's idiotic. Yet it's right. We trust *it* and *it* trusts us."

"Did you notice, after you drank just so much of the wine-water, you didn't want more? A world of moderation."

They lay listening to something like the great heart of this earth beating slowly and warmly under their bodies.

Forester thought, I'm thirsty.

A drop of rain splashed on his lips.

He laughed quietly.

I'm lonely, he thought.

Distantly, he heard soft, high voices.

He turned his eyes in upon a vision. There was a group of hills from which flowed a clear river, and in the shallows of that river, sending up spray, their faces shimmering, were the beautiful women. They played like children on the shore. And it came to Forester to know about them and their life. They were nomads, roaming the face of this world as was their desire. There were no highways or cities, there were only hills and plains and winds to carry them like white feathers where they wished. As Forester shaped the questions, some invisible answerer whispered the answers. There were no men. These women, alone, produced their race. The men had vanished fifty thousand years ago. And where were these women now? A mile down from the green forest, a mile over on the wine stream by the six white stones, and a third mile to the large river. There, in the shallows, were the women who would make fine wives, and raise beautiful children.

Forester opened his eyes. The other men were sitting up.

"I had a dream."

They had all dreamed.

"A mile down from the green forest . . ."

". . . a mile over on the wine stream . . ."

". . . by the six white stones . . ." said Koestler.

". . . and a third mile to the large river," said Driscoll, sitting there.

Nobody spoke again for a moment. They looked at the silver rocket standing there in the starlight.

"Do we walk or fly, Captain?"

Forester said nothing.

Driscoll said, "Captain let's stay. Let's never go back to Earth. They'll never come and investigate to see what happened to us; they'll think we were destroyed here. What do you say?"

Forester's face was perspiring. His tongue moved again and

again on his lips. His hands twitched over his knees. The crew sat waiting.

"It'd be nice," said the captain.

"Sure."

"But . . ." Forester sighed. "We've got our job to do. People invested in our ship. We owe it to them to go back."

Forester got up. The men still sat on the ground, not listening to him.

"It's such a fine, nice, wonderful night," said Koestler.

They stared at the soft hills and the trees and the rivers running off to other horizons.

"Let's get aboard ship," said Forester, with difficulty.

"Captain . . ."

"Get aboard," he said.

The rocket rose into the sky. Looking back, Forester saw every valley and every tiny lake.

"We should've stayed," said Koestler.

"Yes, I know."

"It's not too late to turn back."

"I'm afraid it is." Forester made an adjustment on the port telescope. "Look now."

Koestler looked.

The face of the world was changed. Tigers, dinosaurs, mammoths appeared. Volcanoes erupted, cyclones and hurricanes tore over the hills in a welter and fury of weather.

"Yes, she was a woman all right," said Forester. "Waiting for visitors for millions of years, preparing herself, making herself beautiful. She put on her best face for us. When Chatterton treated her badly, she warned him a few times, and then, when he tried to ruin her beauty, eliminated him. She wanted to be loved, like every woman, for herself, not for her wealth. So now, after she had offered us everything, we turn our backs. She's the woman scorned. She let us go, yes, but we can never come back. She'll be waiting for us with *those* . . ." He nodded to the tigers and the cyclones and the boiling seas.

"Captain," said Koestler.

"Yes."

"It's a little late to tell you this. But just before we took off, I was in charge of the air lock. I let Driscoll slip away from the ship. He wanted to go. I couldn't refuse him. I'm responsible. He's back there now, on that planet."

They both turned to the viewing port.

After a long while, Forester said, "I'm glad. I'm glad one of us had enough sense to stay."

"But he's dead by now!"

"No, that display down there is for us, perhaps a visual hallucination. Underneath all the tigers and lions and hurricanes, Driscoll is quite safe and alive, because he's her only audience now. Oh, she'll spoil him rotten. He'll lead a wonderful life, he will, while we're slugging it out up and down the system looking for but never finding a planet quite like this again. No, we won't try to go back and 'rescue' Driscoll. I don't think 'she' would let us anyway. Full speed ahead, Koestler, make it full speed."

The rocket leaped forward into greater accelerations.

And just before the planet dwindled away in brightness and mist, Forester imagined that he could see Driscoll very clearly, walking away down from the green forest, whistling quietly, all of the fresh planet around him, a wine creek flowing for him, baked fish lolling in the hot springs, fruit ripening in the midnight trees, and distant forests and lakes waiting for him to happen by. Driscoll walked away across the endless green lawns near the six white stones, beyond the forest, to the edge of the large bright river. . . .

THE STRAWBERRY WINDOW

In his dream he was shutting the front door with its straw-berry windows and lemon windows and windows like white clouds and windows like clear water in a country stream. Two dozen panes squared round the one big pane, colored of fruit wines and gelatins and cool water ices. He remem-bered his father holding him up as a child. "Look!" And through the green glass the world was emerald, moss, and summer mint. "Look!" The lilac pane made livid grapes of all the passers-by. And at last the strawberry glass perpetually bathed the town in roseate warmth, carpeted the world in pink sunrise, and made the cut lawn seem imported from some Persian rug bazaar. The strawberry window, best of all, cured people of their paleness, warmed the cold rain, and set the blowing, shifting February snows afire.

"Yes, yes! There—!"

He awoke.

He heard his boys talking before he was fully out of his dream and he lay in the dark now, listening to the sad sound their talk made, like the wind blowing the white sea-bottoms into the blue hills, and then he remembered.

We're on Mars, he thought.

"What?" His wife cried out in her sleep.

He hadn't realized he had spoken; he lay as still as he possibly could. But now, with a strange kind of numb reality, he saw his wife rise to haunt the room, her pale face staring through the small, high windows of their quonset hut at the clear but unfamiliar stars.

"Carrie," he whispered.

She did not hear.

"Carrie," he whispered. "There's something I want to tell

Copyright 1954 by Ray Bradbury

you. For a month now I've been wanting to say . . . tomorrow . . . tomorrow morning, there's going to be . . ."

But his wife sat all to herself in the blue starlight and would not look at him.

If only the sun stayed up, he thought, if only there was no night. For during the day he nailed the settlement town together, the boys were in school, and Carrie had cleaning, gardening, cooking to do. But when the sun was gone and their hands were empty of flowers or hammers and nails and arithmetics, their memories, like night birds, came home in the dark.

His wife moved, a slight turn of her head.

"Bob," she said at last. "I want to go home."

"Carrie!"

"This isn't home," she said.

He saw that her eyes were wet and brimming. "Carrie, hold on awhile."

"I've got no fingernails from holding on now!"

As if she still moved in her sleep, she opened her bureau drawers and took out layers of handkerchiefs, shirts, underclothing, and put it all on top of the bureau, not seeing it, letting her fingers touch and bring it out and put it down. The routine was long familiar now. She would talk and put things out and stand quietly awhile, and then later put all the things away and come, dry-faced, back to bed and dreams. He was afraid that some night she would empty every drawer and reach for the few ancient suitcases against the wall.

"Bob . . ." Her voice was not bitter, but soft, featureless, and as uncolored as the moonlight that showed what she was doing. "So many nights for six months I've talked this way; I'm ashamed. You work hard building houses in town. A man who works so hard shouldn't have to listen to a wife gone sad on him. But there's nothing to do but talk it out. It's the little things I miss most of all. I don't know—silly things. Our front-porch swing. The wicker rocking chair, summer nights. Looking at the people walk or ride by those evenings, back in Ohio. Our black upright piano, out of tune. My Swedish cut glass. Our parlor furniture—oh, it was like a herd of elephants, I know, and all of it old. And the Chinese hanging crystals that hit when the wind blew. And talking to neighbors there on the front porch, July nights. All those crazy, silly things . . . they're not important. But it seems those are things that come to mind around three in the morning. I'm sorry."

"Don't be," he said. "Mars is a far place. It smells funny, looks funny, and feels funny. I think to myself nights too. We came from a nice town."

"It was green," she said. "In the spring and summer. And yellow and red in the fall. And ours was a nice house; my, it was old, eighty-ninety years or so. Used to hear the house talking at night, whispering away. All the dry wood, the banisters, the front porch, the sills. Wherever you touched, it talked to you. Every room a different way. And when you had the whole house talking, it was a family around you in the dark, putting you to sleep. No other house, the kind they build nowadays, can be the same. A lot of people have got to go through and live in a house to make it mellow down all over. This place here, now, this hut, it doesn't know I'm in it, doesn't care if I live or die. It makes a noise like tin, and tin's cold. It's got no pores for the years to sink in. It's got no cellar for you to put things away for next year and the year after that. It's got no attic where you keep things from last year and all the other years before you were born. If we only had a little bit up here that was familiar, Bob, then we could make room for all that's strange. But when everything, *every single thing* is strange, then it takes forever to make things familiar."

He nodded in the dark. "There's nothing you say that I haven't thought."

She was looking at the moonlight where it lay upon the suitcases against the wall. He saw her move her hand down toward them.

"Carrie!"

"What?"

He swung his legs out of bed. "Carrie, I've done a crazy lame-brain thing. All these months I heard you dreaming away, scared, and the boys at night and the wind, and Mars out there, the sea-bottoms and all, and . . ." He stopped and swallowed. "You got to understand what I did and why I did it. All the money we had in the bank a month ago, all the money we saved for ten years, I spent."

"Bob!"

"I threw it away, Carrie, I swear, I threw it away on nothing. It was going to be a surprise. But now, tonight, there you are, and there are those blasted suitcases on the floor and . . ."

"Bob," she said, turning around. "You mean we've gone

through all *this*, on Mars, putting away extra money every week, only to have you burn it up in a few hours?"

"I don't know," he said. "I'm a crazy fool. Look, it's not long till morning. We'll get up early. I'll take you down to see what I've done. I don't want to tell you, I want you to see. And if it's no go then, well, there's always those suitcases and the rocket to Earth four times a month."

She did not move. "Bob, Bob," she murmured.

"Don't say any more," he said.

"Bob, Bob . . ." She shook her head slowly, unbelievingly. He turned away and lay back down on his own side of the bed, and she sat on the other side, looking at the bureau where her handkerchiefs and jewelry and clothing lay ready in neat stacks where she had left them. Outside a wind the color of moonlight stirred up the sleeping dust and powdered the air.

At last she lay back, but said nothing more and was a cold weight in the bed, staring down the long tunnel of night toward the faintest sign of morning.

They got up in the very first light and moved in the small quonset hut without a sound. It was a pantomime prolonged almost to the time when someone might scream at the silence, as the mother and father and the boys washed and dressed and ate a quiet breakfast of toast and fruit juice and coffee, with no one looking directly at anyone and everyone watching someone in the reflective surfaces of toaster, glassware, or cutlery, where all their faces were melted out of shape and made terribly alien in the early hour. Then, at last, they opened the quonset door and let in the air that blew across the cold blue-white Martian seas, where only the sand tides dissolved and shifted and made ghost patterns, and they stepped out under a raw and staring cold sky and began their walk toward a town, which seemed no more than a motion-picture set far on ahead of them on a vast, empty stage.

"What part of town are we going to?" asked Carrie.

"The rocket depot," he said. "But before we get there, I've a lot to say."

The boys slowed down and moved behind their parents, listening. The father gazed ahead, and not once in all the time he was talking did he look at his wife or sons to see how they were taking all that he said.

"I believe in Mars," he began quietly. "I guess I believe some day it'll belong to us. We'll nail it down. We'll settle in. We won't turn tail and run. It came to me one day a year ago, right after we first arrived. Why did we come? I asked myself. Because, I said, because. It's the same thing with the salmon every year. The salmon don't know why they go where they go, but they go, anyway. Up rivers they don't remember, up streams, jumping waterfalls, but finally making it to where they propagate and die, and the whole thing starts again. Call it racial memory, instinct, call it nothing, but there it is. And here we are."

They walked in the silent morning with the great sky watching them and the strange blue and steam-white sands sifting about their feet on the new highway.

"So here we are. And from Mars where? Jupiter, Neptune, Pluto, and on out? Right. *And on out*. Why? Some day the sun will blow up like a leaky furnace. Boom—there goes Earth. But maybe Mars won't be hurt; or if Mars is hurt maybe Pluto won't be, or if Pluto's hurt, then where'll *we* be, our sons' sons, that is?"

He gazed steadily up into that flawless shell of plum-colored sky.

"Why, we'll be on some world with a number maybe; planet 6 of star system 97, planet 2 of system 99! So darn far off from here you need a nightmare to take it in! We'll be gone, do you see, gone off away and safe! And I thought to myself, ah, ah. So that's the reason we came to Mars, so *that's* the reason men shoot off their rockets."

"Bob—"

"Let me finish; not to make money, no. Not to see the sights, no. Those are the lies men tell, the fancy reasons they give themselves. Get rich, get famous, they say. Have fun, jump around, they say. But all the while, inside, something else is ticking along the way it ticks in salmon or whales, the way it ticks, oh, Lord, in the smallest microbe you want to name. And that little clock that ticks in everything living, you know what it says? It says get away, spread out, move along, keep swimming. Run to so many worlds and build so many towns that *nothing* can ever kill man. You *see*, Carrie? It's not just us come to Mars, it's the race, the whole darn human race, depending on how *we* make out in our lifetime. This thing is so big I want to laugh, I'm so scared stiff of it."

He felt the boys walking steadily behind him and he felt

Carrie beside him and he wanted to see her face and how she was taking all this, but he didn't look there, either.

"All this is no different than me and Dad walking the fields when I was a boy, casting seed by hand when our seeder broke down and we'd no money to fix it. It had to be done, somehow, for the later crops. Why now, Carrie, why, do you *remember* those Sunday-supplement articles. THE EARTH WILL FREEZE IN A MILLION YEARS! I bawled once, as a boy, reading articles like that. My mother asked why. I'm bawling for all those poor people up ahead, I said. Don't worry about them, Mother said. But, Carrie, that's my whole point; we *are* worrying about them. Or we wouldn't be here. It matters if Man with a capital M keeps going. There's nothing better than Man with a capital M in my books. I'm prejudiced, of course, because I'm one of the breed. But if there's any way to get hold of that immortality men are always talking about, this is the way—spread out—seed the universe. Then you got a harvest against crop failures anywhere down the line. No matter if Earth has famines or the rust comes in. You got the new wheat lifting on Venus or where-in-blazes-ever man gets to in the next thousand years. I'm crazy with the idea, Carrie, crazy. When I finally hit on it I got so excited I wanted to grab people, you, the boys, and tell them. But well, I knew that wasn't necessary. I knew a day or night would come when you'd hear that ticking in yourselves too, and then you'd see, and no one'd have to say anything again about all this. It's big talk, Carrie, I know, and big thoughts for a man just short of five feet five, but by all that's holy, it's true."

They moved through the deserted streets of the town and listened to the echoes of their walking feet.

"And this morning?" said Carrie.

"I'm coming to this morning," he said. "Part of *me* wants to go home too. But the other part says if we go, everything's lost. So I thought, what bothers us most? Some of the things we once had. Some of the boys' things, your things, mine. And I thought, if it takes an old thing to get a new thing started, why then, I'll use the old thing. I remember from history books that a thousand years ago they put charcoals in a hollowed out cow horn, blew on them during the day, so they carried their fire on marches from place to place, to start a fire every night with the sparks left over from morning. Always a new fire, but always something of the old in it. So

I weighed and balanced it off. Is the Old worth all our money? I asked. No! It's only the things we *did* with the Old that have any worth. Well, then, is the New worth *all* our money? I asked. Do you feel like investing in the day after the middle of next week? Yes! I said. If I can fight this thing that makes us want to go back to Earth, I'd dip my money in kerosene and strike a match!"

Carrie and the two boys did not move. They stood on the street, looking at him as if he were a storm that had passed over and around, almost blowing them from the ground, a storm that was now dying away.

"The freight rocket came in this morning," he said, quietly. "Our delivery's on it. Let's go and pick it up."

They walked slowly up the three steps into the rocket depot and across the echoing floor toward the freight room that was just sliding back its doors, opening for the day.

"Tell us again about the salmon," said one of the boys.

In the middle of the warm morning they drove out of town in a rented truck filled with great crates and boxes and parcels and packages, long ones, tall ones, short ones, flat ones, all numbered and neatly addressed to one Robert Prentiss, New Toledo, Mars.

They stopped the truck by the quonset hut and the boys jumped down and helped their mother out. For a moment Bob sat behind the wheel, and then slowly got out himself to walk around and look into the back of the truck at the crates.

And by noon all but one of the boxes were opened and their contents placed on the sea-bottom where the family stood among them.

"Carrie . . ."

And he led her up the old porch steps that now stood uncrated on the edge of town.

"Listen to 'em, Carrie."

The steps squeaked and whispered underfoot.

"What do they say, tell me what they say?"

She stood on the ancient wooden steps, holding to herself, and could not tell him.

He waved his hand. "Front porch here, living room there, dining room, kitchen, three bedrooms. Most we'll build new, part we'll bring. Of course all we got here now is the front steps, some parlor furniture, and the old bed."

"All that money, Bob!"

He turned, smiling. "You're not mad, now, look at me!

You're not mad. We'll bring it up, next year, five years! The cut-glass vases, that Armenian carpet your mother gave us in 1975! Just *let* the sun explode!"

They looked at the other crates, numbered and lettered: Front-porch swing, front-porch wicker rocker, hanging Chinese crystals . . .

"I'll blow them myself to make them ring."

And then they set the front door, with its little panes of colored glass, on the top of the stairs, and Carrie looked through the strawberry window.

"What do you see?"

But he knew what she saw, for he gazed through the colored glass, too. And there was Mars, with its cold sky warmed and its dead seas fired with color, with its hills like mounds of strawberry ice, and its sand like burning charcoals sifted by wind. The strawberry window, the strawberry window, breathed soft rose colors on the land and filled the mind and the eye with the light of a never-ending dawn. Bent there, looking through, he heard himself say:

"The town'll be out this way in a year. This'll be a shady street, you'll have your porch, and you'll have friends. You won't *need* all this so much, then. But starting right here, with this little bit that's familiar, watch it spread, watch Mars change so you'll know it as if you've known it all your life."

He ran down the steps to the last and as-yet unopened canvas-covered crate. With his pocket knife he cut a hole in the canvas. "Guess!" he said.

"My kitchen stove? My sewing machine?"

"Not in a million years." He smiled very gently. "Sing me a song," he said.

"Bob, you're clean off your head."

"Sing me a song worth all the money we had in the bank and now don't have, but who gives a blast in hades," he said.

"I don't know anything but 'Genevieve, Sweet Genevieve!'"

"Sing that," he said.

But she could not open her mouth and start the song. He saw her lips move and try, but there was no sound.

He ripped the canvas wider and shoyed his hand into the crate and touched around for a quiet moment, and started to sing the words himself until he moved his hand a last time and then a single clear piano chord sprang out on the morning air.

"There," he said. "Let's take it right on to the end. Everyone! Here's the harmony."

THE DRAGON

The night blew in the short grass on the moor; there was no other motion. It had been years since a single bird had flown by in the great blind shell of sky. Long ago a few small stones had simulated life when they crumbled and fell into dust. Now only the night moved in the souls of the two men bent by their lonely fire in the wilderness; darkness pumped quietly in their veins and ticked silently in their temples and their wrists.

Firelight fled up and down their wild faces and welled in their eyes in orange tatters. They listened to each other's faint, cool breathing and the lizard blink of their eyelids. At last, one man poked the fire with his sword.

"Don't idiot; you'll give us away!"

"No matter," said the second man. The dragon can smell us miles off anyway. God's breath, it's cold. I wish I was back at the castle."

"It's death, not sleep we're after. . . ."

"Why? Why? The dragon never sets foot in the town!"

"Quiet, fool! He eats men traveling alone from our town to the next!"

"Let them be eaten and let us get home!"

"Wait now; listen!"

The two men froze.

They waited a long time, but there was only the shake of their horses' nervous skin like black velvet tambourines jingling the silver stirrup buckles, softly, softly.

"Ah." The second man sighed. "What a land of nightmares. Everything happens here. Someone blows out the sun; it's night. And then, and *then*, oh, sweet mortality, listen! This dragon, they say his eyes are fire. His breath a white

Copyright © 1955 by Ray Bradbury

gas; you can see him burn across the dark lands. He runs with sulfur and thunder and kindles the grass. Sheep panic and die insane. Women deliver forth monsters. The dragon's fury is such that tower walls shake back to dust. His victims, at sunrise, are strewn hither thither on the hills. How many knights, I ask, have gone for this monster and failed, even as we shall fail?"

"Enough of that!"

"More than enough! Out here in this desolation I cannot tell what year this is!"

"Nine hundred years since the Nativity."

"No, no," whispered the second man, eyes shut. "On this moor is no Time, is only Forever. I feel if I ran back on the road the town would be gone, the people yet unborn, things changed, the castles unquarried from the rocks, the timbers still uncut from the forests; don't ask how I know; the moor knows and tells me. And here we sit alone in the land of the fire dragon, God save us!"

"Be you afraid, then gird on your armor!"

"What use? The dragon runs from nowhere; we cannot guess its home. It vanishes in fog; we know not where it goes. Aye, on with our armor, we'll die well dressed."

Half into his silver corselet, the second man stopped again and turned his head.

Across the dim country, full of night and nothingness from the heart of the moor itself, the wind sprang full of dust from clocks that used dust for telling time. There were black suns burning in the heart of this new wind and a million burnt leaves shaken from some autumn tree beyond the horizon. The wind melted landscapes, lengthened bones like white wax, made the blood roil and thicken to a muddy deposit in the brain. The wind was a thousand souls dying and all time confused and in transit. It was a fog inside of a mist inside of a darkness, and this place was no man's place and there was no year or hour at all, but only these men in a faceless emptiness of sudden frost, storm and white thunder which moved behind the great falling pane of green glass that was the lightning. A squall of rain drenched the turf; all faded away until there was unbreathing hush and the two men waiting alone with their warmth in a cool season.

"There," whispered the first man, "Oh, *there* . . ."

Miles off, rushing with a great chant and a roar—the dragon.

In silence the men buckled on their armor and mounted

their horses. The midnight wilderness was split by a monstrous gushing as the dragon roared nearer, nearer; its flashing yellow glare spurted above a hill and then, fold on fold of dark body, distantly seen, therefore indistinct, flowed over that hill and plunged vanishing into a valley.

"Quick!"

They spurred their horses forward to a small hollow.

"This is where it passes!"

They seized their lances with mailed fists and blinded their horses by flipping the visors down over their eyes.

"Lord!"

"Yes, let us use His name."

On the instant, the dragon rounded a hill. Its monstrous amber eye fed on them, fired their armor in red glints and glitters. With a terrible wailing cry and a grinding rush it flung itself forward.

"Mercy, mercy!"

The lance struck under the unlidded yellow eye, buckled, tossed the man through the air. The dragon hit, spilled him over, down, ground him under. Passing, the black brunt of its shoulder smashed the remaining horse and rider a hundred feet against the side of a boulder, wailing, wailing, the dragon shrieking, the fire all about, around, under it, a pink, yellow, orange sun-fire with great soft plumes of blinding smoke.

"Did you *see* it?" cried a voice. "Just like I told you!"

"The same! The same! A knight in armor, by the Lord Harry! We *hit* him!"

"You goin' to stop?"

"Did once; found nothing. Don't like to stop on this moor. I get the willies. Got a *feel*, it has."

"But we hit *something!*"

"Gave him plenty of whistle; chap wouldn't budge!"

A steaming blast cut the mist aside.

"We'll make Stokely on time. More coal, eh, Fred?"

Another whistle shook dew from the empty sky. The night train, in fire and fury, shot through a gully, up a rise, and vanished away over cold earth toward the north, leaving black smoke and steam to dissolve in the numbed air minutes after it had passed and gone forever.

THE GIFT

Tomorrow would be Christmas, and even while the three of them rode to the rocket port the mother and father were worried. It was the boy's first flight into space, his very first time in a rocket, and they wanted everything to be perfect. So when, at the custom's table, they were forced to leave behind his gift which exceeded the weight limit by no more than a few ounces and the little tree with the lovely white candles, they felt themselves deprived of the season and their love.

The boy was waiting for them in the Terminal room. Walking toward him, after their unsuccessful clash with the Interplanetary officials, the mother and father whispered to each other.

"What shall we do?"

"Nothing, nothing. What *can* we do?"

"Silly rules!"

"And he so wanted the tree!"

The siren gave a great howl and people pressed forward into the Mars Rocket. The mother and father walked at the very last, their small pale son between them, silent.

"I'll think of something," said the father.

"What . . . ?" asked the boy.

And the rocket took off and they were flung headlong into dark space.

The rocket moved and left fire behind and left Earth behind on which the date was December 24, 2052, heading out into a place where there was no time at all, no month, no year, no hour. They slept away the rest of the first "day." Near midnight, by their Earth-time New York watches, the boy awoke and said, "I want to go look out the porthole."

Copyright 1952 by Ray Bradbury

There was only one port, a "window" of immensely thick glass of some size, up on the next deck.

"Not quite yet," said the father. "I'll take you up later."

"I want to see where we are and where we're going."

"I want you to wait for a reason," said the father.

He had been lying awake, turning this way and that, thinking of the abandoned gift, the problem of the season, the lost tree and the white candles. And at last, sitting up, no more than five minutes ago, he believed he had found a plan. He need only carry it out and this journey would be fine and joyous indeed.

"Son," he said, "in exactly one half hour it will be Christmas."

"Oh," said the mother, dismayed that he had mentioned it. Somehow she had rather hoped that the boy would forget.

The boy's face grew feverish and his lips trembled. "I know, I know. Will I get a present, will I? Will I have a tree? You promised—"

"Yes, yes, all that, and more," said the father.

The mother started. "But—"

"I mean it," said the father. "I really mean it. All and more, much more. Excuse me, now. I'll be back."

He left them for about twenty minutes. When he came back he was smiling. "Almost time."

"Can I hold your watch?" asked the boy, and the watch was handed over and he held it ticking in his fingers as the rest of the hour drifted by in fire and silence and unfelt motion.

"It's Christmas *now!* Christmas! Where's my present?"

"Here we go," said the father and took his boy by the shoulder and led him from the room, down the hall, up a rampway, his wife following.

"I don't understand," she kept saying.

"You will. Here we are," said the father.

They had stopped at the closed door of a large cabin. The father tapped three times and then twice in a code. The door opened and the light in the cabin went out and there was a whisper of voices.

"Go on in, son," said the father.

"It's dark."

"I'll hold your hand. Come on, Mama."

They stepped into the room and the door shut, and the room was very dark indeed. And before them loomed a great glass eye, the porthole, a window four feet high and six feet wide, from which they could look out into space.

The boy gasped.

Behind him, the father and the mother gasped with him, and then in the dark room some people began to sing.

"Merry Christmas, son," said the father.

And the voices in the room sang the old, the familiar carols, and the boy moved forward slowly until his face was pressed against the cool glass of the port. And he stood there for a long long time, just looking and looking out into space and the deep night at the burning and the burning of ten billion billion white and lovely candles . . .

FROST AND FIRE

During the night, Sim was born. He lay wailing upon the cold cave stones. His blood beat through him a thousand pulses each minute. He grew, steadily.

Into his mouth his mother with feverish hands put the food. The nightmare of living was begun. Almost instantly at birth his eyes grew alert, and then, without half understanding why, filled with bright, insistent terror. He gagged upon the food, choked and wailed. He looked about, blindly.

There was a thick fog. It cleared. The outlines of the cave appeared. And a man loomed up, insane and wild and terrible. A man with a dying face. Old, withered by winds, baked like adobe in the heat. The man was crouched in a far corner of the cave, his eyes whitening to one side of his face, listening to the far wind trumpeting up above on the frozen night planet.

Sim's mother, trembling now and again, staring at the man, fed Sim pebble-fruits, valley-grasses and ice-nipples broken from the cavern entrances, and eating, eliminating, eating again, he grew larger, larger.

The man in the corner of the cave was his father! The man's eyes were all that was alive in his face. He held a crude stone dagger in his withered hands and his jaw hung loose and senseless.

Then, with a widening focus, Sim saw the old people sitting in the tunnel beyond this living quarter. And as he watched, they began to die.

Their agonies filled the cave. They melted like waxen images, their faces collapsed inward on their sharp bones, their teeth protruded. One minute their faces were mature,

Copyright 1946 by Planet Stories

124

fairly smooth, alive, electric. The next minute a dessication and burning away of their flesh occurred.

Sim thrashed in his mother's grasp. She held him. "No, no," she soothed him, quietly, earnestly, looking to see if this, too, would cause her husband to rise again.

With a soft swift padding of naked feet, Sim's father ran across the cave. Sim's mother screamed. Sim felt himself torn loose from her grasp. He fell upon the stones, rolling, shrieking with his new, moist lungs!

The webbed face of his father jerked over him, the knife was poised. It was like one of those prenatal nightmares he'd had again and again while still in his mother's flesh. In the next few blazing, impossible instants questions flicked through his brain. The knife was high, suspended, ready to destroy him. But the whole question of life in this cave, the dying people, the withering and the insanity, surged through Sim's new, small head. How was it that he understood? A newborn child? Can a newborn child think, see, understand, interpret? No. It was wrong! It was impossible! Yet it was happening! To him. He had been alive an hour now. And in the next instant perhaps dead!

His mother flung herself upon the back of his father, and beat down the weapon. Sim caught the terrific backwash of emotion from both their conflicting minds. "Let me kill him!" shouted the father, breathing harshly, sobbingly. "What has he to live for?"

"No, no!" insisted the mother, and her body, frail and old as it was, stretched across the huge body of the father, tearing at his weapon. "He must live! There may be a future for him! He may live longer than us, and be young!"

The father fell back against a stone crib. Lying there, staring, eyes glittering, Sim saw another figure inside that stone crib. A girl-child, quietly feeding itself, moving its delicate hands to procure food. His sister.

The mother wrenched the dagger from her husband's grasp, stood up, weeping and pushing back her cloud of stiffening gray hair. Her mouth trembled and jerked. "I'll kill you!" she said, glaring down at her husband. "Leave my children alone."

The old man spat tiredly, bitterly, and looked vacantly into the stone crib, at the little girl. "One-eighth of *her* life's over already," he gasped. "And she doesn't know it. What's the use?"

As Sim watched, his own mother seemed to shift and take a tortured, smokelike form. The thin bony face broke

out into a maze of wrinkles. She was shaken with pain and
had to sit by him, shuddering and cuddling the knife to her
shriveled breasts. She, like the old people in the tunnel, was
aging, dying.

Sim cried steadily. Everywhere he looked was horror. A
mind came to meet his own. Instinctively he glanced toward
the stone crib. Dark, his sister returned his glance. Their
minds brushed like straying fingers. He relaxed somewhat.
He began to learn.

The father sighed, shut his lids down over his green eyes.
"Feed the child," he said, exhaustedly. "Hurry. It is almost
dawn and it is our last day of living, woman. Feed him.
Make him grow."

Sim quieted, and images, out of the terror, floated to him.

This was a planet next to the sun. The nights burned with
cold, the days were like torches of fire. It was a violent, impossible world. The people lived in the cliffs to escape the
incredible ice and the day of flame. Only at dawn and sunset was the air breath-sweet, flower-strong, and then the cave
peoples brought their children out into a stony, barren
valley. At dawn the ice thawed into creeks and rivers, at
sunset the day fire died and cooled. In the intervals of even,
livable temperature the people lived, ran, played, loved, free
of the caverns; all life on the planet jumped, burst into life.
Plants grew instantly, birds were flung like pellets across the
sky. Smaller, legged animal life rushed frantically through
the rocks; everything tried to get its living down in the
brief hour of respite

It was an unbearable planet. Sim understood this, a matter
of hours after birth. Racial memory bloomed in him. He
would live his entire life in the caves, with two hours a day
outside. Here, in stone channels of air he would talk, talk
incessantly with his people, sleep never, think, think and lie
upon his back, dreaming; but never sleeping.

And he would live exactly eight days.

The *violence* of this thought! Eight days. Eight *short* days.
It was wrong, impossible, but a fact. Even while in his mother's
flesh some racial knowledge of some strange far wild voice
had told him he was being formed rapidly, shaped and
propelled out swiftly.

Birth was quick as a knife. Childhood was over in a flash.
Adolescence was a sheet of lightning. Manhood was a dream,

maturity a myth, old age an inescapably quick reality, death a swift certainty.

Eight days from now he'd stand half-blind, withering, dying, as his father now stood, staring uselessly at his own wife and child.

This day was an eighth part of his total life! He must enjoy every second of it. He must search his parents' thoughts for knowledge.

Because in a few hours they'd be dead.

This was so impossibly unfair. Was this all of life? In his prenatal state hadn't he dreamed of *long* lives, valleys not of blasted stone but green foliage and temperate clime? Yes! And if he'd dreamed then there must be truth in the visions. How could he seek and find the long life? Where? And how could he accomplish a life mission that huge and depressing in eight short, vanishing days?

How had his people gotten into such a condition?

As if at a button pressed, he saw an image. Metal seeds, blown across space from a distant green world, fighting with long flames, crashing on this bleak planet. From their shattered hulls tumbled men and women.

When? Long ago. Ten thousand days. The crash victims hid in the cliffs from the sun. Fire, ice and floods washed away the wreckage of the huge metal seeds. The victims were shaped and beaten like iron upon a forge. Solar radiations drenched them. Their pulses quickened, two hundred, five hundred, a thousand beats a minute. Their skins thickened, their blood changed. Old age came rushing. Children were born in the caves. Swifter, swifter, swifter the process. Like all this world's wild life, the men and women from the crash lived and died in a week, leaving children to do likewise.

So this is life, thought Sim. It was not spoken in his mind, for he knew no words, he knew only images, old memory, an awareness, a telepathy that could penetrate flesh, rock, metal. Somewhere along the line, they *had* developed telepathy, plus racial memory, the only good gifts, the only hope in all this terror. So thought Sim, I'm the five-thousandth in a long line of futile sons? What can I do to save myself from dying eight days from now? Is there escape?

His eyes widened, another image came to focus.

Beyond this valley of cliffs, on a low mountain lay a perfect, unscarred metal seed. A metal ship, not rusted or touched by the avalanches. The ship was deserted, whole, intact. It was the only ship of all these that had crashed that was still a unit, still usable. But it was so far away. There was no one in it to help. This ship, then, on the far mountain, was the destiny toward which he would grow. There was his only hope of escape.

His mind flexed.

In this cliff, deep down in a confinement of solitude, worked a handful of scientists. To these men, when he was old enough and wise enough, he must go. They, too, dreamed of escape, of long life, of green valleys and temperate weathers. They, too, stared longingly at that distant ship upon its high mountain, its metal so perfect it did not rust or age.

The cliff groaned.

Sim's father lifted his eroded, lifeless face.

"Dawn's coming," he said.

II

Morning relaxed the mighty granite cliff muscles. It was the time of the Avalanche.

The tunnels echoed to running bare feet. Adults, children pushed with eager, hungry eyes toward the outside dawn. From far out, Sim heard a rumble of rock, a scream, a silence. Avalanches fell into valley. Stones that had been biding their time, not quite ready to fall, for a million years let go their bulks, and where they had begun their journey as single boulders they smashed upon the valley floor in a thousand shrapnels and friction-heated nuggets.

Every morning at least one person was caught in the downpour.

The cliff people dared the avalanches. It added one more excitement to their lives, already too short, too headlong, too dangerous.

Sim felt himself seized up by his father. He was carried brusquely down the tunnel for a thousand yards, to where the daylight appeared. There was a shining insane light in his father's eyes. Sim could not move. He sensed what was going to happen. Behind his father, his mother hurried, bringing with her the little sister, Dark. "Wait! Be careful!" she cried to her husband.

Sim felt his father crouch, listening.

High in the cliff was a tremor, a shivering.

"Now!" bellowed his father, and leaped out.

An avalanche fell down at them!

Sim had accelerated impressions of plunging walls, dust, confusion. His mother screamed! There was a jolting, a plunging.

With one last step, Sim's father hurried him forward into the day. The avalanche thundered behind him. The mouth of the cave, where mother and Dark stood back out of the way, was choked with rubble and two boulders that weighed a hundred pounds each.

The storm thunder of the avalanche passed away to a trickle of sand. Sim's father burst out into laughter. "Made it! By the Gods! Made it alive!" And he looked scornfully at the cliff and spat. "Pagh!"

Mother and sister Dark struggled through the rubble. She cursed her husband. "Fool! You might have killed Sim!"

"I may yet," retorted the father.

Sim was not listening. He was fascinated with the remains of an avalanche afront of the next tunnel. Blood trickled out from under a rise of boulders, soaking into the ground. There was nothing more to be seen. Someone else had lost the game.

Dark ran ahead on lithe, supple feet, naked and certain.

The valley air was like a wine filtered between mountains. The heaven was a restive blue; not the pale scorched atmosphere of full day, nor the bloated, bruised black-purple of night, a-riot with sickly shining stars.

This was a tide pool. A place where waves of varying and violent temperatures struck, receded. Now the tide pool was quiet, cool, and its life moved abroad.

Laughter! Far away, Sim heard it. Why laughter? How could any of his people find time for laughing? Perhaps later he would discover why.

The valley suddenly blushed with impulsive color. Plant life, thawing in the precipitant dawn, shoved out from most unexpected sources. It flowered as you watched. Pale green tendrils appeared on scoured rocks. Seconds later, ripe globes of fruit twitched upon the blade-tips. Father gave Sim to his mother and harvested the momentary, volatile crop, thrust scarlet, blue, yellow fruits into a fur sack which hung at his waist. Mother tugged at the moist new grasses, laid them on Sim's tongue.

His senses were being honed to a fine edge. He stored knowledge thirstily. He understood love, marriage, customs, anger, pity, rage, selfishness, shadings and subtleties, realities and reflections. One thing suggested another. The sight of green plant life whirled his mind like a gyroscope, seeking balance in a world where lack of time for explanations made a mind seek and interpret on its own. The soft burden of food gave him knowledge of his system, of energy, of movement. Like a bird newly cracking its way from a shell, he was almost a unit, complete, all-knowing. Heredity and telepathy that fed upon every mind and every wind had done all this for him. He grew excited with his ability.

They walked, mother, father and the two children, smelling the smells, watching the birds bounce from wall to wall of the valley like scurrying pebbles and suddenly the father said a strange thing:

"Remember?"

Remember what? Sim lay cradled. Was it any effort for them to remember, when they'd lived only seven days!

The husband and wife looked at each other.

"Was it only three days ago?" said the woman, her body shaking, her eyes closing to think. "I can't believe it. It is so unfair." She sobbed, then drew her hand across her face and bit her parched lips. The wind played at her gray hair. "Now it is my turn to cry. An hour ago it was you!"

"An hour is half a life."

"Come," she took her husband's arm. "Let us look at everything, because it will be our last looking."

"The sun'll be up in a few minutes," said the old man. "We must turn back now."

"Just one more moment," pleaded the woman.

"The sun will catch us."

"Let it catch me then!"

"You don't mean that."

"I mean nothing, nothing at all," cried the woman.

The sun was coming fast. The green in the valley burnt away. Searing wind blasted from over the cliffs. Far away where sun bolts hammered battlements of cliff, the huge stone faces shook their contents; those avalanches not already powdered down, were now released and fell like mantles.

"Dark!" shouted the father. The girl sprang over the warm floor of the valley, answering, her hair a black flag behind her. Hands full of green fruits, she joined them.

The sun rimmed the horizon with flame, the air convulsed dangerously with it, and whistled.

The cave people bolted, shouting, picking up their fallen

children, bearing vast loads of fruit and grass with them back to their deep hideouts. In moments the valley was bare. Except for one small child someone had forgotten. He was running far out on the flatness, but he was not strong enough, and the engulfing heat was drifting down from the cliffs even as he was half across the valley.

Flowers were burnt into effigies, grasses sucked back into rocks like singed snakes. Flower seeds whirled and fell in the sudden furnace blast of wind, sown far into gullies and crannies, ready to blossom at sunset tonight, and then go to seed and die again.

Sim's father watched that child running, alone, out on the floor of the valley. He and his wife and Dark and Sim were safe in the mouth of their tunnel.

"He'll never make it," said father. "Do not watch him, woman. It's not a good thing to watch."

They turned away. All except Sim, whose eyes had caught a glint of metal far away His heart hammered in him, and his eyes blurred. Far away, atop a low mountain, one of those metal seeds from space reflected a dazzling ripple of light! It was like one of his intra-embryo dreams fulfilled! A metal space seed, intact, undamaged, lying on a mountain! There was his future! There was his hope for survival! There was where he would go in a few days, when he was—strange thought—a grown man!

The sun plunged into the valley like molten lava.

The little running child screamed, the sun burned, and the screaming stopped.

Sim's mother walked painfully, with sudden age, down the tunnel, paused, reached up, broke off two last icicles that had formed during the night. She handed one to her husband, kept the other. "We will drink one last toast. To you, to the children."

"To *you*," he nodded to her. "To the children." They lifted the icicles. The warmth melted the ice down into their thirsty mouths.

III

All day the sun seemed to blaze and erupt into the valley. Sim could not see it, but the vivid pictorials in his parents' minds were sufficient evidence of the nature of the day fire. The light ran like mercury, sizzling and roasting the caves,

poking inward, but never penetrating deeply enough. It lighted the caves. It made the hollows of the cliff comfortably
warm.

Sim fought to keep his parents young. But no matter how
hard he fought with mind and image, they became like
mummies before him. His father seemed to dissolve from one
stage of oldness to another. This is what will happen to me
soon, thought Sim in terror.

Sim grew upon himself. He felt the digestive-eliminatory
movements of his body. He was fed every minute, he was
continually swallowing, feeding. He began to fit words to images and processes. Such a word was love. It was not an ab-
straction, but a process, a stir of breath, a smell of morning
air, a flutter of heart, the curve of arm holding him, the look
in the suspended face of his mother. He saw the processes,
then searched behind her suspended face and there was the
word, in her brain, ready to use. His throat prepared to speak.
Life was pushing him, rushing him along toward oblivion.

He sensed the expansion of his fingernails, the adjustments
of his cells, the profusion of his hair, the multiplication of his
bones and sinew, the grooving of the soft pale wax of his
brain. His brain at birth as clear as a circle of ice, innocent,
unmarked, was, an instant later, as if hit with a thrown rock,
cracked and marked and patterned in a million crevices of
thought and discovery.

His sister, Dark, ran in and out with other little hothouse
children, forever eating. His mother trembled over him, not
eating, she had no appetite, her eyes were webbed shut.

"Sunset," said his father, at last.

The day was over. The light faded, a wind sounded.

His mother arose. "I want to see the outside world once
more . . . just once more. . . ." She stared blindly, shivering.

His father's eyes were shut, he lay against the wall.

"I cannot rise," he whispered faintly. "I cannot."

"Dark!" The mother croaked, the girl came running.
"Here," and Sim was handed to the girl. "Hold to Sim, Dark,
feed him, care for him." She gave Sim one last fondling
touch.

Dark said not a word, holding Sim, her great green eyes
shining wetly.

"Go now," said the mother. "Take him out into the sunset
time. Enjoy yourselves. Pick foods, eat. Play."

Dark walked away without looking back. Sim twisted in

her grasp, looking over her shoulder with unbelieving, tragic eyes. He cried out and somehow summoned from his lips the first word of his existence:

"Why . . . ?"

He saw his mother stiffen. "The child spoke!"

"Aye," said his father. "Did you hear what he said?"

"I heard," said the mother quietly

The last thing Sim saw of his living parents was his mother weakly, swayingly, slowly moving across the floor to lie beside her silent husband. That was the last time he ever saw them move.

IV

The night came and passed and then started the second day.

The bodies of all those who had died during the night were carried in a funeral procession to the top of a small hill. The procession was long, the bodies numerous.

Dark walked in the procession, holding the newly walking Sim by one hand. Only an hour before dawn Sim had learned to walk.

At the top of the hill, Sim saw once again the far off metal seed. Nobody ever looked at it, or spoke of it. Why? Was there some reason? Was it a mirage? Why did they not run toward it? Worship it? Try to get to it and fly away into space?

The funeral words were spoken. The bodies were placed upon the ground where the sun, in a few minutes, would cremate them.

The procession then turned and ran down the hill, eager to have their few minutes of free time running and playing and laughing in the sweet air.

Dark and Sim, chattering like birds, feeding among the rocks, exchanged what they knew of life. He was in his second day, she in her third. They were driven, as always, by the mercurial speed of their lives.

Another piece of his life opened wide.

Fifty young men ran down from the cliffs, holding sharp stones and rock daggers in their thick hands. Shouting, they ran off toward distant black, low lines of small rock cliffs.

"War!"

The thought stood in Sim's brain. It shocked and beat at him. These men were running to fight, to kill, over there in those small black cliffs where other people lived.

But why? Wasn't life short enough without fighting, killing?

From a great distance he heard the sound of conflict, and it made his stomach cold. "Why, Dark, why?"

Dark didn't know. Perhaps they would understand tomorrow. Now, there was the business of eating to sustain and support their lives. Watching Dark was like seeing a lizard forever flicking its pink tongue, forever hungry.

Pale children ran on all sides of them. One beetlelike boy scuttled up the rocks, knocking Sim aside, to take from him a particularly luscious red berry he had found growing under an outcrop.

The child ate hastily of the fruit before Sim could gain his feet. Then Sim hurled himself unsteadily, the two of them fell in a ridiculous jumble, rolling, until Dark pried them, squalling, apart.

Sim bled. A part of him stood off, like a god, and said, "This should not be. Children should not be this way. It is wrong!"

Dark slapped the little intruding boy away. "Get on!" she cried. "What's your name, bad one?"

"Chion!" laughed the boy. "Chion, Chion, Chion!"

Sim glared at him with all the ferocity in his small, unskilled features. He choked. This was his enemy. It was as if he'd waited for an enemy of person as well as scene. He had already understood the avalanches, the heat, the cold, the shortness of life, but these were things of places, of scene —mute, extravagant manifestations of unthinking nature, not motivated save by gravity and radiation. Here, now, in this stridulant Chion he recognized a thinking enemy!

Chion darted off, turned at a distance, taunting:

"Tomorrow I will be big enough to kill you!"

And he vanished around a rock.

More children ran, giggling, by Sim. Which of them would be friends, enemies? How could friends and enemies come about in this impossible, quick life time? There was no time to make either, was there?

Dark, knowing his thoughts, drew him away. As they searched for food, she whispered fiercely in his ear. "Enemies are made over things like stolen foods; gifts of long grasses make friends. Enemies come, too, from opinions and thoughts. In five seconds you've made an enemy for life. Life's so short enemies must be made quickly." And she laughed with an irony strange for one so young, who was growing older before her rightful time. "You must fight to protect yourself. Others, superstitious ones, will try killing you. There is a belief, a ridiculous belief, that if one kills another, the murderer partakes of the life energy of the slain, and therefore will live an extra day. You see? As long as that is believed, you're in danger."

But Sim was not listening. Bursting from a flock of delicate girls who tomorrow would be tall, quieter, and who day after that would become shapely and the next day take husbands, Sim caught sight of one small girl whose hair was a violet-blue flame.

She ran past, brushed Sim, their bodies touched. Her eyes, white as silver coins, shone at him. He knew then that he'd found a friend, a love, a wife, one who would a week from now lie with him atop the funeral pyre as sunlight undressed their flesh from bone.

Only the glance, but it held them in mid-motion, one instant.

"Your name?" he shouted after her.

"Lyte!" she called laughingly back.

"I'm Sim," he answered, confused and bewildered.

"Sim!" she repeated it, flashing on. "I'll remember!"

Dark nudged his ribs. "Here, *eat,*" she said to the distracted boy. "Eat or you'll never get big enough to catch her."

From nowhere, Chion appeared, running by. "Lyte!" he mocked, dancing malevolently along and away. "Lyte! I'll remember Lyte, too!"

Dark stood tall and reed slender, shaking her dark ebony clouds of hair, sadly. "I see your life before you, little Sim. You'll need weapons soon to fight for this Lyte one. Now, hurry—the sun's coming!"

They ran back to the caves.

V

One-fourth of his life was over! Babyhood was gone. He was now a young boy! Wild rains lashed the valley at nightfall. He watched new river channels cut in the valley, out past the mountain of the metal seed. He stored the knowledge for later use. Each night there was a new river, a bed newly cut.

"What's beyond the valley?" wondered Sim.

"No one's ever been beyond it," explained Dark. "All who

tried to reach the plain were frozen to death or burnt. The only land we know's within half an hour's run. Half an hour out and half an hour back."

"No one has ever reached the metal seed, then?"

Dark scoffed. "The Scientists, they try. Silly fools. They don't know enough to stop. It's no use. It's too far."

The Scientists. The word stirred him. He had almost forgotten the vision he had in the moments before and after birth. His voice was eager. "Where are the Scientists?"

Dark looked away from him, "I wouldn't tell you if I knew. They'd kill you, experimenting! I don't want you joining them! Live your life, don't cut it in half trying to reach that silly metal thing on the mountain."

"I'll find out where they are from someone else, then!"

"No one'll tell you! They hate the Scientists. You'll have to find them on your own. And then what? Will you save us? Yes, save us, little boy!" Her face was sullen; already half her life was gone.

"We can't just sit and talk and eat," he protested. "And *nothing* else." He leapt up.

"Go find them!" she retorted acidly. "They'll help you forget. Yes, yes," she spat it out. "Forget your life's over in just a few more days!"

Sim ran through the tunnels, seeking. Sometimes he half imagined where the Scientists were. But then a flood of angry thought from those around him, when he asked the direction to the Scientists' cave, washed over him in confusion and resentment. After all, it was the Scientists' fault that they had been placed upon this terrible world! Sim flinched under the bombardment of oaths and curses.

Quietly he took his seat in a central chamber with the children to listen to the grown men talk. This was the time of education, the Time of Talking. No matter how he chafed at delay, or how great his impatience, even though life slipped fast from him and death approached like a black meteor, he knew his mind needed knowledge. Tonight, then, was the night of school. But he sat uneasily. Only *five* more days of life.

Chion sat across from Sim, his thin-mouthed face arrogant.

Lyte appeared between the two. The last few hours had made her firmer footed, gentler, taller. Her hair shone brighter. She smiled as she sat beside Sim, ignoring Chion. And Chion became rigid at this and ceased eating.

The dialogue crackled, filled the room. Swift as heartbeats, one thousand, two thousand words a minute. Sim learned, his head filled. He did not shut his eyes, but lapsed into a kind of dreaming that was almost intra-embryonic in lassitude and drowsy vividness. In the faint background the words were spoken, and they wove a tapestry of knowledge in his head.

He dreamed of green meadows free of stones, all grass, round and rolling and rushing easily toward a dawn with no taint of freezing, merciless cold or smell of boiled rock or scorched monument. He walked across the green meadow. Overhead the metal seeds flew by in a heaven that was a steady, even temperature. Things were slow, slow, slow.

Birds lingered upon gigantic trees that took a hundred, two hundred, five thousand days to grow. Everything remained in its place, the birds did not flicker nervously at a hint of sun, nor did the trees suck back frightenedly when a ray of sunlight poured over them.

In this dream people strolled, they rarely ran, the heart rhythm of them was evenly languid, not jerking and insane. The grass remained, and did not burn away in torches. The dream people talked always of tomorrow and living and not tomorrow and dying. It all seemed so familiar that when Sim felt someone take his hand he thought it simply another part of the dream.

Lyte's hand lay inside his own. "Dreaming?" she asked.

"Yes."

"Things are balanced. Our minds, to even things, to balance the unfairness of our living, go back in on ourselves, to find what there is that is good to see."

He beat his hand against the stone floor again and again. "It does not make things fair! I hate it! It reminds me that there is something better, something I have missed! Why can't we be ignorant! Why can't we live and die without knowing that this is an abnormal living?" And his breath rushed harshly from his half-open, constricted mouth.

"There is purpose in everything," said Lyte. "This gives us purpose, makes us work, plan, try to find a way."

His eyes were hot emeralds in his face. "I walked up a hill of grass, very slowly," he said.

"The same hill of grass I walked an hour ago?" asked Lyte.

"Perhaps. Close enough to it. The dream is better than the

reality." He flexed his eyes, narrowed them. "I watched people and they did not eat."

"Or talk?"

"Or talk, either. And we always are eating, always talking. Sometimes those people in the dream sprawled with their eyes shut, not moving a muscle."

As Lyte stared down into his face a terrible thing happened. He imagined her face blackening, wrinkling, twisting into knots of agedness. The hair blew out like snow about her ears, the eyes were like discolored coins caught in a web of lashes. Her teeth sank away from her lips, the delicate fingers hung like charred twigs from her atrophied wrists. Her beauty was consumed and wasted even as he watched, and when he seized her, in terror, he cried out, for he imagined his own hand corroded, and he choked back a cry.

"Sim, what's wrong?"

The saliva in his mouth dried at the taste of the words. "Five more days . . ."

"The Scientists."

Sim started. Who'd spoken? In the dim light a tall man talked. "The Scientists crashed us on this world, and now have wasted thousands of lives and time. It's no use. It's no use. Tolerate them but give them none of your time. You only live once, remember."

Where were these hated Scientists? Now, after the Learning, the Time of Talking, he was ready to find them. Now, at least, he knew enough to begin his fight for freedom, for the ship!

"Sim, where're you going?"

But Sim was gone. The echo of his running feet died away down a shaft of polished stone.

It seemed that half the night was wasted. He blundered into a dozen dead ends. Many times he was attacked by the insane young men who wanted his life energy. Their superstitious ravings echoed after him. The gashes of their hungry fingernails covered his body.

He found what he looked for.

A half dozen men gathered in a small basalt cave deep down in the cliff lode. On a table before them lay objects which, though unfamiliar, struck harmonious chords in Sim.

The Scientists worked in sets, old men doing important work, young men learning, asking questions; and at their feet were three small children. They were a process. Every eight days there was an entirely new set of scientists working on any one problem. The amount of work done was terribly inadequate. They grew old, fell dead just when they were beginning their creative period. The creative time of any one individual was perhaps a matter of twelve hours out of his entire span. Three quarters of one's life was spent learning, a brief interval of creative power, then senility, insanity, death.

The men turned as Sim entered.

"Don't tell me we have a recruit?" said the eldest of them.

"I don't believe it," said another, younger one. "Chase him away. He's probably one of those warmongers."

"No, no," objected the elder one, moving with little shuffles of his bare feet toward Sim. "Come in, come in, boy." He had friendly eyes, slow eyes, unlike those of the swift inhabitants of the upper caves. Gray and quiet. "What do you want?"

Sim hesitated, lowered his head, unable to meet the quiet, gentle gaze. "I want to live," he whispered.

The old man laughed quietly. He touched Sim's shoulder. "Are you a new breed? Are you sick?" he queried of Sim, half seriously. "Why aren't you playing? Why aren't you readying yourself for the time of love and marriage and children? Don't you know that tomorrow night you'll be almost grown? Don't you realize that if you are not careful you'll miss all of life?" He stopped.

Sim moved his eyes back and forth with each query. He blinked at the instruments on the table top. "Shouldn't I be here?" he asked.

"Certainly," roared the old man, sternly. "But it's a miracle you are. We've had no volunteers from the rank and file for a thousand days! We've had to breed our own scientists, a closed unit! Count us! Six! Six men! And three children! Are we not overwhelming?" The old man spat upon the stone floor. "We ask for volunteers and the people shout back at us, 'Get someone else!' or 'We have no time!' And you know why they say that?"

"No." Sim flinched.

"Because they're selfish. They'd like to live longer, yes, but they know that anything they do cannot possibly insure their *own* lives any extra time. It might guarantee longer life to some future offspring of theirs. But they won't give up their love, their brief youth, give up one interval of sunset or sunrise!"

Sim leaned against the table, earnestly. "I understand."

"You do?" The old man stared at him blindly. He sighed and slapped the child's arm gently. "Yes, of course, you do. It's too much to expect anyone to understand, any more. You're rare."

The others moved in around Sim and the old man.

"I am Dienc. Tomorrow night Cort here will be in my place. I'll be dead by then. And the night after that someone else will be in Cort's place, and then you, if you work and believe—but first, I give you a chance. Return to your playmates if you want. There is someone you love? Return to her. Life is short. Why should you care for the unborn to come? You have a right to youth. Go now, if you want. Because if you stay you'll have no time for anything but working and growing old and dying at your work. But it is good work. Well?"

Sim looked at the tunnel. From a distance the wind roared and blew, the smells of cooking and the patter of naked feet sounded, and the laughter of young people was an increasingly good thing to hear. He shook his head, impatiently, and his eyes were wet.

"I will stay," he said.

VI

The third night and third day passed. It was the fourth night. Sim was drawn into their living. He learned about that metal seed upon the top of the far mountain. He heard of the original seeds—things called "ships" that crashed and how the survivors hid and dug in the cliffs, grew old swiftly and in their scrabbling to barely survive, forgot all science. Knowledge of mechanical things had no chance of survival in such a volcanic civilization. There was only NOW for each human.

Yesterday didn't matter, tomorrow stared them vividly in their very faces. But somehow the radiations that had forced their aging had also induced a kind of telepathic communication whereby philosophies and impressions were absorbed by the newborn. Racial memory, growing instinctively, preserved memories of another time.

"Why don't we go to that ship on the mountain?" asked Sim.

"It is too far. We would need protection from the sun," explained Dienc.

"Have you tried to make protection?"

"Salves and ointments, suits of stone and bird-wing and, recently, crude metals. None of which worked. In ten thousand more lifetimes perhaps we'll have made a metal in which will flow cool water to protect us on the march to the ship. But we work so slowly, so blindly. This morning, mature, I took up my instruments. Tomorrow, dying, I lay them down. What can one man do in one day? If we had ten thousand men, the problem would be solved. . . ."

"I will go to the ship," said Sim.

"Then you will die," said the old man. A silence had fallen on the room at Sim's words. Then the men stared at Sim. "You are a very selfish boy."

"Selfish!" cried Sim, resentfully.

The old man patted the air. "Selfish in a way I like. You want to live longer, you'll do anything for that. You will try for the ship. But I tell you it is useless. Yet, if you want to, I cannot stop you. At least you will not be like those among us who go to war for an extra few days of life."

"War?" asked Sim. "How can there be war here?"

And a shudder ran through him. He did not understand.

"Tomorrow will be time enough for that," said Dienc. "Listen to me, now."

The night passed.

VII

It was morning. Lyte came shouting and sobbing down a corridor, and ran full into his arms. She had changed again. She was older, again, more beautiful. She was shaking and she held to him. "Sim, they're coming after you!"

Bare feet marched down the corridor, surged inward at the opening. Chion stood grinning there, taller, too, a sharp rock in either of his hands. "Oh, there you are, Sim!"

"Go away!" cried Lyte savagely whirling on him.

"Not until we take Sim with us," Chion assured her. Then, smiling at Sim. "*If* that is, he is with us in the fight."

Dienc shuffled forward, his eye weakly fluttering, his birdlike hands fumbling in the air. "Leave!" he shrilled angrily. "This boy is a Scientist now. He works with us."

Chion ceased smiling. "There is better work to be done. We go now to fight the people in the farthest cliffs." His eyes glittered anxiously. "Of course, you will come with us, Sim?"

"No, no!" Lyte clutched at his arm.

Sim patted her shoulder, then turned to Chion. "Why are you attacking these people?"

"There are three extra days for those who go with us to fight."

"Three extra days! Of living?"

Chion nodded firmly. "If we win, we live eleven days instead of eight. The cliffs they live in, something about the mineral in it that protects you from radiation! Think of it, Sim, three long, good days of life. Will you join us?"

Dienc interrupted. "Get along without him. Sim is my pupil!"

Chion snorted. "Go die, old man. By sunset tonight you'll be charred bone. Who are you to order us? We are young, we want to live longer."

Eleven days. The words were unbelievable to Sim. Eleven days. Now he understood why there was war. Who wouldn't fight to have his life lengthened by almost half its total. So many more days of living! Yes. Why not, indeed!

"Three extra days," called Dienc, stridently, "*if* you live to enjoy them. If you're not killed in battle. *If. If!* You have never won yet. You have always lost!"

"But this time," Chion declared sharply, "we'll win!"

Sim was bewildered. "But we are all of the same ancestors. Why don't we all share the best cliffs?"

Chion laughed and adjusted a sharp stone in his hand. "Those who live in the best cliffs think they are better than us. That is always man's attitude when he has power. The cliffs there, besides, are smaller, there's room for only three hundred people in them."

Three extra days.

"I'll go with you," Sim said to Chion.

"Fine!" Chion was very glad, much too glad at the decision.

Dienc gasped.

Sim turned to Dienc and Lyte. "If I fight, and win, I will be half a mile closer to the Ship. And I'll have three extra days in which to strive to reach the Ship. That seems the only thing for me to do."

Dienc nodded, sadly. "It *is* the only thing. I believe you. Go along now."

"Good-bye," said Sim.

The old man looked surprised, then he laughed as at a little joke on himself. "That's right—I won't see you again, will I? Good-bye, then." And they shook hands.

They went out, Chion, Sim, and Lyte, together, followed by the others, all children growing swiftly into fighting men. And the light in Chion's eyes was not a good thing to see.

Lyte went with him. She chose his rocks for him and carried them. She would not go back, no matter how he pleaded. The sun was just beyond the horizon and they marched across the valley.

"Please, Lyte, go back!"

"And wait for Chion to return?" she said. "He plans that when you die I will be his mate." She shook out her unbelievable blue-white curls of hair defiantly. "But I'll be with you. If you fall, I fall."

Sim's face hardened. He was tall. The world had shrunk during the night. Children packs screamed by hilarious in their food-searching and he looked at them with alien won-. der: could it be only four days ago he'd been like these? Strange. There was a sense of many days in his mind, as if he'd really lived a thousand days. There was a dimension of incident and thought so thick, so multicolored, so richly diverse in his head that it was not to be believed so much could happen in so short a time.

The fighting men ran in clusters of two or three. Sim looked ahead at the rising line of small ebon cliffs. This, then, he said to himself, is my fourth day. And still I am no closer to the Ship, or to anything, not even—he heard the light tread of Lyte beside him—not even to her who bears my weapons and picks me ripe berries.

One-half of his life was gone. Or a third of it—If he won this battle. *If.*

He ran easily, lifting, letting fall his legs. This is the day of my physical awareness, as I run I feed, as I feed I grow and as I grow I turn eyes to Lyte with a kind of dizzying vertigo. And she looks upon me with the same gentleness of thought. This is the day of our youth. Are we wasting it? Are we losing it on a dream, a folly?

Distantly he heard laughter. As a child he'd questioned it. Now he understood laughter. This particular laughter was made of climbing high rocks and plucking the greenest blades and drinking the headiest vintage from the morning ices and eating of the rock-fruits and tasting of young lips in new appetite.

They neared the cliffs of the enemy.

He saw the slender erectness of Lyte. The new surprise of her neck where if you touched you could time her pulse; the fingers which cupped in your own were animate and supple and never still; the . . .

Lyte snapped her head to one side. "Look ahead!" she cried. "See what is to come—look only ahead."

He felt that they were racing by part of their lives, leaving their youth on the pathside, without so much as a glance.

"I am blind with looking at stones," he said, running.

"Find new stones, then!"

"I see stones—" His voice grew gentle as the palm of her hand. The landscape floated under him. Everything was like a fine wind, blowing dreamily. "I see stones that make a ravine that lies in a cool shadow where the stone-berries are thick as tears. You touch a boulder and the berries fall in silent red avalanches, and the grass is very tender . . ."

"I do not see it!" She increased her pace, turning her head away.

He saw the floss upon her neck, like the small moss that grows silvery and light on the cool side of pebbles, that stirs if you breathe the lightest breath upon it. He looked upon himself, his hands clenched as he heaved himself forward toward death. Already his hands were veined and youth-swollen.

Lyte handed him food to eat.

"I am not hungry," he said.

"Eat, keep your mouth full," she commanded sharply, "so you will be strong for battle."

"Gods!" He roared, anguished. "Who cares for battles!"

Ahead of them, rocks hailed down, thudding. A man fell with his skull split wide. The war was begun.

Lyte passed the weapons to him. They ran without another word until they entered the killing ground.

The boulders began to roll in a synthetic avalanche from the battlements of the enemy!

Only one thought was in his mind now. To kill, to lessen the life of someone else so he could live, to gain a foothold here and live long enough to make a stab at the ship. He ducked, he weaved, he clutched stones and hurled them up. His left hand held a flat stone shield with which he diverted the swiftly plummeting rocks. There was a spatting sound everywhere. Lyte ran with him, encouraging him. Two men dropped before him, slain, their breasts cleaved to the bone, their blood springing out in unbelievable founts.

It was a useless conflict. Sim realized instantly how insane the venture was. They could never storm the cliff. A solid wall of rocks rained down. A dozen men dropped with shards of ebony in their brains, a half dozen more showed drooping, broken arms. One screamed and the upthrust white joint of his knee was exposed as the flesh was pulled away by two successive blows of well-aimed granite. Men stumbled over one another.

The muscles in his cheeks pulled tight and he began to wonder why he had ever come. But his raised eyes, as he danced from side to side, weaving and bobbing, sought always the cliffs. He wanted to live there so intensely, to have his chance. He would have to stick it out. But the heart was gone from him.

Lyte screamed piercingly. Sim, his heart panicking, twisted and saw that her hand was loose at the wrist, with an ugly wound bleeding profusely on the back of the knuckles. She clamped it under her armpit to soothe the pain. The anger rose in him and exploded. In his fury he raced forward, throwing his missiles with deadly accuracy. He saw a man topple and flail down, falling from one level to another of the caves, a victim of his shot. He must have been screaming, for his lungs were bursting open and closed and his throat was raw, and the ground spun madly under his racing feet.

The stone that clipped his head sent him reeling and plunging back. He ate sand. The universe dissolved into purple whorls. He could not get up. He lay and knew that this was his last day, his last time. The battle raged around him, dimly he felt Lyte over him. Her hands cooled his head, she tried to drag him out of range, but he lay gasping and telling her to leave him.

"Stop!" shouted a voice. The whole war seemed to give pause. "Retreat!" commanded the voice swiftly. And as Sim watched, lying upon his side, his comrades turned and fled back toward home.

"The sun is coming, our time is up!" He saw their muscled backs, their moving, tensing, flickering legs go up and down. The dead were left upon the field. The wounded cried for help. But there was no time for the wounded. There was only time for swift men to run the gauntlet home and, their lungs aching and raw with heated air, burst into their tunnels before the sun burnt and killed them.

The sun!

Sim saw another figure racing toward him. It was Chion! Lyte was helping Sim to his feet, whispering helpfully to him. "Can you walk?" she asked. And he groaned and said, "I think so." "Walk then," she said. "Walk slowly, and then faster and faster. We'll make it, I know we will."

Sim got to his feet, stood swaying. Chion raced up, a strange expression cutting lines in his cheeks, his eyes shining with battle. Pushing Lyte abruptly aside he seized upon a rock and dealt Sim a jolting blow upon his ankle that laid wide the flesh. All of this was done quite silently.

Now he stood back, still not speaking, grinning like an animal from the night mountains, his chest panting in and out, looking from the thing he had done, to Lyte, and back. He got his breath. "He'll never make it," he nodded at Sim. "We'll have to leave him here. Come along, Lyte."

Lyte, like a cat-animal, sprang upon Chion, searching for his eyes, shrieking through her exposed, hard-pressed teeth. Her fingers stroked great bloody furrows down Chion's arms and again, instantly, down his neck. Chion, with an oath, sprang away from her. She hurled a rock at him. Grunting, he let it miss him, then ran off a few yards. "Fool!" he cried, turning to scorn her. "Come along with me. Sim will be dead in a few minutes. Come along!"

Lyte turned her back on him. "I will go if you carry me."

Chion's face changed. His eyes lost their gleaming. "There is no time. We would both die if I carried you."

Lyte looked through and beyond him. "Carry me, then, for that's how I wish it to be."

Without another word, glancing fearfully at the sun, Chion fled. His footsteps sped away and vanished from hearing. "May he fall and break his neck," whispered Lyte, savagely glaring at his form as it skirted a ravine. She returned to Sim. "Can you walk?"

Agonies of pain shot up his leg from the wounded ankle. He nodded ironically. "We could make it to the cave in two hours, walking. I have an idea, Lyte. Carry me." And he smiled with the grim joke.

She took his arm. "Nevertheless we'll walk. Come."

"No," he said. "We're staying here."

"But why?"

"We came to seek a home here. If we walk we will die. I would rather die here. How much time have we?"

Together they measured the sun. "A few minutes," she said, her voice flat and dull. She held close to him.

The black rocks of the cliff were paling into deep purples and browns as the sun began to flood the world.

What a fool he was! He should have stayed and worked with Dienc, and thought and dreamed.

With the sinews of his neck standing out defiantly he bellowed upward at the cliff holes.

"Send me down one man to do battle!"

Silence. His voice echoed from the cliff. The air was warm.

"It's no use," said Lyte, "They'll pay no attention."

He shouted again. "Hear me!" He stood with his weight on his good foot, his injured left leg throbbing and pulsating with pain. He shook a fist. "Send down a warrior who is no coward! I will not turn and run home! I have come to fight a fair fight! Send a man who will fight for the right to his cave! Him I will surely kill!"

More silence. A wave of heat passed over the land, receded.

"Oh, surely," mocked Sim, hands on naked hips, head back, mouth wide, "surely there's one among you not afraid to fight a cripple!" Silence. "No?" Silence.

"Then I have miscalculated you. I'm wrong. I'll stand here, then, until the sun shucks the flesh off my bone in black scraps, and call you the filthy names you deserve."

He got an answer.

"I do not like being called names," replied a man's voice.

Sim leaned forward, forgetting his crippled foot.

A huge man appeared in a cave mouth on the third level.

"Come down," urged Sim. "Come down, fat one, and kill me."

The man scowled seriously at his opponent a moment, then lumbered slowly down the path, his hands empty of any weapons. Immediately every cave above clustered with heads. An audience for this drama.

The man approached Sim. "We will fight by the rules, if you know them."

"I'll learn as we go," replied Sim.

This pleased the man and he looked at Sim warily, but not unkindly. "This much I will tell you," offered the man generously. "If you die, I will give your mate shelter and she will live as she pleases, because she is the wife of a good man."

Sim nodded swiftly. "I am ready," he said.

"The rules are simple. We do not touch each other, save
with stones. The stones and the sun will do either of us in.
Now is the time—"

VIII

A tip of the sun showed on the horizon. "My name is
Nhoj," said Sim's enemy, casually taking up a handful of pebbles and stones, weighing them. Sim did likewise. He was
hungry. He had not eaten for many minutes. Hunger was the
curse of this planet's peoples—a perpetual demanding of
empty stomachs for more, more food. His blood flushed
weakly, shot tinglingly through veins in jolting throbs of heat
and pressure, his rib cage shoved out, went in, shoved out
again, impatiently.

"Now!" roared the three hundred watchers from the cliffs.
"Now!" they clamored, the men and women and children
balanced, in turmoil on the ledges. "Now! Begin!"

As if at a cue, the sun arose. It smote them a blow as with
a flat, sizzling stone. The two men staggered under the
molten impact, sweat broke from their naked thighs and loins,
under their arms and on their faces was a glaze like fine glass.

Nhoj shifted his huge weight and looked at the sun as if
in no hurry to fight. Then, silently, with no warning, he
snapped out a pebble with a startling trigger-flick of thumb
and forefinger. It caught Sim flat on the cheek, staggered him
back, so that a rocket of unbearable pain climbed up his
crippled foot and burst into nervous explosion at the pit of
his stomach. He tasted blood from his bleeding cheek.

Nhoj moved serenely. Three more flicks of his magical
hands and three tiny, seemingly harmless bits of stone flew
like whistling birds. Each of them found a target, slammed
it. The nerve centers of Sim's body! One hit his stomach so
that ten hours' eating almost slid up his throat. A second
got his forehead, a third his neck. He collapsed to the boiling
sand. His knee made a wrenching sound on the hard earth.
His face was colorless and his eyes, squeezed tight, were
pushing tears out from the hot, quivering lids. But even as he
had fallen he had let loose, with wild force, his handful of
stones!

The stones purred in the air. One of them, and only one,
struck Nhoj. Upon the left eyeball. Nhoj moaned and laid
his hands in the next instant to his shattered eye.

Sim choked out a bitter, sighing laugh. This much triumph he had. The eye of his opponent. It would give him . . . Time. Oh, gods, he thought, his stomach retching sickly, fighting for breath, this is a world of time. Give me a little more, just a trifle!

Nhoj, one-eyed, weaving with pain, pelted the writhing body of Sim, but his aim was off now, the stones flew to one side or if they struck at all they were weak and spent and lifeless.

Sim forced himself half erect. From the corners of his eyes he saw Lyte, waiting, staring at him, her lips breathing words of encouragement and hope. He was bathed in sweat, as if a rain spray had showered him down.

The sun was now fully over the horizon. You could smell it. Stones glinted like mirrors, the sand began to roil and bubble. Illusions sprang up everywhere in the valley. Instead of one warrior Nhoj he was confronted by a dozen, each in an upright position, preparing to launch another missile. A dozen irregular warriors who shimmered in the golden menace of day, like bronze gongs smitten, quivered in one vision!

Sim was breathing desperately. His nostrils flared and sucked and his mouth drank thirstily of flame instead of oxygen. His lungs took fire like silk torches and his body was consumed. The sweat spilled from his pores to be instantly evaporated. He felt himself shriveling, shriveling in on himself, he imagined himself looking like his father, old, sunken, slight, withered! Where was the sand? Could he move? Yes. The world wriggled under him, but now he was on his feet.

There would be no more fighting.

A murmur from the cliff told this. The sunburnt faces of the high audience gaped and jeered and shouted encouragement to their warrior. "Stand straight, Nhoj, save your strength now! Stand tall and perspire!" they urged him. And Nhoj stood, swaying lightly, swaying slowly, a pendulum in an incandescent fiery breath from the skyline. "Don't move, Nhoj, save your heart, save your power!"

"The Test, The Test!" said the people on the heights. "The test of the sun."

And this was the worst part of the fight. Sim squinted painfully at the distorted illusion of cliff. He thought he saw his parents; father with his defeated face, his green eyes burning, mother with her hair blowing like a cloud of gray smoke in the fire wind. He must get up to them, live for and with them!

Behind him, Sim heard Lyte whimper softly. There was a whisper of flesh against sand. She had fallen. He did not dare turn. The strength of turning would bring him thundering down in pain and darkness.

His knees bent. If I fall, he thought, I'll lie here and become ashes. Where was Nhoj? Nhoj was there, a few yards from him, standing bent, slick with perspiration, looking as if he were being hit over the spine with great hammers of destruction.

"Fall, Nhoj! Fall!" thought Sim. "Fall, fall! Fall so I can take your place!"

But Nhoj did not fall. One by one the pebbles in his half-loose left hand plummeted to the broiling sands and Nhoj's lips peeled back, the saliva burned away from his lips and his eyes glazed. But he did not fall. The will to live was strong in him. He hung as if by a wire.

Sim fell to one knee!

"Ahh!" wailed the knowing voices from the cliff. They were watching death. Sim jerked his head up, smiling mechanically, foolishly as if caught in the act of doing something silly. "No, no," he insisted drowsily, and got back up again. There was so much pain he was all one ringing numbness. A whirring, buzzing, frying sound filled the land. High up, an avalanche came down like a curtain on a drama, making no noise. Everything was quiet except for a steady humming. He saw fifty images of Nhoj now, dressed in armors of sweat, eyes puffed with torture, cheeks sunken, lips peeled back like the rind of a drying fruit. But the wire still held him.

"Now," muttered Sim, sluggishly, with a thick, baked tongue between his blazing teeth. "Now I'll fall and lie and dream." He said it with slow, thoughtful pleasure. He planned it. He knew how it must be done. He would do it accurately. He lifted his head to see if the audience was watching.

They were gone!

The sun had driven them back in. All save one or two brave ones. Sim laughed drunkenly and watched the sweat gather on his dead hands, hesitate, drop off, plunge down toward sand and turn to steam halfway there.

Nhoj fell.

The wire was cut. Nhoj fell flat upon his stomach, a gout

of blood kicked from his mouth. His eyes rolled back into a white, senseless insanity.

Nhoj fell. So did his fifty duplicate illusions.

All across the valley the winds sang and moaned and Sim saw a blue lake with a blue river feeding it and low white houses near the river with people going and coming in the houses and among the tall green trees. Trees taller than seven men, beside the river mirage.

"Now," explained Sim to himself at last, "Now I can fall. Right—into—that—lake."

He fell forward.

He was shocked when he felt the hands eagerly stop him in mid-plunge, lift him, hurry him off, high in the hungry air, like a torch held and waved, ablaze.

"How strange is death," he thought, and blackness took him.

He wakened to the flow of cool water on his cheeks.

He opened his eyes fearfully. Lyte held his head upon her lap, her fingers were moving food to his mouth. He was tremendously hungry and tired, but fear squeezed both of these things away. He struggled upward, seeing the strange cave contours overhead.

"What time is it?" he demanded.

"The same day as the contest. Be quiet," she said.

"The same day!"

She nodded amusedly. "You've lost nothing of your life. This is Nhoj's cave. We are inside the black cliff. We will live three extra days. Satisfied? Lie down."

"Nhoj is dead?" He fell back, panting, his heart slamming his ribs. He relaxed slowly. "I won. I won," he breathed.

"Nhoj is dead. So were we, almost. They carried us in from outside only in time."

He ate ravenously. "We have no time to waste. We must get strong. My leg—" He looked at it, tested it. There was a swath of long yellow grasses around it and the ache had died away. Even as he watched, the terrific pulsings of his body went to work and cured away the impurities under the bandages. It *has* to be strong by sunset, he thought. It *has* to be.

He got up and limped around the cave like a captured animal. He felt Lyte's eyes upon him. He could not meet her gaze. Finally, helplessly, he turned.

She interrupted him. "You want to go on to the ship?" she asked, softly. "Tonight? When the sun goes down?"

He took a breath, exhaled it. "Yes."

"You couldn't possibly wait until morning?"

"No."

"Then I'll go with you."

"No!"

"If I lag behind, let me. There's nothing here for me."

They stared at each other a long while. He shrugged wearily.

"All right," he said, at last. "I couldn't stop you, I know that. We'll go together."

IX

They waited in the mouth of their new cave. The sun set. The stones cooled so that one could walk on them. It was almost time for the leaping out and the running toward the distant, glittering metal seed that lay on the far mountain.

Soon would come the rains. And Sim thought back over all the times he had watched the rains thicken into creeks, into rivers that cut new beds each night. One night there would be a river running north, the next a river running northeast, the third night a river running due west. The valley was continually cut and scarred by the torrents. Earthquakes and avalanches filled the old beds. New ones were the order of the day. It was this idea of the river and the directions of the river that he had turned over in his head for many hours. It might possibly— Well, he would wait and see.

He noticed how living in this new cliff had slowed his pulse, slowed everything. A mineral result, protection against the solar radiations. Life was still swift, but not as swift as before.

"Now, Sim!" cried Lyte.

They ran. Between the hot death and the cold one. Together, away from the cliffs, out toward the distant, beckoning ship.

Never had they run this way in their lives. The sound of their feet running was a hard, insistent clatter over vast oblongs of rock, down into ravines, up the sides, and on again. They raked the air in and out their lungs. Behind them the cliffs faded into things they could never turn back to now.

They did not eat as they ran. They had eaten to the bursting point in the cave, to save time. Now it was only running, a lifting of legs, a balancing of bent elbows, a convulsion of muscles, a slaking in of air that had been fiery and was now cooling.

"Are they watching us?"

Lyte's breathless voice snatched at his ears above the pound of his heart.

Who? But he knew the answer. The cliff peoples, of course. How long had it been since a race like this one? A thousand days? Ten thousand? How long since someone had taken the chance and sprinted with an entire civilization's eyes upon their backs, into gullies, across cooling plain. Were there lovers pausing in their laughter back there, gazing at the two tiny dots that were a man and woman running toward destiny? Were children eating of new fruits and stopping in their play to see the two people racing against time? Was Dienc still living, narrowing hairy eyebrows down over fading eyes, shouting them on in a feeble, rasping voice, shaking a twisted hand? Were there jeers? Were they being called fools, idiots? And in the midst of the name-calling, were people praying them on, hoping they would reach the ship?

Sim took a quick glance at the sky, which was beginning to bruise with the coming night. Out of nowhere clouds materialized and a light shower trailed across a gully two hundred yards ahead of them. Lightning beat upon distant mountains and there was a strong scent of ozone on the disturbed air.

"The halfway mark," panted Sim, and he saw Lyte's face half turn, longingly looking back at the life she was leaving. "Now's the time, if we want to turn back, we still have time. Another minute—"

Thunder snarled in the mountains. An avalanche started out small and ended up huge and monstrous in a deep fissure. Light rain dotted Lyte's smooth white skin. In a minute her hair was glistening and soggy with rain.

"Too late, now," she shouted over the patting rhythm of her own naked feet. "We've got to go ahead!"

And it was too late. Sim knew, judging the distances, that there was no turning back now.

His leg began to pain him. He favored it, slowing. A wind came up swiftly. A cold wind that bit into the skin. But it came from the cliffs behind them, helped rather than hindered them. An omen? he wondered. No.

For as the minutes went by it grew upon him how poorly he had estimated the distance. Their time was dwindling out, but they were still an impossible distance from the ship. He said nothing, but the impotent anger at the slow muscles in his legs welled up into bitterly hot tears in his eyes.

He knew that Lyte was thinking the same as himself. But she flew along like a white bird, seeming hardly to touch ground. He heard her breath go out and in her throat, like a clean, sharp knife in its sheath.

Half the sky was dark. The first stars were peering through lengths of black cloud. Lightning jiggled a path along a rim just ahead of them. A full thunderstorm of violent rain and exploding electricity fell upon them.

They slipped and skidded on moss-smooth pebbles. Lyte fell, scrambled up again with a burning oath. Her body was scarred and dirty. The rain washed over her.

The rain came down and cried on Sim. It filled his eyes and ran in rivers down his spine and he wanted to cry with it.

Lyte fell and did not rise, sucking her breath, her breasts quivering.

He picked her up and held her. "Run, Lyte, please, run!"

"Leave me, Sim. Go ahead!" The rain filled her mouth. There was water everywhere. "It's no use. Go on without me."

He stood there, cold and powerless, his thoughts sagging, the flame of hope blinking out. All the world was blackness, cold falling sheaths of water, and despair.

"We'll walk, then," he said. "And keep walking, and resting."

They walked for fifty yards, easily, slowly, like children out for a stroll. The gully ahead of them filled with water that went sliding away with a swift wet sound, toward the horizon.

Sim cried out. Tugging at Lyte he raced forward. "A new channel," he said, pointing. "Each day the rain cuts a new channel. Here, Lyte!" He leaned over the floodwaters.

He dived in, taking her with him.

The flood swept them like bits of wood. They fought to stay upright, the water got into their mouths, their noses. The land swept by on both sides of them. Clutching Lyte's fingers with insane strength, Sim felt himself hurled end over end, saw flicks of lightning on high, and a new fierce hope was born in him. They could no longer run—well, then they would let the water do the running for them.

With a speed that dashed them against rocks, split open their shoulders, abraded their legs, the new, brief river carried them. "This way!" Sim shouted over a salvo of thunder and steered frantically toward the opposite side of the gully. The mountain where the ship lay was just ahead. They must not pass it by. They fought in the transporting liquid and were slammed against the far side. Sim leaped up, caught at an overhanging rock, locked Lyte in his legs, and drew himself hand over hand upward.

As quickly as it had come, the storm was gone. The lightning faded. The rain ceased. The clouds melted and fell away over the sky. The wind whispered into silence.

"The ship!" Lyte lay upon the ground. "The ship, Sim. This is the mountain of the ship!"

Now the cold came. The killing cold.

They forced themselves drunkenly up the mountain. The cold slid along their limbs, got into their arteries like a chemical and slowed them.

Ahead of them, with a fresh-washed sheen, lay the ship. It was a dream. Sim could not believe that they were actually so near it. Two hundred yards. One hundred and seventy yards.

The ground became covered with ice. They slipped and fell again and again. Behind them the river was frozen into a blue-white snake of cold solidity. A few last drops of rain from somewhere came down as hard pellets.

Sim fell against the bulk of the ship. He was actually touching it. Touching it! He heard Lyte whimpering in her constricted throat. This was the metal, the ship. How many others had touched it in the long days? He and Lyte had made it!

Then, as cold as the air, his veins were chilled.

Where was the entrance?

You run, you swim, you almost drown, you curse, you sweat, you work, you reach a mountain, you go up it, you hammer on metal, you shout with relief, and then—you can't find the entrance.

He fought to control himself. Slowly, he told himself, but not too slowly, go around the ship. The metal slid under his searching hands, so cold that his hands, sweating, almost froze to it. Now, far around to the side. Lyte moved with him. The cold held them like a fist. It began to squeeze.

The entrance.

Metal. Cold, immutable metal. A thin line of opening at the sealing point. Throwing all caution aside, he beat at it. He felt his stomach seething with cold. His fingers were numb, his eyes were half frozen in their sockets. He began to beat and search and scream against the metal door. "Open up! Open up!" He staggered. He had struck something . . . A *click!*

The air lock sighed. With a whispering of metal on rubber beddings, the door swung softly sidewise and vanished back.

He saw Lyte run forward, clutch at her throat, and drop inside a small shiny chamber. He shuffled after her, blankly.

The air-lock door sealed shut behind him.

He could not breathe. His heart began to slow, to stop.

They were trapped inside the ship now, and something was happening. He sank down to his knees and choked for air.

The ship he had come to for salvation was now slowing his pulse, darkening his brain, poisoning him. With a starved, faint kind of expiring terror, he realized that he was dying.

Blackness.

He had a dim sense of time passing, of thinking, struggling, to make his heart go quick, quick. . . . To make his eyes focus. But the fluid in his body lagged quietly through his settling veins and he heard his pulses thud, pause, thud, pause and thud again with lulling intermissions.

He could not move, not a hand or leg or finger. It was an effort to lift the tonnage of his eyelashes. He could not shift his face even, to see Lyte lying beside him.

From a distance came her irregular breathing. It was like the sound a wounded bird makes with his dry, unraveled pinions. She was so close he could almost feel the heat of her; yet she seemed a long way removed.

I'm getting cold! he thought. Is this death? This slowing of blood, of my heart, this cooling of my body, this drowsy thinking of thoughts?

Staring at the ship's ceiling he traced its intricate system of tubes and machines. The knowledge, the purpose of the ship, its actions, seeped into him. He began to understand in a kind of revealing lassitude just what these things were his eyes rested upon. Slow. Slow.

There was an instrument with a gleaming white dial.

Its purpose?

He drudged away at the problem, like a man underwater. People had used the dial. Touched it. People had repaired it. Installed it. People had dreamed of it before the building, before the installing, before the repairing and touching and using. The dial contained memory of use and manufacture, its very shape was a dream-memory telling Sim why and for what it had been built. Given time, looking at anything, he could draw from it the knowledge he desired. Some dim part of him reached out, dissected the contents of things, analyzed them.

This dial measured time!

Millions of hours of time!

But how could that be? Sim's eyes dilated, hot and glittering. Where were humans who needed such an instrument?

Blood thrummed and beat behind his eyes. He closed them.

Panic came to him. The day was passing. I am lying here, he thought, and my life slips away. I cannot move. My youth is passing. How long before I can move?

Through a kind of porthole he saw the night pass, the day come, the day pass, and again another night. Stars danced frostily.

I will lie here for four or five days, wrinkling and withering, he thought. This ship will not let me move. How much better if I had stayed in my home cliff, lived, enjoyed this short life. What good has it done to come here? I'm missing all the twilights and dawns. I'll never touch Lyte, though she's here at my side.

Delirium. His mind floated up. His thoughts whirled through the metal ship. He smelled the razor-sharp smell of joined metal. He heard the hull contract with night, relax with day.

Dawn.

Already—another dawn!

Today I would have been fully grown. His jaw clenched. I must get up. I must move. I must enjoy this time.

But he didn't move. He felt his blood pump sleepily from chamber to red chamber in his heart, on down and around through his dead body, to be purified by his folding and unfolding lungs.

The ship grew warm. From somewhere a machine clicked. automatically the temperature cooled. A controlled gust of air flushed the room.

Night again. And then another day.

He lay and saw four days of his life pass.

He did not try to fight. It was no use. His life was over.

He didn't want to turn his head now. He didn't want to see Lyte with her face like his tortured mother's—eyelids like gray ash flakes, eyes like beaten, sanded metal, cheeks like eroded stones. He didn't want to see a throat like parched thongs of yellow grass, hands the pattern of smoke risen from a fire, breasts like dessicated rinds and hair stubbly and unshorn as moist gray weeds!

And himself? How did *he* look? Was his jaw sunken, the flesh of his eyes pitted, his brow lined and age-scarred?

His strength began to return. He felt his heart beating so slow that it was amazing. One hundred beats a minute. Impossible. He felt so cool, so thoughtful, so easy.

His head fell over to one side. He stared at Lyte. He shouted in surprise.

She was young and fair.

She was looking at him, too weak to say anything. Her eyes were like tiny silver medals, her throat curved like the arm of a child. Her hair was blue fire eating at her scalp, fed by the slender life of her body.

Four days had passed and still she was young . . . no, younger than when they had entered the ship. She was still adolescent.

He could not believe it.

Her first words were, "How long will this last?"

He replied, carefully, "I don't know."

"We are still young."

"The ship. Its metal is around us. It cuts away the sun and the things that came from the sun to age us."

Her eyes shifted thoughtfully "Then, if we stay here—"

"We'll remain young."

"Six more days? Fourteen more? Twenty?"

"More than that, maybe."

She lay there, silently. After a long time she said, "Sim?"

"Yes."

"Let's stay here. Let's not go back. If we go back now, you know what'll happen to us . . . ?"

"I'm not certain."

"We'll start getting old again, won't we?"

He looked away. He stared at the ceiling and the clock with the moving finger. "Yes. We'll grow old."

"What if we grow old—instantly. When we step from the ship won't the shock be too much?"

"Maybe."

Another silence. He began to move his limbs, testing them. He was very hungry. "The others are waiting," he said.

Her next words made him gasp. "The others are dead," she said. "Or will be in a few hours. All those we knew back there are old."

He tried to picture them old. Dark, his sister, bent and senile with time. He shook his head, wiping the picture away. "They may die," he said. "But there are others who've been born."

"People we don't even know."

"But, nevertheless, *our* people," he replied. "People who'll live only eight days, or eleven days unless we help them."

"But we're *young*, Sim! We can *stay* young!"

He didn't want to listen. It was too tempting a thing to listen to. To stay here. To live. "We've already had more time than the others," he said. "I need workers. Men to heal this ship. We'll get on our feet now, you and I, and find food, eat, and see if the ship is movable. I'm afraid to try to move it myself. It's so big. I'll need help."

"But that means running back all that distance!"

"I know." He lifted himself weakly. "But I'll do it."

"How will you get the men back here?"

"We'll use the river."

"*If* it's there. It *may* be somewhere else."

"We'll wait until there *is* one, then. I've got to go back, Lyte. The son of Dienc is waiting for me, my sister, your brother, are old people, ready to die, and waiting for some word from us—"

After a long while he heard her move, dragging herself tiredly to him. She put her head upon his chest, her eyes closed, stroking his arm. "I'm sorry. Forgive me. You have to go back. I'm a selfish fool."

He touched her cheek, clumsily. "You're human. I understand you. There's nothing to forgive."

They found food. They walked through the ship. It was empty. Only in the control room did they find the remains of a man who must have been the chief pilot. The others had evidently bailed out into space in emergency lifeboats. This pilot, sitting at his controls, alone, had landed the ship on a mountain within sight of other fallen and smashed crafts. Its location on high ground had saved it from the floods. The pilot himself had died, probably of heart failure, soon after landing. The ship had remained here, almost within reach of the other survivors, perfect as an egg, but silent, for—how many thousand days? If the pilot had lived, what a different thing life might have been for the ancestors of Sim and Lyte. Sim, thinking of this, felt the distant, ominous vibration of war. How had the war between worlds come out? Who had won? Or had both planets lost and never

bothered trying to pick up survivors? Who had been right?
Who was the enemy? Were Sim's people of the guilty or innocent side? They might never know.

He checked the ship hurriedly. He knew nothing of its
workings, yet as he walked its corridors, patted its machines, he learned from it. It needed only a crew. One man
couldn't possibly set the whole thing running again. He laid
his hand upon one round, snoutlike machine. He jerked his
hand away, as if burnt.

"Lyte!"

"What is it?"

He touched the machine again, caressed it, his hand trembled violently, his eyes welled with tears, his mouth opened
and closed, he looked at the machine, loving it, then looked
at Lyte.

"With this machine—" he stammered, softly, incredulously. "With— With this machine I can—"

"What, Sim?"

He inserted his hand into a cuplike contraption with a
lever inside. Out of the porthole in front of him he could
see the distant line of cliffs. "We were afraid there might
never be another river running by this mountain, weren't
we?" he asked, exultantly.

"Yes, Sim, but—"

"There *will* be a river. And I *will* come back, tonight!
and I'll bring men with me. Five hundred men! Because
with this machine I can blast a river bottom all the way to
the cliffs, down which the waters will rush, giving myself
and the men a swift, sure way of traveling back!" He rubbed
the machine's barrellike body. "When I touched it, the life
and method of it burnt into me! Watch!" He depressed the
lever.

A beam of incandescent fire lanced out from the ship,
screaming.

Steadily, accurately, Sim began to cut away a riverbed for
the storm waters to flow in. The night was turned to day
by its hungry eating.

The return to the cliffs was to be carried out by Sim
alone. Lyte was to remain in the ship, in case of any mishap.
The trip back seemed, at first glance, to be impossible.
There would be no river rushing to cut his time, to sweep
him along toward his destination. He would have to run the

entire distance in the dawn, and the sun would get him, catch him before he'd reached safety.

"The only way to do it is to start *before* sunrise."

"But you'd be frozen, Sim."

"Here." He made adjustments on the machine that had just finished cutting the riverbed in the rock floor of the valley. He lifted the smooth snout of the gun, pressed the lever, left it down. A gout of fire shot toward the cliffs. He fingered the range control, focused the flame end three miles from its source. Done. He turned to Lyte. "But I don't understand," she said.

He opened the air-lock door. "It's bitter cold out, and half an hour yet till dawn. If I run parallel to the flame from the machine, close enough to it, there'll not be much heat, but enough to sustain life, anyway."

"It doesn't sound safe," Lyte protested.

"*Nothing* does, on this world." He moved forward. "I'll have a half-hour start. That should be enough to reach the cliffs."

"But if the machine should fail while you're still running near its beam?"

"Let's not think of that," he said.

A moment later he was outside. He staggered as if kicked in the stomach. His heart almost exploded in him. The environment of his world forced him into swift living again. He felt his pulse rise, kicking through his veins.

The night was cold as death. The heat ray from the ship sliced across the valley, humming, solid and warm. He moved next to it, very close. One misstep in his running and—

"I'll be back," he called to Lyte.

He and the ray of light went together.

In the early morning the people in the caves saw the long finger of orange incandescence and the weird whitish apparition floating, running along beside it. There was muttering and moaning and many sighs of awe.

And when Sim finally reached the cliffs of his childhood he saw alien peoples swarming there. There were no familiar faces. Then he realized how foolish it was to expect familiar faces. One of the older men glared down at him. "Who're you?" he shouted. "Are you from the enemy cliff? What's your name?"

"I am Sim, the son of Sim!"

"Sim!"

An old woman shrieked from the cliff above him. She came hobbling down the stone pathway "Sim, Sim, it *is* you!"

He looked at her frankly bewildered. "But I don't know you," he murmured.

"Sim, don't you recognize me? Oh, Sim, it's me! Dark!"

"Dark!"

He felt sick at his stomach. She fell into his arms. This old, trembling woman with the half-blind eyes, his sister.

Another face appeared above. That of an old man. A cruel, bitter face. It looked down at Sim and snarled. "Drive him away!" cried the old man. "He comes from the cliff of the enemy. He's lived there! He's still young! Those who go there can never come back among us. Disloyal beast!" And a rock hurtled down.

Sim leaped aside, pulling the old woman with him.

A roar came from the people. They ran toward Sim, shaking their fists. "Kill him, kill him!" raved the old man, and Sim did not know who he was.

"Stop!" Sim held out his hands. "I come from the ship!"

"The ship?" The people slowed. Dark clung to him, looking up into his young face, puzzling over its smoothness.

"Kill him, kill him, kill him!" croaked the old man, and picked up another rock.

"I offer you ten days, twenty days, thirty more days of life!"

The people stopped. Their mouths hung open. Their eyes were incredulous.

"Thirty days?" It was repeated again and again. "How?"

"Come back to the ship with me. Inside it, one can live forever!"

The old man lifted high a rock, then, choking, fell forward in an apoplectic fit, and tumbled down the rocks to lie at Sim's feet.

Sim bent to peer at the ancient one, at the raw, dead eyes, the loose, sneering lips, the crumpled, quiet body.

"Chion!"

"Yes," said Dark behind him, in a croaking, strange voice. "Your enemy. Chion."

That night two hundred men started for the ship. The water ran in the new channel. One hundred of them were drowned or lost behind in the cold. The others, with Sim, got through to the ship.

Lyte awaited them, and threw wide the metal door.

The weeks passed. Generations lived and died in the cliffs, while the scientists and workers labored over the ship, learning its functions and its parts.

On the last day, two dozen men moved to their stations within the ship. Now there was a destiny of travel ahead.

Sim touched the control plates under his fingers.

Lyte, rubbing her eyes, came and sat on the floor next to him, resting her head against his knee, drowsily. "I had a dream," she said, looking off at something far away. "I dreamed I lived in caves in a cliff on a cold-hot planet where people grew old and died in eight days."

"What an impossible dream," said Sim. "People couldn't possibly live in such a nightmare. Forget it. You're awake now."

He touched the plates gently. The ship rose and moved into space.

Sim was right.

The nightmare was over at last.

UNCLE EINAR

"It will take only a minute," said Uncle Einar's sweet wife.

"I refuse," he said. "And that takes but a *second*."

"I've worked all morning," she said, holding to her slender back, "and you won't help? It's drumming for a rain."

"Let it rain," he cried, morosely. "I'll not be pierced by lightning just to air your clothes."

"But you're so quick at it."

"Again, I refuse." His vast tarpaulin wings hummed nervously behind his indignant back.

She gave him a slender rope on which were tied four dozen fresh-washed clothes. He turned it in his fingers with distaste. "So it's come to this," he muttered, bitterly. "To this, to this, to this." He almost wept angry and acid tears.

"Don't cry; you'll wet them down again," she said. "Jump up, now, run them about."

"Run them about." His voice was hollow, deep, and terribly wounded. "I say: let it thunder, let it pour!"

"If it was a nice, sunny day I wouldn't ask," she said, reasonably. "All my washing gone for nothing if you don't. They'll hang about the house—"

That *did* it. Above all, he hated clothes flagged and festooned so a man had to creep under on the way across a room. He jumped up. His vast green wings boomed. "Only so far as the pasture fence!"

Whirl: up he jumped, his wings chewed and loved the cool air. Before you'd say Uncle Einar Has Green Wings he sailed low across his farmland, trailing the clothes in a vast fluttering loop through the pounding concussion and backwash of his wings!

"Catch!"

Copyright 1947 by Ray Bradbury

164

Back from the trip, he sailed the clothes, dry as popcorn, down on a series of clean blankets she'd spread for their landing.

"Thank you!" she cried.

"Gahh!" he shouted, and flew off under the apple tree to brood.

Uncle Einar's beautiful silk-like wings hung like sea-green sails behind him, and whirred and whispered from his shoulders when he sneezed or turned swiftly. He was one of the few in the Family whose talent was visible. All his dark cousins and nephews and brothers hid in small towns across the world, did unseen mental things or things with witch-fingers and white teeth, or blew down the sky like fire-leaves, or loped in forests like moon-silvered wolves. They lived comparatively safe from normal humans. Not so a man with great green wings.

Not that he hated his wings. Far from it! In his youth he'd always flown nights, because nights were rare times for winged men! Daylight held dangers, always had, always would; but nights, ah, nights, he had sailed over islands of cloud and seas of summer sky. With no danger to himself. It had been a rich, full soaring, an exhilaration.

But now he could not fly at night.

On his way home to some high mountain pass in Europe after a Homecoming among Family members in Mellin Town, Illinois (some years ago) he had drunk too much rich crimson wine. "I'll be all right," he had told himself, vaguely, as he beat his long way under the morning stars, over the moon-dreaming country hills beyond Mellin Town. And then —crack out of the sky—

A high-tension tower.

Like a netted duck! A great sizzle! His face blown black by a blue sparkler of wire, he fended off the electricity with a terrific back-jumping percussion of his wings, and fell.

His hitting the moonlit meadow under the tower made a noise like a large telephone book dropped from the sky.

Early the next morning, his dew-sodden wings shaking violently, he stood up. It was still dark. There was a faint bandage of dawn stretched across the east. Soon the bandage would stain and all flight would be restricted. There was nothing to do but take refuge in the forest and wait out the day in the deepest thicket until another night gave his wings a hidden motion in the sky.

In this fashion he met his wife.

During the day, which was warm for November first in Illinois country, pretty young Brunilla Wexley was out to udder a lost cow, for she carried a silver pail in one hand as she sidled through thickets and pleaded cleverly to the unseen cow to please return home or burst her gut with unplucked milk. The fact that the cow would have most certainly come home when her teats really needed pulling did not concern Brunilla Wexley. It was a sweet excuse for forest-journeying, thistle-blowing, and flower chewing; all of which Brunilla was doing as she stumbled upon Uncle Einar.

Asleep near a bush, he seemed a man under a green shelter.

"Oh," said Brunilla, with a fever. "A man. In a camp-tent."

Uncle Einar awoke. The camp-tent spread like a large green fan behind him.

"Oh," said Brunilla, the cow-searcher. "A man with wings."

That was how she took it. She was startled, yes, but she had never been hurt in her life, so she wasn't afraid of anyone, and it was a fancy thing to see a winged man and she was proud to meet him. She began to talk. In an hour they were old friends, and in two hours she'd quite forgotten his wings were there. And he somehow confessed how he happened to be in this wood.

"Yes, I noticed you looked banged around," she said. "That right wing looks very bad. You'd best let me take you home and fix it. You won't be able to fly all the way to Europe on it, anyway. And who wants to live in Europe these days?"

He thanked her, but he didn't quite see how he could accept.

"But I live alone," she said. "For, as you see, I'm quite ugly."

He insisted she was not.

"How kind of you," she said. "But I am, there's no fooling myself. My folks are dead, I've a farm, a big one, all to myself, quite far from Mellin Town, and I'm in need of talking company."

But wasn't she afraid of him? he asked.

"Proud and jealous would be more near it," she said. *"May* I?" And she stroked his large green membraned veils with careful envy. He shuddered at the touch and put his tongue between his teeth.

So there was nothing for it but that he come to her house

for medicaments and ointments, and my! what a burn across his face, beneath his eyes! "Lucky you weren't blinded," she said. "How'd it happen?"

"Well . . ." he said, and they at her farm, hardly noticing they'd walked a mile, looking at each other.

A day passed, and another, and he thanked her at her door and said he must be going, he much appreciated the ointment, the care, the lodgings. It was twilight and between now, six o'clock, and five the next morning, he must cross an ocean and a continent. "Thank you; good-bye," he said, and started to fly off in the dusk and crashed right into a maple tree.

"Oh!" she screamed, and ran to his unconscious body.

When he waked the next hour he knew he'd fly no more in the dark again ever; his delicate night-perception was gone. The winged telepathy that had warned him where towers, trees, houses and hills stood across his path, the fine clear vision and sensibility that guided him through mazes of forest, cliff, and cloud, all were burnt forever by that strike across his face, that blue electric fry and sizzle.

"How?" he moaned softly. "How can I go to Europe? If I flew by day, I'd be seen and—miserable joke—maybe shot down! Or kept for a zoo perhaps, what a life *that'd* be! Brunilla, tell me, what shall I do?"

"Oh," she whispered, looking at her hands. "We'll think of something. . ."

They were married.

The Family came for the wedding. In a great autumnal avalanche of maple, sycamore, oak, elm leaf they hissed and rustled, fell in a shower of horse chestnut, thumped like winter apples on the earth, with an overall scent of farewell-summer on the wind they made in their rushing. The ceremony? The ceremony was brief as a black candle lit, blown out, and smoke left still on the air. Its briefness, darkness, upside-down and backward quality escaped Brunilla, who only listened to the great tide of Uncle Einar's wings faintly murmuring above them as they finished out the rite. And as for Uncle Einar, the wound across his nose was almost healed and, holding Brunilla's arm, he felt Europe grow faint and melt away in the distance.

He didn't have to see very well to fly straight up, or come straight down. It was only natural that on this night of their wedding he take Brunilla in his arms and fly right up into the sky.

A farmer, five miles over, glanced at a low cloud at midnight, saw faint glows and crackles.

"Heat lightning," he observed, and went to bed.

They didn't come down till morning, with the dew.

The marriage took. She had only to look at him, and it lifted her to think she was the only woman in the world married to a winged man. "Who else could say it?" she asked her mirror. And the answer was: "No one!"

He, on the other hand, found great beauty behind her face, great kindness and understanding. He made some changes in his diet to fit her thinking, and was careful with his wings about the house; knocked porcelains and broken lamps were nerve-scrapers, he stayed away from them. He changed his sleeping habits, since he couldn't fly nights now anyhow. And she in turn fixed chairs so they were comfortable for his wings, put extra padding here or took it out there, and the things she said were the things he loved her for. "We're in our cocoons, all of us. See how ugly I am?" she said. "But one day I'll break out, spread wings as fine and handsome as you."

"You broke out long ago," he said.

She thought it over. "Yes," she had to admit. "I know just which day it was, too. In the woods when I looked for a cow and found a tent!" They laughed, and with him holding her she felt so beautiful she knew their marriage had slipped her from her ugliness, like a bright sword from its case.

They had children. At first there was fear, all on his part, that they'd be winged.

"Nonsense, I'd love it!" she said, "Keep them out from under foot."

"Then," he exclaimed, "they'd be in your *hair!*"

"Ow!" she cried.

Four children were born, three boys and a girl, who, for their energy, seemed to have wings. They popped up like toadstools in a few years, and on hot summer days asked their father to sit under the apple tree and fan them with his cooling wings and tell them wild starlit tales of island clouds and ocean skies and textures of mist and wind and how a star tastes melting in your mouth, and how to drink cold mountain air, and how it feels to be a pebble dropped from Mt. Everest, turning to a green bloom, flowering your wings just before you strike bottom!

This was his marriage.

And today, six years later, here sat Uncle Einar, here he was, festering under the apple tree, grown impatient and unkind; not because this was his desire, but because after the long wait, he was still unable to fly the wild night sky; his extra sense had never returned. Here he sat despondently, nothing more than a summer sun-parasol, green and discarded, abandoned for the season by the reckless vacationers who once sought the refuge of its translucent shadow. Was he to sit here forever, afraid to fly by day because someone might see him? Was his only flight to be as a drier of clothes for his wife, or a fanner of children on hot August noons? His one occupation had *always* been flying Family errands, quicker than storms. A boomerang, he'd whickled over hills and valleys and like a thistle, landed. He had always had money; the Family had good use for their winged man! But now? Bitterness! His wings jittered and whisked the air and made a captive thunder.

"Papa," said little Meg.

The children stood looking at his thought-dark face.

"Papa," said Ronald. "Make more thunder!"

"It's a cold March day, there'll soon be rain and plenty of thunder," said Uncle Einar.

"Will you come watch us?" asked Michael.

"Run on, run on! Let papa brood!"

He was shut of love, the children of love, and the love of children. He thought only of heavens, skies, horizons, infinities, by night or day, lit by star, moon, or sun, cloudy or clear, but always it was skies and heavens and horizons that ran ahead of you forever when you soared. Yet here he was, sculling the pasture, kept low for fear of being seen.

Misery in a deep well!

"Papa, come watch us; it's March!" cried Meg. "And we're going to the Hill with all the kids from town!"

Uncle Einar grunted. "What hill is that?"

"The Kite Hill, of course!" they all sang together.

Now he looked at them.

Each held a large paper kite, their faces sweating with anticipation and an animal glowing. In their small fingers were balls of white twine. From the kites, colored red and blue and yellow and green; hung caudal appendages of cotton and silk strips.

"We'll fly our kites!" said Ronald. "Won't you come?"

"No," he said, sadly. "I mustn't be seen by anyone or there'd be trouble."

"You could hide and watch from the woods," said Meg. "We made the kites ourselves. Just because we know how."

"How do you know how?"

"You're our father!" was the instant cry. "That's why!"

He looked at his children for a long while. He sighed. "A kite festival, is it?"

"Yes, sir!"

"I'm going to win," said Meg.

"No, *I'm!*" Michael contradicted.

"Me, *me!*" piped Stephen.

"Wind up the chimney!" roared Uncle Einar, leaping high with a deafening kettledrum of wings. "Children! Children, I love you dearly!"

"Father, what's wrong?" said Michael, backing off.

"Nothing, nothing, nothing!" chanted Einar. He flexed his wings to their greatest propulsion and plundering. Whoom! they slammed like cymbals. The children fell flat in the backwash! "I have it, I *have* it! I'm free again! Fire in the flue! Feather on the wind! Brunilla!" Einar called to the house. His wife appeared. "I'm free!" he called, flushed and tall, on his toes. "Listen, Brunilla, I don't need the night anymore! I can fly by day! I don't need the night! I'll fly *every* day and *any* day of the year from now on!—but I waste time, talking. Look!"

And as the worried members of his family watched, he seized the cotton tail from one of the little kites, tied it to his belt behind, grabbed the twine ball, held one end in his teeth, gave the other end to his children, and up, up into the air he flew, away into the March wind!

And across the meadows and over the farms his children ran, letting out string to the daylit sky, bubbling and stumbling, and Brunilla stood back in the farmyard and waved and laughed to see what was happening; and her children marched to the far Kite Hill and stood, the four of them, holding the ball of twine in their eager, proud fingers, each tugging and directing and pulling. And the children from Mellin Town came running with *their* small kites to let up on the wind, and they saw the great green kite leap and hover in the sky and exclaimed:

"Oh, oh, what a kite! What a kite! Oh, I wish I'd a kite like that! Where, where did you *get* it!"

"Our father made it!" cried Meg and Michael and Stephen and Ronald, and gave an exultant pull on the twine and the humming, thundering kite in the sky dipped and soared and made a great and magical exclamation mark across a cloud!

THE TIME MACHINE

"Seems like the town is full of machines," said Douglas, running. "Mr. Auffmann and his Happiness Machine, Miss Fern and Miss Roberta and their Green Machine. Now, Charlie, what you handing me?"

"A Time Machine!" panted Charlie Woodman, pacing him. "Mother's, scout's, Injun's honor!"

"Travels in the past and future?" John Huff asked, easily circling them.

"Only in the past, but you can't have everything. Here we are."

Charlie Woodman pulled up at a hedge.

Douglas peered in at the old house. "Heck, that's Colonel Freeleigh's place. Can't be no Time Machine in there. He's no inventor, and if he was, we'd known about an important thing like a Time Machine years ago."

Charlie and John tiptoed up the front-porch steps. Douglas snorted and shook his head, staying at the bottom of the steps.

"Okay, Douglas," said Charlie. "Be a knucklehead. Sure, Colonel Freeleigh didn't *invent* this Time Machine. But he's got a proprietary interest in it, and it's been here all the time. We were too darned dumb to notice! So long, Douglas Spaulding, to you!"

Charlie took John's elbow as though he was escorting a lady, opened the front-porch screen and went in. The screen door did not slam.

Douglas had caught the screen and was following silently.

Charlie walked across the enclosed porch, knocked, and opened the inside door. They all peered down a long dark

Copyright © 1957 by Ray Bradbury

hall toward a room that was lit like an undersea grotto, soft green, dim, and watery.

"Colonel Freeleigh?"

Silence.

"He don't hear so good," whispered Charlie. "But he told me to just come on in and yell. *Colonel!*"

The only answer was the dust sifting down and around the spiral stair well from above. Then there was a faint stir in that undersea chamber at the far end of the hall.

They moved carefully along and peered into a room which contained but two pieces of furniture—an old man and a chair. They resembled each other, both so thin you could see just how they had been put together, ball and socket, sinew and joint. The rest of the room was raw floor boards, naked walls and ceiling, and vast quantities of silent air.

"He looks dead," whispered Douglas.

"No, he's just thinking up new places to travel to," said Charlie, very proud and quiet. "Colonel?"

One of the pieces of brown furniture moved and it was the colonel, blinking around, focusing, and smiling a wild and toothless smile. "Charlie!"

"Colonel, Doug and John here came to—"

"Welcome, boys; sit down, sit down!"

The boys sat, uneasily, on the floor.

"But where's the—" said Douglas. Charlie jabbed his ribs quickly.

"Where's the what?" asked Colonel Freeleigh.

"Where's the point in *us* talking, he means." Charlie grimaced at Douglas, then smiled at the old man. "We got nothing to say. Colonel, *you* say something."

"Beware, Charlie, old men only lie in wait for people to ask them to talk. Then they rattle on like a rusty elevator wheezing up a shaft."

"Ching Ling Soo," suggested Charlie casually.

"Eh?" said the colonel.

"Boston," Charlie prompted, "1910."

"Boston, 1910 . . ." The colonel frowned. "Why, Ching Ling Soo, of course!"

"Yes, sir, Colonel."

"Let me see, now . . ." The colonel's voice murmured, it drifted away on serene lake waters. "Let me see . . ."

The boys waited.

Colonel Freeleigh closed his eyes.

"October first, 1910, a calm cool fine autumn night, the

Boston Variety Theatre, yes, there it *is*. Full house, all waiting. Orchestra, fanfare, curtain! Ching Ling Soo, the great Oriental Magician! There he is, on stage! And there I am, front row center! 'The Bullet Trick!' he cries. 'Volunteers!' The man next to me goes up. 'Examine the rifle!' says Ching. 'Mark the bullet!' says he. 'Now, fire this marked bullet from this rifle, using my face for a target, and,' says Ching, 'at the far end of the stage I will catch the bullet in my *teeth!*' "

Colonel Freeleigh took a deep breath and paused.

Douglas was staring at him, half puzzled, half in awe. John Huff and Charlie were completely lost. Now the old man went on, his head and body frozen, only his lips moving.

" 'Ready, aim, fire!' cries Ching Ling Soo. Bang! The rifle cracks. Bang! Ching Ling Soo shrieks, he staggers, he falls, his face all red. Pandemonium. Audience on its feet. Something wrong with the rifle. 'Dead,' someone says. And they're right. Dead. Horrible, horrible . . . I'll always remember . . . his face a mask of red, the curtain coming down fast and the women weeping . . . 1910 . . . Boston . . . Variety Theatre . . . poor man . . . poor man . . ."

Colonel Freeleigh slowly opened his eyes.

"Boy, Colonel," said Charlie, "that was fine. Now how about Pawnee Bill?"

"Pawnee Bill . . . ?"

"And the time you was on the prairie way back in seventy-five."

"Pawnee Bill . . ." The colonel moved into darkness. "Eighteen seventy-five . . . yes, me and Pawnee Bill on a little rise in the middle of that prairie, waiting. 'Sh!' says Pawnee Bill. 'Listen.' The prairie like a big stage all set for the storm to come. Thunder. Soft. Thunder again. Not so soft. And across that prairie as far as the eye could see this big ominous yellow-dark cloud full of black lightning, somehow sunk to earth, fifty miles wide, fifty miles long, a mile high, and no more than an inch off the ground. 'Lord!' I cried, 'Lord!'—from up on my hill—'Lord!' The earth pounded like a mad heart, boys, a heart gone to panic. My bones shook fit to break. The earth shook: rat-a-tat rat-a-tat, boom! Rumble. That's a rare word: rumble. Oh, how that mighty storm rumbled along down, up, and over the rise, and all you could see was the cloud and nothing inside. 'That's them!' cried Pawnee Bill. And the cloud was dust! Not vapors or rain, no, but prairie dust flung up from the tinder-dry grass like fine cornmeal, like pollen all blazed with sunlight now, for the sun had come out. I shouted again! Why? Because in all that hell-fire filtering dust now a veil moved aside and I saw them, I swear it! The grand army of the ancient prairie: the bison, the buffalo!"

The colonel let the silence build, then broke it again.

"Heads like giant Negroes' fists, bodies like locomotives! Twenty, fifty, two hundred thousand iron missiles shot out of the west, gone off the track and flailing cinders, their eyes like blazing coals, rumbling toward oblivion!

"I saw that the dust rose up and for a little while showed me that sea of humps, of dolloping manes, black shaggy waves rising, falling . . . 'Shoot!' says Pawnee Bill. 'Shoot!' And I cock and aim. 'Shoot!' he says. And I stand there feeling like God's right hand, looking at that great vision of strength and violence going by, going by, midnight at noon, like a glinty funeral train all black and long and sad and forever and you don't fire at a funeral train, now do you, boys? *do* you? All I wanted then was for the dust to sink again and cover the black shapes of doom which pummeled and jostled on in great burdensome commotions. And, boys, the dust came down. The cloud hid the million feet that were drumming up the thunder and dusting out the storm. I heard Pawnee Bill curse and hit my arm. But I was glad I hadn't touched that cloud or the power within that cloud with so much as a pellet of lead. I just wanted to stand watching time bundle by in great trundlings all hid by the storm the bison made and carried with them toward eternity.

"An hour, three hours, six, it took for the storm to pass on away over the horizon toward less kind men than me. Pawnee Bill was gone, I stood alone, stone deaf. I walked all numb through a town a hundred miles south and heard not the voices of men and was satisfied not to hear. For a little while I wanted to remember the thunder. I hear it still, on summer afternoons like this when the rain shapes over the lake; a fearsome, wondrous sound . . . one I wish you might have heard. . . ."

The dim light filtered through Colonel Freeleigh's nose which was large and like white porcelain which cupped a very thin and tepid orange tea indeed.

"Is he asleep?" asked Douglas at last.

"No," said Charlie. "Just recharging his batteries."

Colonel Freeleigh breathed swiftly, softly, as if he'd run a long way. At last he opened his eyes.

"Yes, *sir!*" said Charlie, in admiration.

"Hello, Charlie." The colonel smiled at the boys puzzledly.

"That's Doug and that's John," said Charlie.

"How-de-do, boys."

The boys said hello.

"But—" said Douglas. "Where is the—?"

"My gosh, you're dumb!" Charlie jabbed Douglas in the arm. He turned to the colonel. "You were saying, sir?"

"*Was* I?" murmured the old man.

"The Civil War," suggested John Huff quietly. "Does he remember that?"

"Do I remember?" said the colonel. "Oh, I do, I do!" His voice trembled as he shut up his eyes again. "Everything! Except . . . which side I fought on. . . ."

"The *color* of your uniform—" Charlies began.

"Colors begin to run on you," whispered the colonel. "It's gotten hazy. I see soldiers with me, but a long time ago I stopped seeing color in their coats or caps. I was born in Illinois, raised in Virginia, married in New York, built a house in Tennessee and now, very late, here I am, good Lord, back in Green Town. So you see why the colors run and blend. . . ."

"But you remember which side of hills you fought on?" Charlie did not raise his voice. "Did the sun rise on your left or right? Did you march toward Canada or Mexico?"

"Seems some mornings the sun rose on my good right hand, some mornings over my left shoulder. We marched all directions. It's most seventy years since. You forget suns and mornings that long past."

"You remember winning, don't you? A battle won, somewhere?"

"No," said the old man, deep under. "I don't remember anyone winning anywhere any time. War's never a winning thing, Charlie. You just lose all the time, and the one who loses last asks for terms. All I remember is a lot of losing and sadness and nothing good but the end of it. The end of it, Charles, that was a winning all to itself, having nothing to do with guns. But I don't suppose that's the kind of victory you boys mean for me to talk on."

"Antietam," said John Huff. "Ask about Antietam."

"I was there."

The boys' eyes grew bright. "Bull Run, ask him Bull Run . . ."

"I was there." Softly.

"What about Shiloh?"

"There's never been a year in my life I haven't thought, what a lovely name and what a shame to see it only on battle records."

"Shiloh, then. Fort Sumter?"

"I saw the first puffs of powder smoke." A dreaming voice, "So many things come back, oh, so many things. I remember songs. 'All's quiet along the Potomac tonight, where the soldiers lie peacefully dreaming; their tents in the rays of the clear autumn moon, or the light of the watchfire, are gleaming.' Remember, remember . . . 'All quiet along the Potomac tonight; no sound save the rush of the river; while soft falls the dew on the face of the dead—the picket's off duty forever!' . . . After the surrender, Mr. Lincoln, on the White House balcony asked the band to play, 'Look away, look away, look away, Dixie land . . .' And then there was the Boston lady who one night wrote a song will last a thousand years: 'Mine eyes have seen the glory of the coming of the Lord; He is trampling out the vintage where the grapes of wrath are stored.' Late nights I feel my mouth move singing back in another time. 'Ye Cavaliers of Dixie! Who guard the Southern shores . . .' 'When the boys come home in triumph, brother, with the laurels they shall gain . . .' So many songs, sung on both sides, blowing north, blowing south on the night winds. 'We are coming, Father Abraham, three hundred thousand more . . .' 'Tenting tonight, tenting tonight, tenting on the old camp ground.' 'Hurrah, hurrah, we bring the Jubilee, hurrah, hurrah, the flag that makes us free . . .' "

The old man's voice faded.

The boys sat for a long while without moving. Then Charlie turned and looked at Douglas and said, "Well, is he or isn't he?"

Douglas breathed twice and said, "He sure *is*."

The colonel opened his eyes.

"I sure am *what?*" he said.

"A Time Machine," murmured Douglas. "A Time Machine."

The colonel looked at the boys for a full five seconds. Now it was his voice that was full of awe.

"Is that what you boys call me?"

"Yes, sir, Colonel."

"Yes, sir."

The colonel sat slowly back in his chair and looked at the

boys and looked at his hands and then looked at the blank
wall beyond them steadily.

Charlie arose. "Well, I guess we better go. So long and
thanks, Colonel."

"What? Oh, so long, boys."

Douglas and John and Charlie went on tiptoe out the door.
Colonel Freeleigh, though they crossed his line of vision,
did not see them go.

In the street, the boys were startled when someone shouted
from a first-floor window above, "Hey!"

They looked up.

"Yes, sir, Colonel?"

The colonel leaned out, waving one arm.

"I thought about what you said, boys!"

"Yes, sir?"

"And—you're right! Why didn't I *think* of it before! A
Time Machine, praise heaven, a Time Machine!"

"Yes, sir."

"So long, boys. Come aboard any time!"

At the end of the street they turned again and the colonel
was still waving. They waved back, feeling warm and good,
then went on.

"Chug-a-chug," said John. "I can travel twelve years into
the past. Wham-chug-ding!"

"Yeah," said Charlie, looking back at that quiet house, "but
you can't go a hundred years."

"No," mused John, "I can't go a hundred years. That's
really traveling. That's really some machine."

They walked for a full minute in silence, looking at their
feet. They came to a fence.

"Last one over this fence," said Douglas, "is a girl."

All the way home they called Douglas "Dora."

THE SOUND OF SUMMER RUNNING

Late that night, going home from the show with his mother and father and his brother Tom, Douglas saw the tennis shoes in the bright store window. He glanced quickly away, but his ankles were seized, his feet suspended, then rushed. The earth spun; the shop awnings slammed their canvas wings overhead with the thrust of his body running. His mother and father and brother walked quietly on both sides of him. Douglas walked backward, watching the tennis shoes in the midnight window left behind.

"It was a nice movie," said Mother.

Douglas murmured, "It was. . . ."

It was June and long past time for buying the special shoes that were quiet as a summer rain falling on the walks. June and the earth full of raw power and everything everywhere in motion. The grass was still pouring in from the country, surrounding the sidewalks, stranding the houses. Any moment the town would capsize, go down and leave not a stir in the clover and weeds. And here Douglas stood, trapped on the dead cement and the red-brick streets, hardly able to move.

"Dad!" He blurted it out. "Back there in that window, those Cream-Sponge Para Litefoot Shoes . . ."

His father didn't even turn. "Suppose you tell me why you need a new pair of sneakers. Can you do that?"

"Well . . ."

It was because they felt the way it feels every summer when you take off your shoes for the first time and run in

Copyright © 1957 by Ray Bradbury

the grass. They felt like it feels sticking your feet out of the hot covers in wintertime to let the cold wind from the open window blow on them suddenly and you let them stay out a long time until you pull them back in under the covers again to feel them, like packed snow. The tennis shoes felt like it always feels the first time every year wading in the slow waters of the creek and seeing your feet below, half an inch further downstream, with refraction, than the real part of you above water.

"Dad," said Douglas, "it's hard to explain."

Somehow the people who made tennis shoes knew what boys needed and wanted. They put marshmallows and coiled springs in the soles and they wove the rest out of grasses bleached and fired in the wilderness. Somewhere deep in the soft loam of the shoes the thin hard sinews of the buck deer were hidden. The people that made the shoes must have watched a lot of winds blow the trees and a lot of rivers going down to the lakes. Whatever it was, it was in the shoes, and it was summer.

Douglas tried to get all this in words.

"Yes," said Father, "but what's wrong with last year's sneakers? Why can't you dig *them* out of the closet?"

Well, he felt sorry for boys who lived in California where they wore tennis shoes all year and never knew what it was to get winter off your feet, peel off the iron leather shoes all full of snow and rain and run barefoot for a day and then lace on the first new tennis shoes of the season, which was better than barefoot. The magic was always in the new pair of shoes. The magic might die by the first of September, but now in late June there was still plenty of magic, and shoes like these could jump you over trees and rivers and houses. And if you wanted, they could jump you over fences and sidewalks and dogs.

"Don't you see?" said Douglas. "I just *can't* use last year's pair."

For last year's pair were dead inside. They had been fine when he started them out, last year. But by the end of summer, every year, you always found out, you always knew, you couldn't really jump over rivers and trees and houses in them, and they were dead. But this was a new year, and he felt that this time, with this new pair of shoes, he could do anything, anything at all.

They walked up on the steps to their house. "Save your money," said Dad. "In five or six weeks—"

"Summer'll be over!"

Lights out, with Tom asleep, Douglas lay watching his feet, far away down there at the end of the bed in the moonlight, free of the heavy iron shoes, the big chunks of winter fallen away from them.

"Reasons. I've got to think of reasons for the shoes."

Well, as anyone knew, the hills around town were wild with friends putting cows to riot, playing barometer to the atmospheric changes, taking sun, peeling like calendars each day to take more sun. To catch those friends, you must run much faster than foxes or squirrels. As for the town, it steamed with enemies grown irritable with heat, so remembering every winter argument and insult. *Find friends, ditch enemies!* That was the Cream-Sponge Para Litefoot motto. *Does the world run too fast? Want to be alert, stay alert? Litefoot, then! Litefoot!*

He held his coin bank up and heard the faint small tinkling, the airy weight of money there.

Whatever you want, he thought, you got to make your own way. During the night now, let's find that path through the forest. . . .

Downtown, the store lights went out, one by one. A wind blew in the window. It was like a river going downstream and his feet wanting to go with it.

In his dreams he heard a rabbit running running running in the deep warm grass.

Old Mr. Sanderson moved through his shoe store as the proprietor of a pet shop must move through his shop where are kenneled animals from everywhere in the world, touching each one briefly along the way. Mr. Sanderson brushed his hands over the shoes in the window, and some of them were like cats to him and some were like dogs; he touched each pair with concern, adjusting laces, fixing tongues. Then he stood in the exact center of the carpet and looked around, nodding.

There was a sound of growing thunder.

One moment, the door to Sanderson's Shoe Emporium was empty. The next, Douglas Spaulding stood clumsily there, staring down at his leather shoes as if these heavy things could not be pulled up out of the cement. The thunder had stopped when his shoes stopped. Now, with painful slowness, daring to look only at the money in his cupped hand, Douglas moved out of the bright sunlight of Saturday noon. He made careful stacks of nickels, dimes, and quarters on the counter, like someone playing chess and worried if the next move carried him out into sun or deep into shadow.

"Don't say a word!" said Mr. Sanderson.

Douglas froze.

"First, I know just what you want to buy," said Mr. Sanderson. "Second, I see you every afternoon at my window; you think I don't see? You're wrong. Third, to give it its full name, you want the Royal Crown Cream-Sponge Para Litefoot Tennis Shoes: 'LIKE MENTHOL ON YOUR FEET!' Fourth, you want credit."

"No!" cried Douglas, breathing hard, as if he'd run all night in his dreams. "I got something better than credit to offer!" he gasped. "Before I tell, Mr. Sanderson, you got to do me one small favor. Can you remember when was the last time you yourself wore a pair of Litefoot sneakers, sir?"

Mr. Sanderson's face darkened. "Oh, ten, twenty, say, thirty years ago. Why . . . ?"

"Mr. Sanderson, don't you think you owe it to your customers, sir, to at least try the tennis shoes you sell, for just one minute, so you know how they feel? People forget if they don't keep testing things. United Cigar Store man smokes cigars, don't he? Candy-store man samples his own stuff, I should think. So . . ."

"You may have noticed," said the old man, "I'm wearing shoes."

"But not sneakers, sir! How you going to sell sneakers unless you can rave about them and how you going to rave about them unless you know them?"

Mr. Sanderson backed off a little distance from the boy's fever, one hand to his chin. "Well . . ."

"Mr. Sanderson," said Douglas, "you sell me something and I'll sell you something just as valuable."

"Is it absolutely necessary to the sale that I put on a pair of the sneakers, boy?" said the old man.

"I sure wish you could, sir!"

The old man sighed. A minute later, seated panting quietly, he laced the tennis shoes to his long narrow feet. They looked detached and alien down there next to the dark cuffs of his business suit. Mr. Sanderson stood up.

"How do they *feel?*" asked the boy.

"How do they feel, he asks; they feel fine." He started to sit down.

"Please!" Douglas held out his hand. "Mr. Sanderson, now

could you kind of rock back and forth a little, sponge around, bounce kind of, while I tell you the rest? It's this: I give you my money, you give me the shoes, I owe you a dollar. But, Mr. Sanderson, *but*—soon as I get those shoes on, you know what *happens?*"

"What?"

"Bang! I deliver your packages, pick up packages, bring you coffee, burn your trash, run to the post office, telegraph office, library! You'll see twelve of me in and out, in and out, every minute. Feel those shoes, Mr. Sanderson, *feel* how fast they'd take me? All those springs inside? Feel all the running inside? Feel how they kind of grab hold and can't let you alone and don't like you just *standing* there? Feel how quick I'd be doing the things you'd rather not bother with? You stay in the nice cool store while I'm jumping all around town! But it's not me really, it's the shoes. They're going like mad down alleys, cutting corners, and back! There they go!"

Mr. Sanderson stood amazed with the rush of words. When the words got going the flow carried him; he began to sink deep in the shoes, to flex his toes, limber his arches, test his ankles. He rocked softly, secretly, back and forth in a small breeze from the open door. The tennis shoes silently hushed themselves deep in the carpet, sank as in a jungle grass, in loam and resilient clay. He gave one solemn bounce of his heels in the yeasty dough, in the yielding and welcoming earth. Emotions hurried over his face as if many colored lights had been switched on and off. His mouth hung slightly open. Slowly he gentled and rocked himself to a halt, and the boy's voice faded and they stood there looking at each other in a tremendous and natural silence.

A few people drifted by on the sidewalk outside, in the hot sun.

Still the man and boy stood there, the boy glowing, the man with revelation in his face.

"Boy," said the old man at last, "in five years, how would you like a job selling shoes in this emporium?"

"Gosh, thanks, Mr. Sanderson, but I don't know what I'm going to be yet."

"Anything you want to be, son," said the old man, "you'll be. No one will ever stop you."

The old man walked lightly across the store to the wall of ten thousand boxes, came back with some shoes for the boy, and wrote up a list on some paper while the boy was lacing the shoes on his feet and then standing there, waiting.

The old man held out his list. "A dozen things you got to do for me this afternoon. Finish them, we're even Stephen, and you're fired."

"Thanks, Mr. Sanderson!" Douglas bounded away.

"Stop!" cried the old man.

Douglas pulled up and turned.

Mr. Sanderson leaned forward. "How do they *feel?*"

The boy looked down at his feet deep in the rivers, in the fields of wheat, in the wind that already was rushing him out of the town. He looked up at the old man, his eyes burning, his mouth moving, but no sound came out.

"Antelopes?" said the old man, looking from the boy's face to his shoes. "Gazelles?"

The boy thought about it, hesitated, and nodded a quick nod. Almost immediately he vanished. He just spun about with a whisper and went off. The door stood empty. The sound of the tennis shoes faded in the jungle heat.

Mr. Sanderson stood in the sun-blazed door, listening. From a long time ago, when he dreamed as a boy, he remembered the sound. Beautiful creatures leaping under the sky, gone through brush, under trees, away, and only the soft echo their running left behind.

"Antelopes," said Mr. Sanderson. "Gazelles."

He bent to pick up the boy's abandoned winter shoes, heavy with forgotten rains and long-melted snows. Moving out of the blazing sun, walking softly, lightly, slowly, he headed back toward civilization. . . .